Ashes of Her Name

by

Aaron Nash

First published in Great Britain 2026

Dedicated to my beautiful daughter Willow

and

all those that have supported me through my journey.

PROLOGUE:

Before the town, there was a child.

The night was like a choked throat; tight and breathless.

New Grayson was a place that didn't sleep, so much as it waited still and watching. Craven Lane stretched out in silence on the outskirts of the town, street lights flickering like dying stars, their electric hum almost loud enough to cover the distant sound of hurried footsteps through the low bearing fog.

A young girl in a white dress, ran down the centre of the road. Her bare feet cut and bloody from the uneven street. Red hair cascaded down her face, wild and unruly, hiding the tears running down her cheeks. Her little legs were too small to keep going for much longer.

"Momma!" the girl sobbed to no-one in particular.

The street behind her lay empty, but her little eyes scanned frantically for help, flicking left and right at the shadows. Her breath steamed in the air as the panic increased. She was desperate for somebody, anybody to help her.

The wind shifted, carrying with it the faintest echo of footsteps.

Willow paused as she tried to work out where she was.

Her eyes locked on a porch light down the street flickering weakly.

She banged on the door. "HELP! He's coming!"

A shuffle. Then a tired gruff voice. "You need to go."

"He's going to kill me!" Willow kept looking over her shoulder expecting to see her pursuers.

"I can't help you."

"Please sir."

Another voice from inside. A woman's. "Who is it?"

"It's no-one. Get back to bed."

Willow shifted from foot to foot with anxiety. She knocked again.

"I said no. Just go home."

"But my momma's dead!"

There was a pause as the man took in those words.

"I'm sorry but get off our property."

Willow turned, her heart pounding. Tears cascaded from her eyes and then she saw them in the distance.

Shapes in the dark like living shadows. They hadn't seen her yet.

Willow ran door to door, banging as hard as she could. No answer. Curtains twitched, then shut.

Finally a door cracked open. A man, young and nervous scans Willow up and down.

"Please sir," Willow begged. "They're trying to kill me."

The man froze and crouched in front of her.

"Where are your parents?"

"I think he killed her. I ran, she told me too."

Tears continued to flood down Willow's cheeks.

"He? Who killed her?"

"I don't know. It was the man from the church. He was acting funny. There were other people too." Willow whispered with a tiny voice.

The man's gaze froze.

"They're coming." She pointed up the road.

Looking past Willow he saw the figures in the distance emerging from the fog. They were clearly looking for the girl.

"Get inside!"

They rushed in. The man slammed the door and bolted the lock. Inside the house, everything felt like it was holding its breath. On the sofa sat a woman who turned, confused.

"James! What's going on?" She studied Willow and her voice softened. "Who's this?"

James was looking through the peephole.

Willow approached, shaking and hesitant. "I'm Willow. I'm eight. Who are you?"

The lady stood up then crouched in front of her clearly concerned.

"My names Cathy. Where's your Mummy?"

Willow's tears started again. Cathy instinctively pulled her in close.

James's hands trembled as he slid them in his pockets. He knew if they were really after the girl a basic bolt on a door wouldn't be enough to keep them out.

Willow's tiny voice broke through her tears. "She's dead."

Cathy looked to James worried.

"Is there anyone else out there?"

James nodded. "There's a group walking down the road. They look like they're looking for something or someone."

Cathy stood. "I'll call the police." She went to the kitchen to use the phone.

Through the peephole James watched the group continue to scour the street and the alleys.

Cathy ran back into the room. "They're on their way." She grabbed willow and brought her close.

James picked up a baseball bat from beside the door.

"What the hell are you doing?" Cathy's face showed a concern she'd never experienced before.

"I need to find out what's going on. If they don't tell me at least it'll hold them up until the police arrive."

"No! What if something happens to you. What about Rebecca? What about me?"

Willow turns confused. "Who's Rebecca?"

Cathy looks down at her and fakes a smile. "Rebecca's our daughter, well stepdaughter."

"Stepdaughter?" Willow scrunched her face in confusion.

Cathy gave a small smile. "We adopted her."

James looked at the Willow and Cathy conversing and took a deep breath.

"I can't just do nothing." He walked over and kissed Cathy deeply then unbolted the door.

"If anything happens to me, you keep Rebecca safe. Willow's also going to need some help. Lock the door behind me and no matter what happens, do not come out."

He smiled at Willow.

Willow gave a small smile back.

Cathy tried to protest but James raised a hand before quickly sliding out of the door and pulling it closed. She ran to the door locking it and stared through the peephole.

James walked down the road towards the group.

Willow pulled the curtain to one side to see what was happening. She saw the group that had been after her.

The leader of the group; a young looking man from the church, saw James and moved towards him. The others fell in line behind him. James stopped in front of the man and seemed to be talking. The conversation was getting heated as James shook his head. The other man hesitated before launching at James with a knife.

James threw himself forward knocking him sideways. The sirens were coming. The police station wasn't far. James turned to run but they were still there. The group descended on him blocking his escape.

The man swung a blade, his knife severing James's windpipe. He grabbed his throat and dropped to his knees. The bat fell to his feet. Willow looked on from the window as Cathy viewed in horror through the peephole.

The blade rose again as the group encircled him. The sirens and lights were almost there.

The knife came down into James's skull. He dropped to the floor. The man turned and glanced around.

Willow saw the lights illuminating the buildings in the distance. The man stood and wiped his blade before turning to his followers. One pointed to the oncoming police cars before telling the leader something. They all looked down at James before running down the street.

Willow looked through the gap in the window as blood spread from James's body. She couldn't hear the sirens outside. All she could hear was Cathy's frantic screams.

Outside, New Grayson held its breath again.

PART I:

Like a moth to a flame.

CHAPTER ONE

<u>*15 years later.*</u>

The tires hummed over the highway like a lullaby caught in a broken loop. Not peaceful but rhythmic enough to numb the edges of thought. Outside the window, the world stretched into nothingness; Dry, wide fields, skeletal fenceposts and telephone wires sagging like tired veins across the sky.

Kira sat in the front passenger seat with her head tilted against the window, her breath fogging a faint circle on the glass that kept disappearing and returning with every breath. She wasn't watching the fields. Not really. She was looking through them. Or maybe beyond them into the past.

Back to a time when this stretch of road had meant something different.

Back when she had a family.

Back when she believed there was such a thing as hope.

Her fingers tightened around her phone, knuckles pale against the black plastic case. She hadn't looked at it in miles, but still clutched it like a tether to the present.

In the driver's seat, Miles guided the car with one hand loosely on the wheel. His thumb tapped a steady rhythm on the steering column, trying to match the beat of the worn-out song buzzing from the single working speaker. The sound crackled and dipped. The music was barely there, like it had one foot in the real world and the other in some other realm. Looking at his chiselled features side-on, it was obvious why she'd fallen for him when they'd first met.

He'd been handsome, kind and had made her laugh. What wasn't to like. He'd come up to her in the university bar and made some lame joke. Usually this would've pushed her away but his eyes had caught her off guard. One thing led to another and they were quickly dating. Things had been good but after a year, they'd realised they were better off as good friends. Something just didn't gel between them. Sometimes she wondered what it would've been like if they hadn't split.

"You sure you're okay?" he asked.

It wasn't the first time. He didn't expect a real answer any more but felt he needed to ask anyway.

Kira gave him the same one she'd done the whole trip "I'm fine."

He shot her a glance, then returned his eyes to the road. "You've barely said anything since we left the gas station. I'm just saying if you're not okay, I get it."

"I said I'm fine."

Behind them, Amy hadn't moved in almost an hour.

Kira looked at her like her little sister that she needed to protect. She and Amy had grown up in care together. Where Amy was quiet and withdrawn, Kira was more outgoing and upbeat. Being so close it was no surprise they went to university together and ended up having the same choice in boys. Glancing back at Miles she could see why he and Amy were a good fit for each other. Miles provided the balance that Amy needed in her life. She remembered when Miles and Amy had first told her. They expected her to be angry, but she was happy for them.

Amy sat in the back seat with her legs drawn up, arms wrapped around her knees, her forehead pressed lightly against the window. She looked like a doll someone had forgotten to animate. Pale, silent, absent. But her eyes were open, watching something outside the car. Or maybe something inside herself.

She hadn't spoken since they got back on the road. Not a single word. Not even a hum to the music. Miles had tried a few light questions earlier; What do you want to eat? Are you warm enough? but she hadn't answered, hadn't even blinked.

Kira hadn't pushed her. Not yet.

Miles drummed on the wheel a little louder. "Look, we can still turn around. There's no shame in that. You came this far, that's already something."

Kira's voice was flat. "We're almost there."

"You don't have to go through with it, Kira. Just because she..." he paused, choosing his words "...just because your mom's gone doesn't mean you owe her or this place anything."

"She was my stepmother." Kira said. "Anyway, I'm not doing it for her."

Silence.

Amy didn't move. Didn't blink.

The trees on either side of the road started to lean in, growing closer together as if they were trying to whisper to each other. Their branches scraped at the sky. It had been sunny back at the last town, but now the clouds had thickened, dragging shadows behind them like mourning veils.

A green road sign loomed ahead, cracked but readable:

NEW GRAYSON – 11 MILES

The sight of it made Kira's stomach lurch. Amy's eyes shifted toward the sign and then back to the horizon, unblinking.

Miles let out a low whistle. "This place really as bad as you said?"

Kira laughed. "It's worse."

They passed a rusted-out mailbox with the name faded across it in peeling white letters. The house behind it had long since collapsed, overtaken by weeds and silence. Another mile down, an old church with a sagging steeple stood back from the road, its sign missing most of the letters.

Miles slowed a little as they passed.

"You ever go there?" he asked.

Kira nodded her head. "Once when I was young. I don't remember the sermon. Just the smell."

"The smell?"

"It smelt like spoiled milk."

Miles didn't respond.

They drove another few minutes in quiet. The road narrowed slightly and curved around a shallow hill. The landscape began to change. It was less open now, the trees pressing closer to the edge of the road, as if New Grayson were trying to swallow them before they even arrived.

A crow perched on a rusted fencepost watched the car pass, its head turning slowly, eyes flat and unblinking. Amy's gaze fixed on it as they passed. Kira noticed but didn't say anything. She shifted in her seat. Her fingers ached from holding her phone too tight.

"I used to count crows on this road when I was little," she said suddenly.

Miles glanced at her. "Yeah?"

"Yeah. My step-mom said if I saw just one, I should spit over my left shoulder or I'd get bad luck."

He smiled faintly. "That's charming."

"You don't want to know what I was told to do if I saw more then seven."

Amy blinked. Just once.

Miles adjusted the rear-view mirror, trying to catch her eyes. "Amy, you good back there?"

Amy said nothing.

Kira sighed. "You know she gets like this sometimes. It's okay."

But it wasn't okay. Not really.

Kira hadn't felt right since she got the news that her stepmother had died. Kira reached into her coat pocket and pulled out the envelope again. The handwriting on the front was faded and uneven.

They didn't speak for the next few miles.

Amy stayed silent in the back, her head still resting against the window, face half in shadow. Her reflection blurred and jittered with every bump in the road. She blinked slowly, mechanically, like someone remembering how.

Kira kept one hand curled in her lap and put the letter back in her pocket. She could feel the weight of it through the fabric. It had only arrived three weeks ago, no stamp, no sender, no return address. Just two words on a letter inside; *They know.*

She'd ignored it at first.

Then she'd gotten the news her stepmother died.

No context, no build-up. Just a phone call from a stranger who spoke with authority. "Cathy Peters was found deceased this morning." They'd said, as if they knew Kira would be expecting the call. "We're sorry. It was sudden. The funeral's planned for 2 weeks time. As the sole beneficiary of her will we would like you to come down to go through the paperwork." When she'd tried to query how they'd gotten her number, the line went dead.

Although sudden, it hadn't been unexpected. Cathy had lived a troubled life. Kira hadn't seen her since she'd been sent away. She'd spoken by letter but had never fully forgiven her for abandoning her all those years ago.

Now she was part of the ground, Kira wouldn't have a chance to offer forgiveness.

Miles finally broke the silence. "So what's the plan when we get there?"

Kira's brow furrowed. "We go to the house. Sort through what's left. Say goodbye."

"That's all?"

Kira hesitated. "Yeah. That's all."

But it wasn't all. Not even close. There were the lawyers, the paperwork and then there was...

"The funeral?" Miles looked at her, then back at the road. "What's happening with the funeral?"

"Closed casket."

He nodded slowly. "Is the town taking care of it?"

"Apparently. That or they lied and her body's laying in some shallow grave at the edge of town."

He didn't laugh and neither did she.

Another mile marker passed. They were getting close.

The air changed again. It was almost as if the temperature dropped by a considerable amount. It was much cooler and denser then it had been. The clouds had gathered properly overhead, and the light was strange. Not storm-strange, nor like the end-of-day haze. Just off. Like it had been filtered through some old camera lens that had seen so much through it's lens over the years.

Kira shifted in her seat. "How far?"

Miles pointed ahead. "Coming up on the town limits now."

A faded wooden sign appeared around the bend, the paint almost worn to nothing:

Welcome to New Grayson. Where History Lives Forever.

Amy leaned forward slightly. "We're here."

Her voice was hoarse, her first word in hours.
Both Kira and Miles turned in surprise.

"You okay?" Kira asked.

Amy didn't answer but gave a slight nod and sat back again.

They passed an old gas station with half the roof caved in. Next to it, a convenience store with blacked-out windows. A man stood by the door smoking, his eyes following the car as it rolled past. He didn't wave.

No one waved.

Main Street unfolded slowly. Store fronts shuttered. A barbershop with a spinning red-and-white pole that hadn't spun in years. A post office with a door hanging off its hinges. The diner still had a neon sign, but only the letters "EAT" still lit up.

Kira swallowed hard. "It's worse than I remember."

"You live here long?" Miles asked.

"Until I was ten."

He nodded. "Why'd you leave?"

"I had no choice. Cathy sent me away. Said it was for my own good."

Amy pressed her forehead back to the glass.

Kira looked back at her. "You sure you're okay?"

Amy nodded, but it was a mechanical gesture. Nothing in her body moved with it. Just the neck. Just enough to register motion.

The road narrowed as they reached the southern edge of town. The motel sat ahead of them. It was a squat, low building with peeling turquoise paint and a sign that once read '*Rest Easy Lodge*'. With the years of wear it now read: '*Res E Log*'.

Miles pulled into the lot.

There were only two other cars. Both looked abandoned.

He killed the engine. The silence that followed was immediate and heavy.

"Time to check in?" Miles queried.

"I'll do it," Kira said, already unbuckling.

"I'll come with," he added. "You coming?"

Amy shook her head.

As Kira stepped out, the wind kicked up faint dust and the scent of something metallic; something she remembered but couldn't place.

She glanced around the lot. The cars were dusty, their tires low and flat. No movement in the windows of the motel. No staff in sight. Just the low thrum of the vending machine near the office and the buzz of a single yellow bulb swinging in its casing.

A shiver ran down her spine. It was like a ghost town.

Miles followed her to the office, the bell over the door jangling once as they stepped inside.

A man sat behind the desk. Thin. Hollow-eyed. A cigarette dangling between his fingers, burning low. He didn't get up.

"You're the ones who booked over the phone?" he asked.

"No." Kira said. "We just wondered if you had a room. It'd only be for a few nights."

He stared at her a moment longer than necessary, then slid a clipboard across the counter. "Fill that out. Room 6 is clean."

He rummaged in a drawer then handed a key to Miles.

"Thanks," Miles said, but the man was already looking away. He was peering through the dusty blinds toward the parking lot. Toward Amy.

Kira put the completed form back on the desk and glanced to Miles who just shrugged.

....

Amy stepped inside the room first. She didn't speak, just threw her bag on a bed before walking back to the window. Her reflection ghosted in the glass. Kira set her bag down by the foot of the bed closest to the bathroom. She didn't unpack. Just unzipped the top, took out a half-empty bottle of water, and sat down heavily.

Miles dropped his keys on the small night stand between the beds. "Feels like we rented a room right out of a horror film."

Kira didn't laugh.

The motel room smelled like dust and disinfectant trying to cover mildew. The air conditioning unit rattled loudly in the wall and the beds were the kind you wouldn't want to sit on without a layer of clothes. But it was a place they could rest.

The silence hung.

Then Miles tried again. "We could go grab food? See what's still open. Get our bearings."

Kira shook her head. "You go. I'll stay with Amy."

Amy turned from the window. "I'm fine."

Her voice was flat, but clear.

Kira studied her a moment, then nodded. "Okay. Why don't you both go."

Miles hesitated. "You sure?"

"Yeah. I need a minute alone."

Miles gave her a look, something between concern and resignation, then turned toward Amy. "Wanna come?"

With a small nod Amy followed him out without a word.

Kira waited until the door clicked shut. Then she stood, crossed the room to her bag, and dug beneath the layer of clothes until she found a photo. It was folded and tattered, the edges soft from years of handling. She unfolded it carefully.

Cathy stood in front of the house. Her stepmother. Pale, smiling, arms crossed in front of her like she was shielding herself from the world. The porch sagged behind her. A dead plant sat in a clay pot near her feet. It had been taken not long before she died.

Cathy had mailed it, without a note, without explanation.

The back was blank.

Kira stared at it now, feeling nothing.

She wanted to feel something. Anger. Sadness. Guilt. Anything. But all she felt was the old, familiar numbness. The kind that settled into your bones after growing up in a town like this, then being discarded into the wider world.

She folded the photo again, slipped it back in the bag, then opened the drawer beneath the night stand. A worn Bible sat there. She stared at it for a long moment, then shut the drawer again.

Outside, a screech broke the silence. Sharp and sudden.

Kira froze.

She walked slowly to the window, parted the curtain just enough to peek through. Nothing. Just the lot.

Amy and Miles were now out of view.

She let the curtain fall and sat back on the edge of the bed and stared at the yellowed wallpaper peeling in the corner near the bathroom. Every few minutes, the air conditioner gave a low, wheezing cough, like it was remembering how to be useful yet was failing badly.

She checked her phone.

No signal.

No bars. No messages. Nothing.

She set it down and rubbed at her temples. A tension headache had bloomed there, dull and slow like a bruise rising beneath the skin. Her thoughts were jumbled. She wanted to sleep but knew she couldn't until Amy was back. Something about this place told her that rest wouldn't come easily.

She stood and crossed the room to the window again, lifting the curtain only slightly. The parking lot outside remained empty, bathed in the dull glow of a flickering security light. The motel sign swung slowly on a chain, casting lazy shadows across the lot.

Down the road, past the faded motel sign, sat a row of store fronts. The gas station from earlier, a tax office that probably hadn't seen a client in a decade, a small corner shop and a funeral parlour that from it's exterior seemed to be doing fairly well. Beyond that, just shadowed darkness apart from the faint hint of a church spire.

Kira let the curtain fall again. The motel felt smaller by the second.

She paced the room once, twice, then finally sat back down. This time on the other bed, the one Amy had claimed earlier. It smelled faintly of the industrial cleaner. At least it showed that they'd tried to clean the room between guests.

The memories of her past came uninvited.

She was ten again, sitting in the back of a car, the lady she'd called her mother behind the wheel, face rigid and unreadable. They'd just left New Grayson. Cathy had whispered something under her breath that Kira hadn't understood at the time: "I should have buried it."

Buried what?

She never found out.

Even as they drove away, Cathy never talked about the town. Not once. Even in the years since she'd never mentioned New Grayson in any of her letters. Kira had thought it odd but it'd helped allow her to push her abandonment to the back of her mind.

She lay back on the bed and stared at the ceiling. The lightbulb above her buzzed with a faint, high-pitched whine. She considered turning it off, but the dark felt worse somehow. At least with the light on she could keep the shadows at bay.

A knock startled her.

Three soft taps on the motel door.

She sat up immediately. "Who is it?"

Silence.

She moved slowly to the door, pressed her eye to the peephole.

Nothing. Just the shadowed walkway and the parking lot. She looked back into the room.

Another knock.

Softer this time. More like a whisper on wood.

She stepped back from the door shaking her head. This was just exhaustion.

There was another knock. It was much closer, almost inside her head.

She flung the door open in frustration.

No one was there. She stared out into the night. Cold air slipped past her into the room, and she wrapped her arms around herself. Something shifted near the edge of the lot just in the corner of her vision. She stepped forward leaving the safety of the room for a better look. Her feet echoed around the area with each step. She made it about halfway before one of the motel's lights blinked and died leaving half the parking lot in shadow. It felt like she was being watched by the ghosts of the past.

From somewhere across the street, a crow called. Fear set in and she quickly retreated backwards into the room, slamming the door. Her hands were shaking as she frantically found the bolt.

It was just nerves she told herself. That was all. The town playing tricks on her.

When she turned around, Amy was standing in the doorway of the bathroom.

Kira jumped, hand flying to her chest. "Jesus, Amy!"

Amy stared at her, face unreadable in the half-light.

"I thought you went with Miles."

Amy blinked once. "I did."

"You're back? How did you get in? I was standing right…" She turned back to the door then to Amy.

Amy didn't respond. She just stared.

Kira stepped forward slowly. "Are you okay?"

Amy tilted her head slightly, like she was trying to listen to something far away.

Then, in a quiet hushed voice; "We shouldn't have come here."

Kira froze. "What?"

Amy blinked again and just like that, her posture changed. The dazed fog lifted. "I said, we shouldn't have come here."

Kira frowned. "Why?"

Amy looked confused for a moment, then sat on the bed. She didn't seem to remember the exchange. Her hands went up to her temples in frustration.

Kira stood there a long moment before finally sitting down again. "Where's Miles?"

"Getting food."

"Why aren't you with him?

Amy shrugged. "I told him I was feeling tired. He told me to come back."

Kira shook her head.

"Did you see anything out there?"

Amy shook her head. "Like what?"

"Never mind," Kira muttered. "I'm just tired I guess."

She laid back on the bed and stared at the ceiling again. The lightbulb overhead flickered once, twice, then steadied.

Amy sat still, her hands resting in her lap. Neither of them said anything for a long time. Eventually, Kira closed her eyes.

In the darkness, she saw the front door. Only this time when it opened a shadowed figure stood on the other side. She tried to scream but nothing came out. Then everything was consumed by darkness.

CHAPTER TWO

The sky was grey by morning, an unbroken sheet of cold light stretched over New Grayson. Like the world had forgotten the place. Miles had come back at some point in the night but Kira couldn't recall when. He'd Tried to be quiet but had woken her up. It was a ghost-town he'd said but he had managed to find some food. She'd thanked him before drifting back off to sleep.

Kira stood in front of the mirror in the motel bathroom, running a brush through her hair with slow, distracted strokes. Her black dress hung off her like it belonged to someone else. She'd bought it the day after the phone call. Cheap and wrinkled, but served it's purpose.

Outside, the birds were silent.

Amy sat on the edge of the bed, already dressed in black jeans and a plain grey sweater. She looked too young and too old at the same time. Her hair was still damp from the shower, clinging to the sides of her face like vines.

"Are you ready?" Amy asked, not turning around.

Kira nodded, though she wasn't sure what 'ready' meant anymore.

Miles knocked once before entering. He was clean-shaven, suit jacket too tight across the shoulders, the tie slightly off-centre.

"Car's ready," he said. "The place isn't far."

Kira smoothed the front of her dress and finally turned.

Amy stood and followed.

....

The cemetery sat on a hill just outside the southern edge of town, where the road narrowed and the trees grew thick and hunched. The entrance was marked by a crooked arch with rusted letters.

Gravel crunched beneath the tires as Miles pulled up and parked behind a line of older vehicles. The kind driven by people who'd likely lived in New Grayson their entire lives and would never need to leave.

Kira stepped out into the cold. The wind pushed against her gently. Amy followed, her arms folded, hands clenched into the crooks of her elbows. Her eyes scanned the gathered people like she was trying to recognise them. They made their way toward the small crowd gathered near a casket. The funeral had already begun.

Kira's steps slowed as they approached. She didn't recognize most of the faces. She reckoned they must've known Cathy one way or another. Old neighbours maybe or possibly church friends. All of them wore expressions that looked like sympathy but under the surface felt like a performance.

The preacher stood at the head of the casket. His Bible trembled gently in his hands as he read.

"...and though I walk through the valley of the shadow of death…"

Kira barely heard the words. They came to her muffled and far off, like someone whispering underwater. Amy stood beside and gripped her hand. It gave Kira small comfort. She hadn't expected to feel anything, but standing there she felt the slightest twang of loss.

Miles shifted uncomfortably and moved to the back of the group.

A man near the front turned and studied them. His eyes lingered long looking them up and down. Kira couldn't place him. He gave her a small nod then looked at Amy.

His expression changed. Confusion at first followed by recognition.

Amy stared back at him making him turn away.

The preacher closed the book.

"May she rest, finally, in peace. Does anyone else have anything else they would like to say?"

The gathering quietly looked between one another but no-one spoke up. The Preacher nodded and gave the go ahead for the coffin to be lowered. He stood and began handing flowers to each who went to the grave.

Kira didn't cry as she placed a single flower into the grave but she felt her heart getting slightly heavy.

Amy stepped forward to lay a white flower onto the lid but paused. Without warning, an older woman near the back of the group stepped out of line. Her skin was thin and spotted, her hair pulled tight in a bun.

She marched forward and stopped in front of Amy.

"You don't remember me?" the woman said.

Amy didn't respond.

"You should."

Kira stepped between them. "Excuse me?"

The woman's voice dropped to a near whisper as she looked between Kira and Amy. "You shouldn't be here. You're supposed to be dead."

The woman thrust her finger at their faces, her face clenched in anger. Amy flinched as Kira stood strong.

The woman walked away before either of them could speak.

Kira rubbed her neck and turned to Amy. "What the hell was that?"

Amy shook her head, clearly unnerved.

The crowd dispersed slowly, like smoke drifting through a room. One by one, townsfolk murmured their rehearsed condolences, avoiding eye contact as they passed Kira and Amy. Some offered short nods. A few lingered, hesitating like they wanted to say something then turned away.

No one stayed long.

Not even the preacher.

Once everyone had left, the groundskeeper returned with a shovel and an expression like he'd rather be anywhere else. He didn't greet them. Didn't ask them to leave. Just picked up the ground and dumped it into the grave with wet thuds.

Each impact made Kira flinch.

Amy stood silently beside her still grasping her hand. Her eyes weren't on the casket anymore. They were on the woods that bordered the far side of the cemetery. The trees stood too close together, their limbs tangled together like a natural wall.

Miles came up behind them with two styrofoam cups of gas station coffee they'd bought on the way up.

"Strong as paint thinner, and colder then an Eskimo." he said, offering one to Kira.

She took it, grateful for the distraction, even if it was bitter and lukewarm.

He looked at the grave, then at Amy. She was shaking "You okay?"

Amy nodded, but her eyes didn't leave the treeline.

He turned to Kira "And you?"

Kira gave a faint smile but said nothing. They stood watching the groundskeeper until he had finished. With a wipe of his brow he made his way back to his hut.

Kira finally broke the silence. "What did that woman mean?"

Miles blinked. "Who?"

"That old one with the tight hair. She said Amy should be dead. Seemed angry she wasn't."

He looked from Kira to Amy concerned. "I didn't see. I was at the back."

Amy didn't react. Didn't even seem to have heard her own name.

Kira pressed on as she got Amy's attention. "She seemed to know you. She looked at you like it triggered something."

Amy finally turned her gaze back to Kira. Her face was unreadable.

"You're wrong," Amy said.

Kira frowned. "About what?"

Amy looked back at the trees.

"I don't think she was only talking to me." She turned and started back to the car. Kira and Miles followed giving each other a look of confusion.

The walk back to the car was quiet and sullen. Halfway to the parking lot, Kira spotted a figure leaning against a large bowing tree. He was tall, broad-shouldered, wearing a slate gray suit and a kind smile that didn't quite match his eyes. He made his way over to them.

Kira stiffened.

"A pleasure to see you again."

"I'm sorry, who..."

"Richard Carson," he said, extending a hand. "Mayor of New Grayson."

Miles raised an eyebrow. "They still elect mayors in towns like this?"

Richard chuckled. "Somebody has to maintain the illusion of order."

Kira didn't shake his hand.

He dropped it without offence. "I was very sorry to hear about your mother. She was a lovely lady. Died far too young. She meant a lot to the community here. More than people around here will ever let on."

Kira narrowed her eyes. "You knew her?"

"In a manner of speaking and I remember you from when you were just a little girl. Just look at you now."

Richard tilted his head slightly. "Don't remember me, do you?" He side-eyed Amy.

"I don't remember much about this town," Kira said. Richard's gaze settled back on Kira.

"That's probably for the best," he replied smiling. "Memories are like seeds. Bury them long enough, and you never know what'll grow in the shadows."

There was a long pause.

Then he smiled again, broader this time. "Well, I won't keep you. I just wanted to say welcome home."

They watched as he turned and walked toward his car.

Miles gave a low whistle. "Creepy."

Kira exhaled. "Let's get out of here."

....

As they drove back towards the centre of town the wind picked up. It wasn't strong, barely a breeze, really but it moved in a way that dragged a low fog with it. Loose paper lifted from the street and spun lazily in the street around the car.

Miles gently touched Kira's arm being careful to not let Amy see.

"What was all that with the mayor? Seemed a real creep."

Kira shook her head and shrugged. "I have no idea. But there was something definitely off about him."

"Do you remember him from back when you lived here?"

Kira shook her head. "No. But as I've said, I don't remember much from back then."

"Do you know where the law firm is? I don't want to rush things, but my head is pounding."

Kira pointed up the road. "Shouldn't be too far, I think it's in the main square."

Miles glanced in the rear-view mirror at Amy who sat sullen on the backseat.

"This place has a weird vibe about it. It feels 'off' somehow."

Kira nodded as she rested her arm on the open window. "I know what you mean. Once tomorrows done with we can go and not worry about any of this any more."

Amy's head rose. "Then we can go back home?"

Kira turned to her slightly shocked. "Yeah, we'll head back home once I sort the house out tomorrow. Is that OK?"

Amy smiled and gave a nod.

Kira gave a slight smile. "How are you doing anyway?"

"My head hurts but I'm OK."

Silence settled in the car for the rest of the journey.

....

Braven and Perkins was a small firm, the building was unassuming and clearly didn't get much business. A small bell announced the groups arrival.

An old balding man stepped from the backroom wiping crumbs from his mouth and shirt.

"Sorry, wasn't expecting anyone." He regarded the trio. "Oh, you must be Catherine's daughter."

Kira gave a small nod. He wiped his hands on his shirt and placed it out to in greeting.

"Nigel Braven". Kira took it and smiled.

"I'm Kira. These are my friends Miles and Amy."

He smiled and offered them seats next to his old wooden desk.

"Let me just grab the paperwork and the items she left for you." He vanished out back and started rummaging through boxes.

They each took a seat and sat back. It was fairly welcoming on the inside and looked quite professional. Miles looked to Kira then motioned to the wall. There was a large framed print of an old painting depicting a man crawling from a flaming hole.

Nigel re-entered and saw them looking.

"It's not an original." He made his way to the desk and sat down placing a box in front of him. "It depicts that even in the darkest times, man's perseverance can pull them out of anything."

"It's haunting. It looks like it's a demon exiting hell." They all turned to Amy who was staring at the picture.

Nigel adjusted his glasses. "That's an interesting take on it. That's the good thing about art. We all see something different."

He pulled the lid off the box and started pulling items out, a folder, some photos and some other items. When the box was empty, Nigel placed the box on the floor.

"These are the items that were left in the will, as well as the contents of the house." He handed Kira the folder. "These are the details of her bank accounts and insurance policies. You'll also find bank cards in the pocket at the back."

Kira accepted it and glanced quickly through it.

"Here's some pictures that were in her bag when she was found. Thought you'd appreciate them." As he handed them to Kira, Amy glanced over.

Nigel picked up the keys. "And these are for the house. The big one is the front door. There's also keys for the other rooms and the shed. To be fair, some of them we don't actually know what they're for but they are yours now. Do you know where the house is?"

Kira nodded. "Yes I think I remember."

"Good." He placed the keys in her hands. "This is the paperwork that I need signing." Nigel held up a stapled bundle of paperwork. "I understand if you want to give it a read over first. That's fine, I'm not going anywhere. Feel free to take it with you, read it through then drop it back when signed."

Kira took the papers and placed them in the file. "Thank you."

Nigel smiled. "You're very welcome. I'm sorry again for your loss." He stood and the group did the same. He shook their hands again. "My numbers on a card in the front of the folder if you have any queries."

Kira smiled. "Thanks. I'll get this back to you ASAP."

"I'd appreciate that". Nigel guided them to the door with a warm yet mournful smile. "You take care out there."

Miles nodded "Thank you. Have a good day."

As they stepped outside, they noticed the sun was already going down.

"We should get some food then head back to the motel. I'm knackered and need some sleep."

Kira smiled to Miles and nodded. "Sounds good."

....

Kira woke in panic and looked around suspiciously. Something was wrong.

There had been no noise. No sudden nightmare. Just the sharp, feeling that something had changed.

The motel room was dark.

Not just dim. Almost pitch black.

Even the LED from the alarm clock failed to illuminate much.

She got up slowly, feeling her heartbeat rise in her chest. The blanket slid from her legs. The air in the room was unnaturally cold.

She looked toward the other bed and could just make out Miles curled in the thin blanket.

Amy wasn't there.

"Amy?" she whispered.

No answer.

Kira stood and moved carefully through the dark, hands out, trying not to trip.

She turned slowly toward the bathroom.

The door was ajar.

Pale white light spilled through the gap.

She stepped closer.

"Amy?" she whispered again.

A shadow shifted behind the door.

Kira hesitated then pushed it open.

The bathroom was empty.

No light. No Amy. No sound. The overheard light flickered on illuminating the fogged mirror.

Words traced into the glass with a fingertip: "YOU SHOULD HAVE DIED."

Kira stumbled back, heart pounding.

Then the light flickered.

A burst of static.

....

Kira jolted upright. She felt herself over, sweat covered her face and stained her t-shirt. She took in a deep breath realising it was simply a dream. Light drew her vision towards the bathroom door. Amy stood in the doorway, silhouetted by blue flickering light.

Kira jumped. "Jesus! Amy! Stop doing that!"

Amy didn't react. Kira clutched her chest. "Where were you?"

Amy blinked. "What do you mean? I was asleep."

Kira looked beyond her at the mirror. There were no words any more.

She looked confused at Amy, dream was melding with reality. "Did you write something on the mirror?"

Amy frowned. "No. Why would I?"

Kira opened her mouth to respond but hesitated..

"Never mind."

Amy moved and sat on the edge of the bed. Kira shuffled to the edge next to her.

"Are you sure you're OK? That woman, this place?"

Amy placed her hand on Kira's leg. "I'm fine. Just tired."

The light bulb flickered again.

Kira nodded and placed her head on Amy's shoulder. "I hate this place."

Amy rested her head against Kira's. "Me too."

The next morning brought no clarity.

Just dull gray skies and the taste of something metallic in the air.

Kira sat at the small table near the motel window, flipping through the folder left for her by the lawyer; papers to sign, records to review, some half-legible death certificate with too many blank spaces and not enough answers.

Amy had moved back to her bed in the early hours and still lay there. She was on her side, facing the wall, as if whatever dream she was in was safer than the waking world.

Miles returned with coffee and breakfast sandwiches.

"Town's barely awake out there," he said, tossing the bag onto the table. "Gas station guy stared at me like I was a ghost. Then charged me twelve bucks for this."

"Sounds about right."

He sat across from her and unwrapped a sandwich. "You okay?"

"No. Not really."

He paused mid-bite.

"I don't know what I'm doing here," she added. "This place... it's like it didn't just stay the same it got worse."

"You don't have to stay. We could just up and leave now, just say the word."

Kira gave a small, humourless laugh and shook her head. "Yeah, I do. I need to get all of this signed and all of Cathy's affairs in order first."

Miles didn't push.

After a few minutes, Kira pulled a piece of paper from the folder and turned it around. "You ever heard of this?"

He leaned in. "'Property Disposition Authorization?'"

"Yeah. Cathy apparently signed it the day before she died. It basically gives the town authority to take her house unless I claim it."

Miles blinked. "That's a thing?"

"In New Grayson, apparently. Weird thing is that it doesn't look like her signature going by the other documents."

Amy finally stirred.

She sat up slowly, hair tangled, eyes unfocused.

"Morning sleepyhead," Miles said jokingly.

She nodded then stood and walked to the bathroom, closing the door softly behind her.

They heard the faucet turn on.

Miles leaned forward. "She hasn't said more than a few sentences to me since we got here. What've I done? Why's she pissed at me?"

"You've done nothing wrong." Kira placed her hand on his forearm.

Miles shook his head in confusion. "You think this place is getting to her?"

"It's complicated."

That made him stop.

"What does that mean?"

Kira looked toward the bathroom. The water had stopped.

"She's been here before," Kira whispered.

Miles frowned. "What do you mean?"

"She doesn't remember everything…. And it's probably better that way"

Amy emerged a moment later. She looked better, her pale face hidden behind wet hair. It was the first time since they'd arrive that she looked OK.

Kira stood and grabbed her coat.

"I'm going to the house. We'll talk later." she said.

Miles raised an eyebrow. "You're going to the house now?"

"Yeah. I need to see it. I need to know what she left behind."

Amy stepped forward. "I'm coming with you."

Kira hesitated. "You don't have to."

"I want to."

Her voice was firm.

Kira nodded once.

Miles stood. "Guess that means I'm driving."

They left together, stepping out into the stale morning. The motel door clicked shut behind them.

The fog rolled low as they took to the road.

CHAPTER THREE

The drive to Cathy's house took them through the middle of New Grayson, past rusted stop signs and cracked side-walks, down roads that looked more like veins than streets. The town didn't seem that large, barely a grid, but it folded in on itself like a maze that went on forever with no exit.

Some store fronts stood empty while others had people starting their morning routines. The post office had plywood nailed across its smashed windows, though no one had boarded up the front door. An old man sat on a bench outside the general store, head down, lips moving silently as if praying or rehearsing something he didn't want to forget. He didn't look up when the car passed.

Kira sat in the passenger seat, silent. One hand gripped the edge of the seat like she needed it to stay grounded. Her heart thudded in her chest, loud enough that it almost drowned out the sound of the tires over gravel. She hadn't been in the house since the day she'd been driven away.

Amy sat in the back, unusually upright, hands folded in her lap, her expression unreadable. Her eyes moved like she was counting every turn, every tree, every cracked window as if trying to remember.

Kira noticed.

"It's OK. I'm here" she said glancing back.

Amy blinked and gave a slight smile. "Thanks."

The house appeared after the next turn.

Set back behind an overgrown hedge and two dead trees, the place didn't look too bad. The paint had peeled off over the years and the front porch bowed to one side but somehow it still looked fairly well maintained.

Miles whistled low. "Charming."

Kira didn't respond. She was already out of the car, keys in hand. The porch creaked under her weight. The sound was familiar and hit somewhere in her stomach, the memories started creeping into her mind.

She paused at the door. Amy stepped up beside her.

Kira glanced over. "You okay?"

Amy nodded once. "You?"

Kira hesitated then shrugged even though deep down she knew she wasn't.

The key turned easily and the door opened with a sigh. Inside, the air was stale. Not rotting; Cathy hadn't been gone that long, but flat and untouched. A light dust already coated the surfaces in soft gray layers. A stack of unopened mail lay on the floor just inside.

Kira gripped Amy's hand and gave it a squeeze and stepped inside, slowly.

She passed the living room, the old armchair with the torn armrest, the rug with the coffee stain that had never come out. Her fingers brushed the edge of the side table as she passed like muscle memory and for a second she felt like she'd never left.

Miles and Amy entered behind her.

"No sign of forced entry since… you know," Miles said softly, as if not to disturb the house. "That's... something."

"No one would break into this place," Kira replied. "They'd be afraid of what they might find. The other kids called this the death house."

Miles looked confused. "Death house?"

Kira shifted uncomfortably. "Yeah. Ever since James, Cathy's husband was killed."

"God! That's horrible."

Amy drifted toward the hallway that led to the back of the house. She walked slowly, eyes scanning everything like it was half-familiar. Her fingers dragged along the wall as she passed, pausing over an old torn photograph hanging crookedly.

A younger Cathy. Smiling, but barely and beside her... a little girl.

Amy froze. Miles placed his arm around her and studied the image.

Kira appeared beside her. "That was me."

Amy turned to look at her.

Kira stared at the photo. "Yeah. I was maybe eight. Cathy liked taking pictures. Said they were a way of preserving the world as it was."

Amy's lips moved. But no sound came out.

Then, quietly: "I remember."

Kira didn't answer.

"What was on the torn off section?" Miles pointed at the edge of the picture.

Kira shrugged. "No idea."

Miles headed back down the hallway towards the living room. An uncomfortable silence stretched between the girls.

Miles called from the other room. "Hey guys! This thing's still running."

They followed him back to find him crouched beside an old electric fireplace, its coils glowing faintly. The power light flickered as if unsure whether to keep trying.

"This shouldn't be on," Kira said. "I thought they cut everything."

"They probably did. Probably has a backup generator somewhere."

Amy stepped into the room and stopped abruptly.

She turned toward the fireplace and dropped to her knees.

Kira moved to her immediately. "Amy?!"

Amy didn't respond. Her hands hovered over the floorboards near the base of the fireplace.

Then she touched something.

A square.

Barely visible.

A trapdoor.

Miles crouched. "What the hell?"

Amy looked up at Kira. "You didn't know about this?"

Kira stared. "No. Did you?"

Miles Looked confused. "Why would Amy know about it?"

Kira realised what she'd said. "We can talk about this later. For now I want to know what's down there."

The square was the size of a crawlspace hatch, framed in warped wood. There was no handle, just a thin groove wide enough for fingernails or a flat tool.

Miles tried it but his hands couldn't get purchase. He ventured into the house to find something to help.

Kira stood, backing away slightly while Amy remained still, fingers brushing the edge.

"She kept something here," Amy said. "Something she didn't others to find."

Kira's voice dropped. "How do you know that?"

"I remember someone telling me when I was little." Amy whispered.

The trapdoor didn't open. Even with force, no matter how Miles pulled or twisted at the edge with a screwdriver he'd found in the kitchen drawer, it didn't budge. It was flush with the floor, sealed as if it had never been meant to open at all. The wood was warped, dry, and gray, but it held like concrete.

Amy sat back against the fireplace surround, breathing shallowly.

Miles stood up and wiped sweat from his forehead with the back of his hand. "This thing's sealed like a tomb."

Kira turned and stepped back from the living room. The air in the house had grown heavier. She could feel it pressing against her lungs. Everything smelled like dust, old paper, and something faintly metallic like old blood.

"I want to see her bedroom," Kira said suddenly.

Amy looked up, startled. "Why?"

"Because I need to."

The staircase leading upstairs was narrow, and every floorboard groaned underfoot. On the wall were photographs from another life; Cathy in a graduation gown, Cathy standing with James whose face had faded in the print, and one of Cathy and her in a place Kira didn't recognize.

They reached the top of the stairs and saw the door to Cathy's room was closed. Kira stood before it, hand on the knob, her body rigid. Amy hovered behind her, arms wrapped around herself, watching silently.

"You don't have to go in there," Amy said.

"I do."

Kira turned the handle and pushed the door open. The room looked like it hadn't been touched in years. The bed was neatly made, a quilt pulled tight over stiff sheets. Dust lightly coated the surface like morning frost. On the night stand was a small ceramic lamp with roses painted along the base, unplugged. The blinds were shut tight, and light filtered through the gaps like prison bars.

Kira stepped inside slowly. She remembered this room. Every detail. The way the wallpaper peeled behind the dresser. The way the floor dipped slightly just past the closet. The way Cathy always locked the drawers in her night stand but left the closet wide open. Even though she'd only lived with Cathy for a short time all of the memories were so vivid.

She crossed to the blinds first and opened them. Dust fell like shadowed snow.

Inside the closet hung some smart blouses, a winter coat, and an empty hanger swinging slightly even though the air was still. She reached out and stopped it with one finger.

Amy stood in the doorway, not entering but also not retreating.

Kira turned to the dresser. She pulled open the drawers one by one; socks, perfume bottles, a framed picture of two children tucked beneath a stack of worn T-shirts depicting band logos from the 80's and 90's and a journal. Black leather and small. The kind you could fit in a coat pocket.

She pulled it out and turned it over in her hands. No name on the cover. Just initials 'C.P.' etched in worn gold lettering. The pages were brittle. When she opened it, the spine cracked as if it hadn't been opened in a long time.

Most of the entries had dates, scrawled with increasingly frantic handwriting:

March 8: He's watching again. From the trees this time. Same place as last year.

March 12: I found another stone on the porch. It was warm with blood.

March 25: They came to the house again. They just stood at the edge of the yard, waiting. For what, I don't know.

Kira turned the page and stopped.

There was a sketch; rough and drawn in charcoal. A figure all in black with a mask over his face. His hands were ablaze in fire. Behind him, rows of people with their faces erased and at his feet a small body in white.

Amy stepped inside the room slowly, noticing Kira absorbed in the book.

"What's that?" she asked, pointing at the drawing.

Kira didn't hear and turned to the next page.

One line filled the paper;

There is no town. There is only the gate.

Amy's breath hitched.

Kira looked up sharply. "What is it?"

Amy didn't speak. She backed up a step, suddenly pale.

Kira pocketed the journal and moved to her. "Amy?"

"I remember this room," Amy whispered.

"It's OK."

"I remember that smell. I remember that book. Even the sound the closet door makes when it sticks."

Kira turned toward the closet.

It had been open when she left it. Now it was shut.

Miles's voice echoed from downstairs. "Guys? You might want to see this."

Kira and Amy hurried out of the room and followed his voice to the back door.

He stood just inside the threshold, pointing out through the window.

At the edge of the woods, four figures stood.

Still and unmoving.

Too far away to see clearly, but close enough that Kira knew they were being watched. She looked at Amy who looked scared.

Amy whispered, "It's happening again."

Miles looked to her. "What's happening again?"

The girls ignored him.

They stood at the back door for a long moment, just watching.

The figures didn't move.

They didn't wave or shift or pace. They just stood there, perfectly still at the tree line, wrapped in coats too dark for the season, their silhouettes stretched in the fog, as if each one had been drawn from memory by someone who'd never seen a person up close.

"Locals?" Miles guessed, though even he didn't believe it.

Amy pressed her hand against the windowpane. Her breath fogged the glass, but her eyes never blinked. "They're waiting."

"For what?" Miles asked.

Amy didn't answer.

Kira let the curtain fall.

"Lock the doors," she said. "All of them."

"And then what?" Miles was annoyed. "Please can someone just explain what the hell is happening?"

Kira gently touched his arm and looked him in the eyes. "Once they're gone."

They checked the windows first. Then the front and back doors. Then every possible latch or panel they hadn't touched since arriving.

The house groaned as if in protest.

"I don't like this," Miles said under his breath, fiddling with the back door lock again. "This town, this house, those people. This is starting to feel like something out of a movie. And not the good kind."

"Let's move further into the house. At least that way we know they can't see us."

Amy stood near the fireplace again, eyes fixed on the trapdoor in the floor. She hadn't looked away from it since the moment they'd returned from the kitchen.

"She wanted to keep it closed," she said.

Kira turned. "Who? Cathy?"

Amy nodded. "But not for her sake. For ours."

Miles glanced down at the seam in the floor. "What do you reckon is under it?"

"I don't know," Amy said. "But I don't think it's anything good."

Before Kira or Miles could reply, someone knocked on the front door.

Three short, deliberate knocks.

They froze.

Miles took a step toward the door, then hesitated.

Kira whispered, "Don't."

The knock came again louder this time. Amy stepped toward the hallway, toward the door.

Kira moved in front of her. "No."

Amy's eyes were glassy. "He's here."

Kira's skin went cold.

"Who?"

Amy blinked but continued.

Another knock.

Amy glanced through the peephole but the porch was empty. Kira joined her and opened the door slowly. No one was there.

Just the fading echo of footsteps in the gravel. At the edge of the street Kira glimpsed a group of three people just standing and staring at her.

She quickly closed the door and watched as Amy returned to the trapdoor, almost like she was being drawn to it by an unknown force. Amy stood there, staring at it like she could hear something the others couldn't. Like it was whispering directly to her.

The rest of the house was quiet now. The strange rhythm of the knocking had faded. The hallway was still. The fireplace was flickering desperate to stay alight.

Kira approached slowly from the hall, her pulse thick in her ears. She stopped behind Amy, letting her eyes drop to the floor beneath her feet.

Kira crouched beside Amy, fingers brushing the edge of the trapdoor. The seam was tighter now. Almost invisible. If she hadn't already known it was there, she wouldn't have seen it at all. Like the house had tried to close it.

She reached for it but jolted at Miles' voice.

"I found this," Miles said, stepping into the room, crowbar in hand.

Kira looked up.

"Now is someone going to fill me in on what's happening?"

Kira pulled the photo of the two girls from her pocket and handed it to him. He took it and examined it closely.

"This you?" He smiled.

"Yes."

"Who's the other girl?"

Kira glanced to Amy.

Amy looked up to Miles. "That's me."

He paused and looked to the girls. "You both knew each other before?"

Kira nodded solemnly. "We're sisters. Kinda."

He handed the photo back. "What?! Sisters? When... No!"

"Cathy took us both in."

He shook his head, running his hands through his hair. "We'll discuss this later when my mind isn't as frazzled."

Miles paused and pointed to the trap door.

"Are we sure we want to open that? We should just go." he asked.

Amy didn't reply with words. She just nodded once. Miles shrugged awkwardly and placed the crowbar in the slight gap. The metal squealed against the floor as he wedged it into place. The boards pushed back at first, like they didn't want to give. Then with a jolt and a sharp crack, the trapdoor shifted upward about half an inch.

Dust billowed out from the seam, dry and sour, carrying with it the stench of old rot.

Kira covered her mouth.

Amy didn't flinch.

....

Miles crouched beside her as the two of them heaved the door upward. The hinges shrieked as it opened. The boards groaned like they were being ripped apart with a bold reluctance.

Beneath the hatch was no proper basement.

It was a hole. A tunnel.

Hand-dug long ago, narrow and uneven, the walls packed with dirt and splintered roots, sloping downward into darkness. The light from the room above barely penetrated past the first few feet.

A small wooden staircase led down into the shadows.

"That's not a basement," Miles muttered.

"No," Kira said. "It's not."

She leaned forward, trying to peer inside without getting too close.

The air that came up from below was colder than it should've been. Wet. It smelled like a river that hadn't flowed in years.

Amy knelt beside them, her face close to the opening.

"There's a room down there, deep into the tunnel." she said. Her voice was strange but certain.

Miles looked at her sharply. "You've been down there?"

Amy shook her head. "No. But I'm sure I've seen it."

Kira stared at her.

"What else is down there?"

Amy's eyes flicked toward Kira's.

"I don't think we want to know."

A chill raced up Kira's spine. She turned back to the hole and looked into the black. It wasn't just dark. It was complete nothingness. Whatever was down there was waiting and had been for a long time.

Kira stood up and took a step back. Miles followed suit, shutting the trapdoor slowly. The hinges groaned, but the wood settled shut.

None of them said anything.

Amy remained kneeling, fingers pressed lightly to the wood.

Kira looked at her.

"We're not going down there. I think we need to get out of here right now."

Amy nodded but her gaze didn't leave the floor.

Kira backed toward the couch. The room felt heavier now. Denser. She could almost feel the pressure in the air shift with the door closed. Like whatever lay beneath was now contained.

Miles ran a hand through his hair, eyes still fixed on the centre of the floor.

"I hate this place."

"I know," Kira said. "Me too."

They sat for a long time thinking of what their next move would be. Minutes turned to hours.

Amy stood finally, slow and quiet. Miles went over and put his arm around her, she settled into his grasp. They walked to the window. Outside, the trees were still. The wind had died down. The air hung motionless like the world was holding its breath.

Kira joined them.

"The people are gone," she said.

Amy nodded.

"They were real, right?" Kira asked. "We all saw them?"

Amy turned her head slightly. "They're still out there. Just not where we can see them."

Kira stared at her for a long moment before turning from the window and pulling out the journal again.

Cathy's handwriting on the crumpled pages brought more questions.

The last entry though still stood out: *There is no town. There is only the gate.*

Kira traced the words with her fingertip. She didn't know what it meant yet but she was starting to feel like she would.

"What's that?"

Kira turned to see Miles looking over her shoulder.

"It was Cathy's. It seems to be a diary."

"Does it explain any of this?" Miles motioned around the room and towards the trapdoor

Kira shook her head. "I'm not sure yet but I really hope so."

CHAPTER FOUR

The door clicked shut behind them.

They stood on the porch in silence for a long moment, the sky overhead a flat slate of cloud and dimming light. The day had gotten away from them and inside the house hours had felt like minutes. It wasn't quite evening but neither was it day. That in-between time, when shadows stretch and horizons blur.

Amy stood with her back to the house. She hadn't spoken properly since they closed the trapdoor.

Kira locked the door slowly, her fingers trembling slightly as she turned the key. She hadn't even realized how tightly she'd been holding her breath until she let it out in one long, cold exhale.

Miles broke the silence. "Whatever that tunnel was, it looks like it's been here longer then the house."

Kira didn't answer.

"It definitely wasn't there when I…" She looked to Amy. "…When we lived here."

Amy gave a slight nod. "It was but she never wanted you to know."

She stared out past the front yard, across the weedy path that led back to the road, and then beyond, to the town just starting to flicker to life in the distance.

They drove slowly back toward the motel. The roads had grown narrower since they'd last passed through, or maybe it just felt that way. Like the trees had leaned in just a little more. Like the shadows had stretched wider.

Something had changed. As the rest of the world was beginning to get ready to rest New Grayson seemed to be fully waking up. The town square, once silent and still as a photograph, now breathed with movement. Porch lights flickered on like blinking firebugs. Figures emerged slowly from buildings moving with purpose.

Miles followed her gaze. "Looks like people are coming out."

Amy whispered something, her voice flat. Miles strained to hear but missed it. Kira heard it though and didn't like it.

Kira watched the side-walks as they passed. The townsfolk were there now, walking stiffly. Heads turned as the car crawled past, but no one smiled. No one waved. Just stares, blank, glassy and prolonged. There was something uniform in the way they walked. Like the rhythm of the place had found them again and folded them into it.

Miles gripped the steering wheel tighter.

"Looks like they're all going somewhere?"

Kira looked closer.

The people weren't just wandering. They were converging toward the heart of town. Toward the church.

They passed the old diner. The windows were fogged from the inside. Shapes moved behind them. Shadows in the evening. Next was the fire station. The doors were open. Inside, the trucks were covered in tarps. The walls were lined with rusted tools. But barely any firemen.

A man stood just outside the doorway, face painted with soot. He didn't blink as they passed.

Kira pressed her back into the seat and looked straight ahead.

The road opened slightly, near the square, revealing the church steeple in the distance. The bell wasn't ringing but it swayed as though it had just recently stopped.

As they drove into the square they noticed people were filing in through the large double doors of the church.

Two at a time. In silence.

"At least they don't seem to be watching us any more." Miles stated.

Amy turned her head but said nothing.

Kira glanced at her in the mirror, Amy was staring out the window. They drove on.

The gas station lot was empty now. The pump handle hung loose. The front door stood open, swinging slightly in the wind.

A shape stood behind the counter but Kira couldn't make out any features.

She looked away.

They passed the sheriff's office. The windows were black. A cruiser sat outside, tires flat, wind shield cracked. The door had been propped open with a single brick. A figure leaned against the wall just inside. Kira glanced at him; a gun belt, weathered boots and a downcast face.

As they passed, he looked up.

The sheriff's eyes met Kira's for a fraction of a second.

His mouth moved.

One word:

"Run."

They reached the motel just as the sun disappeared behind the horizon.

The air was colder now, biting and electric. Kira stepped out of the car, immediately feeling the weight of the town pressing in. The neon sign flickered overhead. Another of the letters burned out as she looked at it.

She opened the door to the room with a dull groan. The lights inside flickered once, then steadied.

Amy stepped in last and closed the door gently behind her.

Miles grabbed his bag from the corner. "Okay. So we're leaving now, right?"

Kira didn't answer right away. She walked to the window and pushed the curtain aside.

Across the square, the church doors were closed now. The building pulsed from inside with flickering candlelight.

"They're gathering for something." she said.

"For what?"

"I don't know," she replied. "But maybe it'll give us answers?"

Miles looked around. "To What?"

Amy sat on the bed, hands folded in her lap.

She stared at the floor.

"They've done this before," she said.

Miles turned. "How do you know that?"

"I'm sure I saw something similar when I was last here."

He didn't question it any more.

Kira stood at the window, watching the flickering lights outside the church at the far end of the square.

"Screw this. We should just get out of here." Miles threw his things in his bag and headed out to the car. The girls hesitated before following.

Kira tried to protest. "We need to find out what's going on."

Miles was already in the driver's seat. "Fuck that. I'm not dying in some backwater town."

"I need answers."

He smashed his fist into the steering wheel.

"Fuck!"

Kira placed her hand on his shoulder.

"Let's get some rest and reevaluate in the morning. I don't like it here any more then you do but for now, this place seems safer then any of us sitting behind that wheel. We'll leave soon."

Miles looked up sullenly.

Kira tried a small smile. "I promise."

They made their way back to the room and bolted the door.

....

Kira didn't sleep that night.

She sat at the edge of the motel bed, eyes fixed on the gap in the curtain, watching the church. Hours passed. The lights never flickered out. At some point, the rain started, not hard, but persistent. A thin, steady drizzle that slicked the pavement and ran in slow slivers down the windows. It dulled everything and brought a strange calm to her.

Amy had returned to her silence.

She curled into the corner of the bed closest to the window, knees drawn up to her chest, her face unreadable. Not blank, just removed from reality. She wasn't absent in just that moment. She was somewhere much deeper. Eventually she'd drifted off to sleep.

Miles paced for a while, then gave up and sat in the armchair by the bathroom door. His knee bounced with anxiety, as his fingers tapped the armrest in an uneven rhythm. It was the only sound besides the rain.

Outside, the church bell rang once. The sound wasn't loud as it was dulled under the rain. Kira glanced at her watch. It was just after 3am.

Amy sat up suddenly making the others jump. Kira turned back to the window. The church doors had opened. One by one, the townsfolk exited moving slowly, quietly. Their faces were passive. Their eyes wide. No one spoke.

They held flaming torches. Each flame moved in unison, flickering in the rain.

Miles stood beside Kira now. "Where the hell are they going?"

Amy approached the window too.

The line of townspeople crossed the square. They moved in two single-file rows, winding between the buildings. Kira watched them disappear down one of the alleys between the old butcher shop and the antiques store.

Then the last person passed.

The square was empty again.

Only the church remained, lit softly from within.

"What do we do?" Miles asked. "We can't just sit here."

"We need to leave." Amy was scared.

Kira shook her head. "I need to know what all this means. You two are free to stay here or you can just leave."

"We aren't letting you go by yourself. What are you going to do?"

Kira nodded slowly. "I'm going to follow them."

....

The rain eased as they stepped outside. Not quite a break but just enough to see clearer.

The side-walk was slick beneath their feet. Kira led the way across the street, past the fountain that hadn't worked in decades, past the statue of the town's founder, whose plaque had been defaced so many times it was now just a smear of scratched metal. The alley where the procession had vanished was empty but not silent.

A low hum drifted up from somewhere beneath them. Amy knelt near the edge of the alley, pressing her palm to the concrete.

She flinched.

"What's wrong?" Kira asked.

Amy looked up. "It's warm."

Miles crouched beside her, placing his hand where hers had been.

He jerked it back instantly. "Jesus, yeah it is."

Kira touched it too.

She looked around. "There has to be a way down."

They moved through the alley, silently checking doors and windows. Most were locked. Some looked so old that even if they were unlocked they couldn't be opened.

Then Amy stopped.

Her hand rested on a metal panel bolted into the side of an old hotel's outer wall. A delivery hatch. Old. Rusted. But it looked like it had been recently opened.

She reached for the handle. It opened with a groan. Below it, stairs led into an uncomfortable darkness.

Amy's fingers hovered just over the hatch handle when the voice came from behind them firm, tired, and authoritative.

"Don't."

All three froze.

Kira turned first, hand instinctively moving to shield Amy, though she had nothing to defend with. Miles stood straighter, but he didn't move any further.

A man stepped out from the shadows, boots soft on the slick concrete. He was broad-shouldered, well into his forties, his uniform soaked from the rain but buttoned neat, not a thread out of place. The five-pointed badge on his chest was dull and unpolished, the holster at his side worn but still functional.

His voice was steady, but his eyes told another story red-rimmed, tired, and suspicious of everything.

"Step away from there." He said again.

Amy backed off without a word. Kira gently grabbed her arm.

The Sheriff stopped a few feet from them, hands resting on his hips.

"What do you three think you're doing?"

Miles spoke up, forcing casualness. "We saw some people enter the alley. We wanted to know where they were going."

"People?" the Sheriff asked. "Or shadows you wanted to be people?"

Kira narrowed her eyes. "They were real. They were carrying torches. They walked into this alley. We followed."

"Did you see where they went?" the Sheriff asked.

Kira hesitated. "No."

He nodded slowly. "Then let's keep it that way."

"Who are you?" Amy asked, her voice almost too calm.

He turned toward her. "Sheriff Alan Barker."

He studied the girls then gestured back down the alley. "I think we should talk."

"We are talking," Miles muttered.

"Not here." His voice was hushed.

Amy stared at him a moment longer, then nodded once.

··················

The police station hadn't changed much from the outside.

Still the same sagging roof, the cracked sheriff's star painted on the glass door, the porch light flickering with the determination of a dying star. Inside, the station was warm, dimly lit, and too quiet. A single desk lamp cast long shadows over papers stacked on the counter.

Barker led them into a back room that might have once been an interview space, or maybe a break room, judging by the coffee pot with fossilized grounds inside.

He offered them seats. None of them took them.

"You're Cathy Peters' daughter," he said to Kira.

"Stepdaughter."

Amy was about to speak but Kira grabbed her hand. Barker saw this and nodded.

"I liked your mother," Barker said. "Didn't always understand her, but she didn't deserve what she got."

Kira folded her arms. "And what did she get?"

"Too many years in this place. Too many things she tried to fix on her own."

He looked back to Kira.

'They're going to come for you."

Kira stepped back shocked. "What?"

"Because you're the key."

63

Amy tilted her head. "To what?"

"To everything they're planning."

Miles leaned forward. "Look, we didn't come here to stir anything up. We just came for the funeral and now we want to leave."

"And yet," Barker said, "you're already digging into places no one's supposed to go."

"That hatch wasn't locked," Kira snapped. "You're not exactly keeping the town's secrets locked tight."

Barker sighed and rubbed his temples. "The people here, they don't think it's a secret. They think it's protection. They believe what they do down there keeps everything above from falling apart."

"So what are they doing?" Miles asked. "Rituals? Gatherings?"

"They don't call them that. They call them tradition."

Kira's voice was low. "What do they want from me?"

Barker rubbed his face and sat down. The silence in the room thickened.

Kira remained standing, her back rigid, arms still crossed tight. Miles leaned in the doorway, arms loosely folded but ready to move. Amy hadn't sat either; she lingered just behind Kira's shoulder, still and unreadable.

Sheriff Barker sat across from them, resting his weight against the table as if he hadn't slept in days.

"You need to understand," he said, voice low, "This town... is complicated."

He looked up, first at Kira, then Amy, then Miles.

"The people too. It never used to be this way but over the years the townsfolk have changed. They never used to be actively doing these things. Now I'm not too sure."

Miles scoffed. "So you're saying what? That the townspeople know what's going on? That they know they are acting like extras in some cheap horror movie?"

Barker gave a small, bitter smile. "Not all of them. Not most. But enough."

Kira stepped forward. "Enough for what?"

He sighed. "To keep the rituals alive. To keep the cycle going. Every few years, it stirs. And when it does, people start... remembering. Dreams. Symbols. They feel drawn to the church. They call it tradition. But it's older than that."

"And Cathy?" Kira asked. "Where did she fit in?"

"She tried to stop it," Barker said simply.

The words landed like a stone dropped into deep water.

"She was younger. You'd been sent away and were a faint memory to some. I wasn't sheriff back then, but my old man was. He said she came into the station one night; barefoot, bleeding, wild-eyed and told him she saw the ground breathe."

Kira said nothing, but her hand clenched slowly.

"She talked about fire. About figures in the trees. About a little girl consumed in fire."

Barker looked to Amy.

"She tried to get people to listen but nobody did. Or maybe they did, but they were already part of it. People called her crazy."

"Part of what?" Kira asked.

Barker's eyes darkened. "There's a place under this town. Under all of us. Something they found. Something old."

Amy broke her silence. "She told me that once."

Both Kira and Miles turned.

"You must be Cathy's other daughter." The sheriff rubbed his cheek.

Amy didn't look at them. Her voice was soft.

"She didn't say it directly. But before sending me away she said it was to protect us from something that was stirring."

"She was right," Barker said.

Miles paced once across the back of the room. He let out a chuckle. "So what we're dealing with is some buried demon? An old god? A cult?"

"All of the above," Barker said. "And none of it. I don't have the words for what it really is. Only that the ground here was never clean. That before this town, before settlers, before anything, the land was wrong. It got worse when Carson appeared." There was no humour in his voice.

Kira stared at him. "Why are you telling us this?"

"Because you've already stirred the dirt," he said. "You saw what was in Cathy's house. You found the tunnel didn't you? You've seen the people moving at night. You were never going to stay out of it. Warning you is all I can do. I owe Cathy that much."

Amy's voice dropped to almost a whisper. "They were heading underground."

"I know," Barker replied. "There's an old network of tunnels beneath town. Some were dug for mining. Others... not so much. They connect most of the houses to the church, the mayors office, the hotel, the graveyard. Places that matter to them."

He looked tired now.

Kira stepped closer. "If Cathy tried to stop it, what happened to her?"

Barker looked away.

"She got close," he said. "After she sent you two away, she was determined to bring an end to it all no matter how long it was going to take. She blamed the rituals, blamed the church for the death of her husband, James. Your stepfather."

"She discarded us." Amy said, voice flat.

Barker nodded slowly. "Maybe. Or maybe she was trying to protect you. Sometimes it's hard to tell the difference."

Kira finally sat down. "Why the church?"

"She said they were looking for a girl...You! A group of them. Claimed they were being led by the new priest who'd come to town. James stopped them. I was a minute too late. They'd already gone and he was… he was dead."

Kira sat up. "And it was them who killed James?"

Amy was quiet.

"It'd seem so. After that event, the town started to change. People started to whisper, people started to claim the town was haunted. I think that's why Cathy sent you both away. People had heard the history of the town and thought it a joke, but after that some started to take it more seriously."

Silence settled again.

Then Kira asked, "How do we stop it?"

Barker's eyes flicked toward the window, where the night pressed thick against the glass.

"I don't know if you can. We'd be better off trying to get you out of this town."

"But you just said Cathy..."

"She delayed it," he said. "But now she's gone. Something's being opened. I've felt it. The ground's been moving again. The dreams are back. The birds won't nest in the square. I've seen people walking out of their homes at night, their eyes black as coal."

Kira felt a shiver ripple through her spine then slowly turned between Amy and the Sheriff. "Why me?"

Barker shook his head. "I don't know. But as soon as you three came to town, the whisperings seemed to start."

Miles spoke. "So what now? Are you going to help us?"

Barker considered this for a long moment.

"I'd suggest you leave town now, but I think it's too late, I fear you're stuck here now. If you are, I can't fully protect you but I can show you the books Cathy gave me before she died. She didn't trust anyone else with them."

"Why can't we just leave?"

Barker shook his head. "Because the town won't let you."

Miles laughed. "You talk like the town is alive."

"I'm not saying it's not."

Barker stood.

"I think she knew you'd come back."

Kira met his eyes. "She was right."

"Try to get some rest and come back in the morning once the sun's up. I'll dig out the files and have them ready." Barker guided them towards the door. "Stay safe and don't let them know you've seen things."

CHAPTER FIVE

The motel room hadn't changed. The walls were still yellowed. The carpet still damp in one corner. The mirror above the sink had a hairline crack that ran through the reflection of anyone who looked in it. Miles sat on the edge of the bed, Cathy's old leather-bound notebook in his lap. He looked up as the girls entered holding the bags from the car.

"Anything?" Kira asked.

"Lots of rambling," Miles replied. "Some of it coherent. Some of it... not."

He flipped the book open to a page halfway through.

"She keeps referring to 'the vessel.' Over and over. She thought someone, maybe multiple people, were being used as conduits."

Amy looked uneasy.

Kira noticed. "You okay?"

Amy nodded quickly and sat on the chair near the window.

Miles continued. "Listen to this:"

> *"The town speaks through its children. Through its quiet ones. It chooses not by blood but by memory. It picks those who have been forgotten and gives them shape again."*

He looked up. "What does that sound like to you?"

"Reincarnation?" Kira guessed.

Miles shrugged. "Or indoctrination.'"

No one spoke.

Miles shut the journal quietly.

"We need to get more out of Barker," he said. "He said he had more of Cathy's records."

Kira nodded. "He said to go back in the morning. Let's just rest up and revaluate when the sun's up. If they were going to do anything to us tonight, they'd have done it by now. Surely?"

Amy stood suddenly and walked to the mirror above the sink. She stared at her reflection, the thin hairline crack splitting her face in two.

Kira watched her from across the room. "Amy?"

Amy touched the glass with her fingertips.

"I don't like it here. We should go."

Kira stood. "You're just exhausted. We all are. Give it until morning."

Amy turned, slowly and gave a sad nod.

....

They returned to the station the next morning.

The fog hadn't lifted. If anything, it had thickened, clinging to the buildings like a mould that was growing. It turned every figure into a silhouette and every shadow into a question. The town was busier with people going about their usual business, the haunted memories of the night a faint memory.

Sheriff Barker was already in his office when they arrived. He looked worse than before; less like a lawman and more like a man trying to survive. A cold cup of coffee sat untouched beside a radio that hissed softly.

He didn't greet them with a smile.

"Lock the door." he said.

Miles turned the deadbolt. Amy moved to stand near the window. Kira sat across from the desk.

"You said you had files, that you had Cathy's books." She began.

Barker nodded slowly, then reached beneath his desk and pulled out a cardboard storage box. It was old. Water-damaged along the edges. The top corner bore Cathy's name scrawled in fading ink.

He set it down carefully.

"Cathy gave this to me around a year ago," he said. "Told me not to open it unless she vanished or died. She thought someone was after her."

Kira's breath caught. "You think she was murdered?"

"I think she knew the town wouldn't let her leave and was going to do what she could to stop it all before the town stopped her."

He opened the box.

Inside were journals, smaller than the one Kira already had and a mess of yellowed papers, photographs and newspaper clippings. He pulled out the top journal and handed it to Kira.

"She started writing these after the fire."

Kira flipped through it. Dates. Symbols. Names she didn't recognize. Every few pages were marked with deep scratches across the handwriting, as if Cathy had gone back and tried to censor herself.

"What fire?" Miles asked.

Barker looked toward the window, as if remembering.

"It happened around five years ago. A small house on the south edge of town. No one lived there officially, it wasn't on any map. Locals called it the Red House. Said it was cursed. One night it just... burned. No firefighters came. No one reported it. Cathy showed up at the ruins a day later, digging through ash with her bare hands."

"And?" Kira asked.

"She found bones," he said. "Small ones. Child-sized."

Amy turned from the window slowly.

Kira's stomach dropped. "Jesus."

"She never told anyone else. Just me." Barker went on. "Said the town buried the fire like it buried everything else. But that wasn't the worst part."

He handed Kira a photo from the box. Burned and warped from the heat. But still visible.

A circular stone structure, half buried in the ground.

A ring of ash around it.

Symbols etched into the stone crude, primal markings that twisted and turned the longer you looked at them.

"This was under the house, in one of the tunnels" he said. "Cathy called it a gate."

Amy's voice was barely audible.

"It's not the only one though is it?"

Barker nodded. "No. There are others. Hidden under the buildings that hold meaning. The church, the school, the community centre. Places we gather. Places we teach. Places we feed. The biggest one is beneath the church."

"Why?" Kira asked.

"To keep us close to them," Barker replied. "To keep it fed."

Miles stepped forward, looking at the photograph. "And what is 'It'?"

Barker gave the smallest shake of his head. "Cathy called it a rot. A disease that fed on memory, pain and fear. The more you gave it, the deeper it grew."

"And the townspeople know this?" Kira asked.

"Most not consciously, but some do know." Barker said. "But something in them remembers. When the season turns, when the veil thins, they feel it in their bones."

Amy's hand moved slowly toward an envelope that sat amongst the books.

Barker saw her hesitation and nodded.

Kira watched as Amy broke the seal and pulled the contents free.

A single sheet of paper. Typed.

She read Cathy's words aloud.

If you're reading this, it means the hunger has begun to stir again. I tried to stop it with fire. But it always finds its voice again.

There was a girl once. I took her in and raised her alongside my other daughter. Gave her a new name. Hid her from the town and from herself.

But she's mine. Not really. She never was. I sent her away. I sent them both away to keep them safe.

If the veil breaks again, she'll be the first to feel it. When she remembers who she is, she'll need to make the choice.

The rest of the page was torn and missing. No one spoke. Amy folded the page and handed it back.

Kira's hands trembled slightly. "What the hell does that mean?"

"She's got to be writing about someone else?" Miles said quickly, too quickly.

Amy sat back in the chair and looked down at her hands.

"I don't think so. I think the girl is one of us. I think I might be that girl."

They all looked to her but didn't say anything.

CHAPTER SIX

The sky had turned the colour of wet ash. Even from the sheriff's station, Kira could hear the wind shifting over the rooftops, a hollow, low moan that seemed to carry more than just weather with it. Amy stood just outside the front door, unmoving. The fog pressed in around her, blurring the shape of her body like she was vanishing a little at a time.

Inside, Kira stared down at the final sentence of Cathy's letter again.

> *"When she remembers who she is she'll need to make the choice."*

She wanted to tear the page in half, or scream, or throw the whole box against the wall. But she did none of those things. Instead, she folded the letter and tucked it into the front pocket of her jacket.

Miles sat nearby, drumming his fingers against the wood grain of the desk. The phone rang and Barker went off to answer it. Miles watched him as he walked past. He strained to overhear the phone call but only heard muffled voices.

"We can't keep letting this town set the pace," Miles muttered. "We're always reacting. That's how people disappear. You've seen all the films. A group enter a town and then before long they're all dead."

Kira looked him in the eye. "The difference is we know something is up and they don't know we're onto them."

Barker placed the phone down heavily.

"I'm sorry, I've been asked to take you somewhere." Barker said from the doorway, rubbing his temple with two fingers.

"Where?" Kira asked.

"To the Mayor's office" he said. "Carson has requested to meet you. There's little point in pretending your not here."

He glanced to Amy.

"It might be best she stays here for now."

Kira nodded.

……………………..

Mayor Richard Carson's office was above the old post office, a clean, renovated space with windows that overlooked the entire square. From up there, the town looked almost normal. Brick store fronts. A dusty main road. Trees just starting to shift toward autumn. Like any place you might pass through on the way to somewhere else. Staff went about their business as usual, as if everything was normal.

Richard himself stood at the window when they entered, hands clasped behind his back, spine ramrod straight. His reflection in the glass was precise; hair combed, dark suit pressed, shoes polished to a dull gleam. He didn't turn around when the door opened.

"Alan," he said. "You always knock like you're announcing judgment day."

"Habit," Barker said hesitantly.

Richard turned.

He had a politician's smile; all teeth and posture, with nothing behind the eyes. Kira felt it the moment he faced them. That strange hollowness.

Still, he spoke warmly.

"You're Catherine's daughter," he said, extending a hand. "Kira, right?"

She hesitantly shook it. His grip was firm. Cold.

"We met at the funeral." Kira stated.

"Oh yes. How could I forget."

"This is Miles." Barker said.

Richard nodded toward him, then looked beyond them, toward the empty space in the hall. "There was another, wasn't there? Another girl?"

"She couldn't come, she's not feeling too well." Kira said quickly.

Richard's smile didn't falter. "Shame. I'd hoped to talk to her."

He gestured to the chairs arranged neatly before his desk.

"Please, sit. I won't keep you long."

Kira paused, then sat. Miles followed while Barker remained standing.

Richard took his seat behind the desk and steepled his fingers.

"Catherine and I had... differing views on this town," he said. "But I respected her. Truly. She was a woman of strong convictions."

Kira tilted her head slightly. "You mean she didn't agree with the 'traditional' methods."

Richard chuckled. "She didn't agree with my optimism. She believed in replacing rotten foundations. I believe in reinforcing them."

"She thought this town was cursed," Kira said. "You don't?"

Barker looked to Richard who's composure didn't falter.

"I think this town has scars," Richard replied. "Old ones. And like all scars, they itch from time to time. With special care they can be managed. If you give up, the scars heal badly. But curses? That sounds like something you'd tell bad children."

"She didn't give up," Kira said coldly.

Richard nodded, accepting the tension without flinching.

"No," he said. "She didn't. But she's not with us anymore."

Kira's eyes narrowed.

He leaned back, still relaxed. "I'm not your enemy. Despite what you might think. I'm just trying to keep this town from unravelling. There are lots of old tales in this town. I'd be careful how much stock you put in old stories."

"They're starting to feel pretty real," Miles said.

Richard smiled at him. "You're not from here, are you?"

"No."

"Then you can expect more of those feelings."

He gave a little wink before turning to Kira again.

"I'd very much like to see you and the other girl...Amy was it?.. again before you leave town."

Kira looked him in the eye. Something was hidden behind this facade.

"I'm sure we'll see each other again."

The conversation ended politely. Richard shook their hands again, escorted them to the door himself. But even as they stepped out into the cold, Kira could still feel his gaze.

....

Back at the station, Amy was sitting on the edge of the steps leading up to the porch when they arrived. The wind tugged gently at her hair.

"He wanted to see you," Kira said as they approached.

"I know." Amy replied.

Kira looked down at her. "How?"

Amy didn't answer.

Barker lingered by the door.

"I brought you to him so you'd see," he said. "The town doesn't work without him now. They trust him. Worship him, even. He's changed this place, shaped it. He has a way with words"

"And he's hiding something," Kira added.

Barker nodded. "Of course he is. But he's smart enough to know how to smile while he does it."

"What do you think he is?" Miles asked.

Barker chuckled. "Right now? Just a man. A dangerous one. But still a man."

"And later?"

Barker looked out across the town.

"I don't know. I never believed in demons before becoming sheriff. Now though… They're what keeps me awake at night."

....

They walked in silence back to the motel. Barker walked with them before peeling off at the corner, muttering something about a meeting with the town clerk. Kira suspected it was a lie. The way he'd avoided Richard's eyes during the meeting, the tension in his shoulders. He was afraid. Of what, she wasn't sure. But the sheriff of a place like New Grayson didn't seem to scare easy.

The town square was busy now, for the first time since they'd arrived. People moved through it in small clusters talking, carrying groceries, tending plants in rusted side-walk planters that hadn't bloomed in years. Kids ran beneath the dead oak tree near the statue, laughing as if nothing strange had ever happened here.

It looked like a normal town. It even felt like one.

Kira watched a woman pause outside the pharmacy, then slowly reach up and lay a hand against the window, palm flat, eyes shut. Just standing there, unmoving. Almost praying. A moment later, she stepped back and walked on.

Miles noticed too.

"You see that?"

"Yeah."

"That's not normal."

"No," Kira muttered to herself. "It's not."

Amy, walking a few steps behind, glanced up at a window on the second floor of the bar. A man stood behind it, watching them. He didn't look away when she noticed. Just stood, arms at his sides, face empty.

Amy didn't react.

The man turned and vanished into the room.

They reached the motel and were surprised to see the front desk was unmanned. The place felt like a relic waiting for demolition.

Kira dropped her bag by the door and peeled off her jacket. Miles had left Cathy's journal open on the small table. She stared at it for a moment, debating whether she had the energy to dig again.

Miles poured himself a glass of water and offered one to Amy, who took it. She was still looking out the window, this time toward the church. There was something about it that felt overwhelming yet comforting at the same time.

That afternoon, they walked back into town. Kira needed to move. Needed air. The motel walls were starting to feel like skin that was too tight.

They passed the diner, now glowing faintly from inside. It was the first time they'd seen it busy. Music drifted from the cracked door. A waitress swept the front step, her movements slow and mechanical. She didn't greet them, but looked up with interest as they passed.

Amy stopped outside the general store. In the window sat a row of porcelain dolls, old and stiff, each with black pinprick eyes and mouths painted into soft little ovals. One had red hair. Another had a tear trailing down its cheek.

"They weren't there yesterday when we came this way." Amy said.

"They're damn creepy. Just like everything else in this damn town." Miles muttered.

Kira nodded. "We'll get out of here tonight."

They crossed through the square. The statue of the founder stood tall, one hand raised toward heaven, the other resting on a book. Then made their way to the edge of town, past the overgrown baseball field and the old sawmill. The moon was rising now, pale and swollen behind drifting clouds. The woods whispered softly in the distance.

They turned onto another street and found themselves in front of an old, crumbling house Kira didn't recognize. But Amy stopped in her tracks.

"I've been here." she said.

Miles looked up at the darkened windows. "This place looks condemned?"

"Maybe," Amy whispered. "But I've been inside. I remember the wallpaper. It had birds on it."

Kira frowned. "Amy, we've never..."

Amy touched the rusted gate and pushed it open. "I've been here in my dreams."

It shrieked as she stepped inside the yard.

Miles glanced at Kira, but they quickly followed.

The front door was half open. The hinges snapped and sighed as Amy stepped through.

Inside, dust coated everything. Furniture covered in sheets. A fireplace choked with old ash. On the far wall: the wallpaper Amy described now faded and peeling, but still there. Tiny birds flying amongst clouds.

Kira's voice was quiet. "You really remember this?"

Amy nodded. "I played on that rug."

She pointed toward the moth-eaten carpet in the centre of the room.

Kira moved to a nearby table, lifting a photo in a tarnished frame.

It showed a woman, red-haired, holding a child with a half-hidden face. Neither smiled. Behind them, the house they now stood in.

On the back, something was written.

"Willow age 4."

Kira stared.

She dropped the photo back to the table as if it had burned her.

Miles turned. "What is it?"

"Nothing," Kira said. Too quickly.

Amy walked deeper into the house, running her fingers along the wall.

Kira stared at the photo before stepping after her, suddenly uneasy.

In the next room, Amy stopped.

A trapdoor.

Smaller than the one in Cathy's house. Older.

Covered by a thin rug.

Amy knelt.

"We shouldn't." Kira said.

"I know." Amy whispered.

She pulled back the rug anyway.

Beneath, a wood panel marked with the same sigils Kira had seen in Cathy's journal.

Symbols that made her eyes ache.

Amy's fingers hovered just above them.

Then someone spoke from the doorway behind them.

"You shouldn't be here."

They turned.

Mayor Richard Carson stood in the shadowed threshold, his hands folded behind his back.

He didn't look angry. He looked... disappointed.

"I think you should all leave. It's for your own safety, you see this place has been falling down for years. We really should just knock it down."

Miles turned, "What happened to the owner?"

"They unfortunately died many years ago. Was a horrible accident."

Kira looked to Amy then to Richard.

He pointed to the door. "Please leave."

They left the house in silence.

None of them spoke as the front door swung shut behind them, or as the rusted gate groaned closed. Amy walked a few paces ahead, her shoulders rigid, her gaze fixed forward. She hadn't said another word since Richard appeared. He walked ahead and got back in his car. He didn't leave until they'd stepped from the yard.

Kira pulled out the photo she'd quickly slipped into her coat pocket as they left.

She didn't know why. She told herself it was just evidence, something to help make sense of the strange way this town breathed beneath its surface. But deep down, it was the name that rattled her most: Willow. It was something she'd kept hidden all these years. Nobody else knew.

The way Amy had moved through the house shocked Kira and scared her more than she wanted to admit. What if she found out?

Miles walked beside her, hands buried in his jacket pockets, kicking at the loose gravel in the road.

"You okay?" he asked under his breath.

Kira nodded.

A lie.

....

They made it back to the motel just after sunset. The square had emptied again. The store fronts were still lit, but dim.

Amy went straight into the room and sat on the bed. Her hair fell in front of her face.

Kira pulled the photo from her coat and stared at it again.

It didn't make sense. Cathy had told her to keep the secret. The truth about who she was. Cathy said they needed to change her name to keep her safe. It wasn't long after that when Amy had been sent away. Kira holding the secret would follow a few years later

Miles leaned on the door frame. "We need to leave."

Kira looked up.

He'd said it with complete seriousness now. No sarcasm. No bravado. Just fact.

She nodded. "Yeah. We've stayed too long."

She crossed the room and shook Amy's shoulder gently. "Come on. We're getting out of here. Tonight."

Amy looked up, her eyes heavy. "Okay."

They packed quickly. Not that there was much to take. Kira's bag. Miles's duffel. Amy's coat. No one said goodbye to the motel. They didn't check out formally, they simply threw the keys on the counter. The attendant didn't even look up. As they walked across the lot, Kira looked back just once. The sign still glowed dimly in the darkness. But as she watched, it flickered, once, twice and went out.

Miles slid behind the wheel and twisted the key in the ignition. The engine gave a low groan. Then another. Then silence.

He tried again. This time, nothing. No click. No cough. No sign of life. Kira felt a spike of panic crawl into her chest.

"Try again."

Miles did but still nothing.

Amy sat in the back seat, arms folded tightly across her stomach. She didn't speak. She just stared out the side window, expression unreadable.

Kira leaned forward. "Battery?"

"No. We drove it yesterday, remember? Everything was fine. Nothing's been left on."

He popped the hood and climbed out. Kira followed, more out of helplessness than hope. They stared into the engine bay. Miles jiggled wires and checked the oil.

"Looks fine," he muttered.

Kira rubbed her arms. The air had grown colder. The wind had stilled. It was too quiet. Even the crickets had gone silent. Amy stepped out of the car and stood by the passenger side door.

"There's no way out," she said quietly.

Miles looked up. "We just need a jump. Or another vehicle. Or..."

"No," Amy said again. "It won't let us leave. The Sheriff was right"

Kira turned toward her. "What won't?"

Amy looked at her. "The town."

For a second, just a second, she seemed so far away. Kira stepped back from the car and ran a hand through her hair. "Okay. Okay. Let's not spiral. We walk to the station. Barker might have jumper cables, or maybe his cruiser?"

"His cruiser looked pretty banged up," Miles said. "You saw it. Tires were flat."

Kira felt her chest tighten.

"But there are cars in this town. Surely someone has a garage or something?"

No one answered her.

The square was empty. No headlights. No movement. No signs of life.

Amy said softly, "Even if someone does... do you really think they'll help?"

Kira opened her mouth to argue but stopped. She wasn't sure any more. They walked through the square, past the diner and past the church. Every window was dark now.

Kira looked up toward the second floor of the bar. The man from before, the one Amy had noticed was back watching. This time it was Kira who stared back.

His eyes never wavered.

....

At the station, the front door was locked. Barker didn't seem to be inside. There was no note on the door. Through the window they could make out a single light on in the back room flickering weakly through the office blinds.

Miles tried the door again.

"Nothing."

Amy stood by the flagpole, staring at the sky.

"The stars look wrong," she said suddenly.

Kira turned. "What?"

"They're not in the right places."

Kira looked up. They seemed normal to her. But then again... had she really been paying attention?

"Come on we need to go."

Kira stepped back from the steps.

The walk back from the sheriff's station was heavier. Not just because the building had been locked up tight, or because there'd been no sign of Barker, but because of the silence that was tightening around them. The town was quieter than it had any right to be. Even at night, a place had a rhythm; dogs barking, crickets humming, late-night traffic humming on distant roads. But New Grayson had none of that, it was simply still.

They reached the edge of the square, stopping beneath the one flickering streetlamp outside the diner.

Miles exhaled sharply and shook his head. "This is insane."

Kira ignored him. She pulled out her phone again, no bars. She hadn't expected any.

Amy sat on the curb, her arms wrapped tightly around her knees.

Kira crouched beside her. "We'll figure it out, okay? Maybe we're just being paranoid. Maybe the battery really did die."

"What about the Sheriff?"

Kira smiled. "Maybe the sheriff's just asleep. It is late."

Kira felt the chill again, sliding up her spine. The kind that made you want to look over your shoulder.

But then a noise echoed through the square. A sudden clang of metal from down the street. They all jumped.

Miles turned, fists clenched.

Another noise. A rhythmic clang–clang–clang, metal on metal, echoing up the road. It came from a squat, low building behind the gas station; a garage, lit from within by a single yellow bulb. The sound rang from somewhere behind the wide bay doors, half-open, leaking light into the dark.

Kira stood. "Come on."

Miles hesitated. "Or we could wait till morning."

Kira was already walking. "We need help to get out of here, I don't like what's going on. You got any better ideas?"

Miles shook his head and sighed as he walked behind her.

Amy followed.

They crossed the street, gravel crunching beneath their shoes. As they got closer, the sound became clearer, the deliberate hammering of metal against metal, the scratch of a wrench turning, the groan of an old engine trying to come back to life.

Kira stepped into the pool of yellow light and knocked gently on the side of the garage door. The noise stopped instantly and footsteps followed.

A moment later, the door creaked and a man stepped into view.

He was maybe in his late fifties, hair gone white but still thick, face lined with soot and age. His hands were streaked with oil, and a cigarette hung loosely from the corner of his mouth.

His name was stencilled onto his coveralls, the letters flaking from years of wear; WILLIAM.

He eyed them for a moment before exhaling a slow stream of smoke and saying, "Y'all look like you've seen a ghost."

Kira stepped forward. "We're trying to get out of town. Our car's dead and we need to get back home. We thought maybe you could help."

He raised one greasy eyebrow. "Visitors, huh? That's rare."

"Is that a problem?"

"No," he said. "Just uncommon."

He reached for a rag, wiped his hands. "You're staying at the motel?" He motioned in it's direction.

Kira nodded. "We were. Now we're trying to leave."

William scratched his jaw. "Engine dead you said?"

"Won't turn. At all. Not even a click."

"Battery?"

"Fine."

"Hmm"

William turned and walked back inside. He motioned the group to follow.

The garage was cluttered but surprisingly clean. The tools were hung in a careful order, parts were labelled in neat handwriting. An old Buick sat half-disassembled in the middle, its hood propped open, wires dangling like veins.

William moved to a battered mini-fridge and pulled out three sodas, offering them with a shrug.

Miles took his cautiously. Amy held hers without opening it. Kira shook her head with a small smile.

"I've been fixing engines here since '83," William said, settling onto a stool. "Worked on every car in this town. Every truck, too. Even the preacher's old motorcycle. It's amazing how often the town stops them from working."

He sipped from his bottle and leaned back.

"You're not the first to try and leave like this."

Kira froze. "Excuse me?"

William looked at her. Not cruel. Not mocking..

"Sometimes folks come through, think they'll stay the night and move on. Sometimes they get stuck. Car won't start. Tires go flat. Or they say roads seem to loop in on themselves in an endless maze."

Kira stepped forward. "Are you saying this happens often?"

"Not often," William said. "But enough that I don't ask questions any more. I just keep trying to fix engines and wait for the season to pass."

"What season?" Miles asked.

"Every few years around this time, things start to happen in this town." William said. "I try and stay out of it. I've been here long enough to know when to keep to myself."

He stood again and moved to a tool chest.

"Where's the car now?"

"At the motel."

William rubbed his head. "OK. I'll take a look and bring it back here. Won't promise it'll work, but if it's mechanical, I'll should be able to fix it. If it's the town, well…" He shrugged. "I'm not a priest."

"How long will it take."

William ran a hand through his hair. "Can't say but sorry to say, you aint goin' nowhere tonight."

Miles lowered his head. "Thanks."

"Come back in the morning and I'll let you know if I have any luck."

As they left the garage, Amy turned to glance back at William through the open door.

He had already returned to the Buick, leaning into the engine like nothing strange had passed between them. But Amy lingered staring back at him.

"What is it?" Kira asked.

Amy shook her head.

"Something about him feels different. I think he can help us."

Kira sighed as they made their way back to the motel. As they entered, the attendant held up their key without looking at them. Kira took it and they made their way back to the room.

CHAPTER SEVEN

The engine sat there like the carcass of a dead animal, exposed beneath the opened hood; still, cold, and silent. No oil leaks. No loose wires. No corroded terminals. Everything clean, everything intact and yet it still wouldn't start.

William leaned over the engine block, a small flash light clenched between his teeth, hands moving with quiet efficiency. He'd asked the group to stay back as he worked, and so they stood now in a semi-circle near the rear of the car, watching from a distance, like mourners at a wake.

The air was sharp with the smell of damp metal and old leaves. Early morning fog clung low across the lot outside.

Kira folded her arms, eyes flicking between William's movements and the silence of the street. She hadn't slept. None of them had. Amy leaned against the fender of the Buick raised up beside them. She hadn't said a word since they arrived. Just stared at the shadows in the corners of the garage like something might crawl out of them if she blinked.

Miles paced. He'd always needed movement to think, it usually settled him but in that moment even pacing didn't feel right. The uneasy sensation within him just wouldn't pass.

William finally straightened, stretched his back, and pulled the flash-light from his mouth. He tapped it once against his palm.

"Well," he said, voice gravel-dry. "That's the cleanest dead engine I've ever seen."

Kira stepped forward. "What does that mean?"

William glanced at her. "Means nothing's wrong. Nothing mechanical, anyway. Battery's strong, fuses good. Spark plugs fine. Starter's not jammed."

"So why won't it start?"

He shrugged, wiping his hands on a red rag that was already more grease than cloth. "Couldn't say. Might be electrical, might be environmental."

Miles stopped pacing. "Environmental?"

William met his eyes. "Town's been known to interfere with things. Like I said yesterday, weird things happen this time of year. You're the ones that came for the funeral aren't you?"

Kira nodded. "Cathy was our stepmother."

He rubbed his brow, "Been a lot of talk about you lot."

Miles stepped forward. "What about us?"

William pondered his answer carefully before answering. "Just rumblings at the moment, but they aren't good ones. You remember old Marla Cartwright?"

Kira shook her head.

"She had a brand-new hybrid brought in from somewhere out of state," William said. "Ran like a dream. Until the week after her husband died. Then it wouldn't turn over. Not even a flicker. Three days later, the car was gone. Said she woke up, went outside, and it had vanished. No tracks. No tow marks. Just... gone. Then two days after that, they found her body, cut from throat to groin."

"That's comforting," Miles muttered. "Hey. Give the engine another go."

Kira moved to the driver's side and leaned in. The key was still in the ignition. She turned it again.

Nothing. No click. No power. No resistance, even.

She turned it back, removed the key and stared at it in her hand.

"Let me ask you something," William said softly.

Kira looked up.

He gestured to the three of them. "What's it like coming back?" There was a genuine interest in his voice.

Kira glanced at Miles, then at Amy. "It's odd."

William nodded. "I figured. Everyone knew Cathy had passed but I don't think anyone expected to see you again. There were even rumours that you were dead. One day you just vanished."

"The funeral was weird," she said. "It felt like no one was actually mourning."

He raised an eyebrow. "You expected them to?"

Kira bristled. "She lived here her whole life."

"But she resisted what was happening here." William said.

Kira paused. "Resisted what?"

He didn't answer. Instead, he moved back toward the hood and dropped it closed with a careful thunk. The sound echoed too far in the morning air.

"You've seen the church," he said.

"Yes," Amy replied, her voice finally surfacing.

"You see how full it gets every night?"

Amy nodded.

William's mouth twitched. Not a smile. Not quite.

"I've been in there before. There's no sermon. No hymns. Just the preacher and a gathering of people. Stillness. Silence. Sometimes a whisper or two. Like they're waiting for someone to speak."

He moved toward the workbench and picked up a thermos, pouring coffee into a dented metal cup.

"Happens each night in this season. Has ever since the mayor came to town."

"Richard Carson?"

William nodded to Miles' question. "Yeah that's him. No-one knows where he came from. Just strolled into town many years back. He was younger back then but carried himself in a manner of someone much older. Since then he's become mayor."

He took a slow sip and exhaled.

"I'm not trying to scare you. Truth is, I've lived here long enough to know how to breathe through it. You hold your breath too long, the town'll take notice and try to take a part of you. If you panic they'll stop you."

Kira narrowed her eyes. "You're saying we should just... ignore it?"

"No," William said. "I'm saying don't provoke it unless you're prepared for what comes next."

Miles leaned against the wall now, watching him. "And what comes next?"

William drained the cup and set it down.

"Depends."

Amy tensed at that. Kira saw it and shifted.

"Why are you helping us?" she asked. "You don't seem like someone who likes visitors."

William smirked. "I don't. But I've seen what this place does to people. What it's done to the townsfolk, the people I once called friends"

He crossed the garage and pulled open a side cabinet. Inside, a row of radios, all labelled, tuned to different channels. He turned one on. Static. Another. More static. A third. Crackle, then silence.

"This town likes to cut the lines," he said. "Always has. But sometimes, something gets through."

He handed Kira a walkie-talkie. "Channel five. I'll keep mine on."

She took it and was surprised by the weight. It was heavier than she'd expected.

"If anything changes with the car, I'll let you know," he said. "I'll keep looking. But don't bet your way out on it. If you can, leave the town ASAP."

Miles shifted. "Can you drive us out with one of these cars?"

"Sorry. I do that and that's the end of old William."

"Can we buy one of the cars off you?"

William laughed. "As soon as the town knows you're trying to leave it'll stop you. Like your car over there."

"This is so messed up." Miles moved towards the door. Amy Joined him, pushing it open an inch wider. The town was waking again. One porch light at a time.

"We'll find another way. Just in case" Kira said.

William didn't answer. He just returned to his workbench and picked up a wrench.

Kira turned to the others.

"Let's go."

....

The streets of New Grayson were deceptively still and as they crossed the square once more, Kira had the distinct feeling that every window watched them. The walk back was shrouded in silence. Amy drifted ahead, her boots crunching softly along the gravel shoulder. Kira trailed close behind, holding the walkie-talkie William had handed her tight. Miles stuck close, eyes flicking across each passing alleyways like he expected someone or something to step out.

The weight of the town pressed in tighter now.

"Still can't believe the car just… stopped." Miles muttered after several minutes. "It's like something's playing with us."

"You heard William. He didn't think it was mechanical." Kira said quietly.

"Yeah, he said it was the town, I didn't think this place was going to be like being stuck in a damn Twilight Zone episode, but here we are."

Amy didn't say anything. She walked stiffly, like the air around her was weighing her down. Kira watched her back, watched her arms folded tightly over her chest.

They passed the diner. The lights were on but the door brandished a crude closed sign.

"We need to go back to Cathy's."

Miles turned to her shocked. "Why the hell would we do that?"

"I need to know the truth. Hell, we might be able to find a way out."

"Or we could just wait at the motel."

Kira went on the defence. "I feel safer on the move. Feel free to wait back there but I'm going."

Miles thought about it for a second then reluctantly nodded. Amy gave the slight impression of listening and gave a small nod.

…………………

It was a long walk but they finally made it back to Craven Lane. Amy stopped and stared across the street towards Cathy's house.

Kira followed her gaze and froze.

The curtains were moving. Just slightly, a ripple in the fabric of the front window. Then, behind it, a shape. Not distinct. Just the edge of a shoulder, or maybe an elbow. The sort of glimpse you catch when someone doesn't want to be seen but miscalculates.

"The house should be empty." Kira said. "I'm the only one with keys."

Miles stepped forward. "You sure we locked the door?"

"Positive." she replied. "I locked it myself. Turned the deadbolt. That thing stuck like hell."

They stood at the edge of the side-walk, staring. Kira ducked and started up the lawn towards the window. Miles shifted uncomfortably.

"Kira! What the hell are you doing? Let's get out of here."

Kira looked back and shook her head. "Stay quiet. If someones in there they're clearly looking for something. I need to know what that is."

Amy quickly followed and grabbed Kira by the shoulder stopping her in her tracks.

Amy's breath left a fog on the cold air. "They're inside."

Kira looked at her. "Who?"

Amy didn't respond, she just stared at the property. The house loomed in front of them. The windows were dark, save for the one at the front where the curtain had twitched. The porch was littered with dead leaves and damp with morning frost. No sound came from inside.

Kira's hand drifted to her coat pocket, where the photo still rested. She could feel the corners curled against the inside of the fabric, warm from her body.

She glanced back at Amy. "You good?"

Amy was already watching her. She shook her head.

"Don't go in." she said quietly. "It's not safe."

"It's fine, I'm just going to peek in the window. You go back to Miles."

Kira kept moving and stopped under the lit window. Glancing back she noticed that neither Amy nor Miles were on the lawn any more. With a deep breath she glanced into the window. There were two hooded figures standing next to the trap door. The door stood wide open. One of them glanced back towards the window.

Kira's heart stopped as she dropped back below the window, pressing her back to the wall awaiting the figure to open the window and find her. After a moment she let out a breath and glanced back through the glass. The figures were gone.

Panic set in and she quickly retreated back down the lawn towards where Miles had been. Where was he? There was no sign of Amy either. She scurried onto the street and suddenly stopped in her tracks.

Miles stood with a figure close behind him. Amy stood behind a car staring.

Sheriff Barker stood behind Miles, hat low over his brow, coat flared from his shoulders. He looked less tired than before… or maybe just more alert. His right hand rested on his hip near his belt, too close to his holster to be casual.

Kira held up her hands instinctively. "I saw someone… There's two people in the house."

"I know," Barker said. "But it's not your concern. You need to go."

Miles narrowed his eyes. "But someone broke in. What are they looking for."

Barker's expression didn't change. "No one broke in. Not exactly"

Kira stepped forward. "We locked the door." she was puzzled "how did you know there were people inside?"

"I'm sure you did lock the house, but it's not the only way in, is it?," Barker said, voice calm but flat. "Now move along, I'll deal with it."

Amy's voice cut through the moment like a blade.

"It's open again isn't it?"

The sheriff turned to her, a flicker of something in his eyes. Recognition revealed a guilt in his eyes. Maybe even fear.

Amy kept speaking.

"You felt it, didn't you? That shift. It wasn't there last night. But it's there now."

Barker said nothing for a long time.

Then, quietly, "You're not wrong. It's why I came down here. I suspected they'd be here and that you'd turn up."

He looked to Kira. "Go back to the motel. Stay there until I say otherwise. And don't go back in that house."

Kira frowned. "Sheriff..."

He raised a hand.

"This isn't about your mother any more. It's bigger. Cathy knew early on when to back off. Be smart and follow her example."

He turned and walked up to the door, the heels of his boots crunching the frost-bitten pathway.

Kira stared after him.

Miles cursed under his breath. "That guy knows way more than he's telling."

Kira turned to her. "What are they looking for?"

Amy nodded slowly. "Whatever it is, I think they've found it."

She didn't want that answer.

"Let's get back to the motel. Hopefully William's closer to fixing the car so we can get the hell out of here."

·················

Back at the motel, they bolted the door. Miles dumped his duffel bag on the floor and started pacing back and forth with rhythmic steps.

Kira stood at the window, pulling the curtain aside just enough to peek out, seeing nothing but hazy shadows in the fog.

Amy sat on the edge of the bed, eyes unfocused.

Miles ran a hand through his hair. "Alright. No working car. The sheriff's gone cryptic. Cathy's house is haunted. The townspeople are giving us the Children of the Corn treatment. So what now?"

Kira turned away from the window. "We need a plan."

"Great. Step one?"

"We wait until dark," she said. "Then we go back."

Miles looked up. "Seriously? Let's just head out on foot. We can just get out of here."

"Did you see how long the road here was, we wouldn't make it far. Anyway we need answers and that house is where they are."

Amy's voice drifted in, soft. "There's more beneath the house, that's how they got in."

Kira met her eyes. "The tunnel?"

Amy nodded. "It goes deeper than you think."

Miles groaned, frustratingly hitting the wall. "Of course it does."

98

Kira crossed the room, pulled Cathy's old journal from the drawer beside the bed and flipped to the middle, where strange symbols had been drawn over a map of the town. She studied the marks;

A circle was marked under Cathy's house.

Another under the Mayor's office.

A third under the house they'd stumbled upon.

And a fourth near the church, but this time instead of a circle it was a red cross.

"What are these?" she murmured.

Amy leaned forward. "Didn't the sheriff say Cathy had talked about gates. It'd make sense that these are them."

Hours went by as they worked their way through the book, trying to make sense of it all. Outside, the sun slipped behind thickening clouds. They'd received no call from William which meant they were stuck another day. The motel room had never felt safe. But that night felt worse. The air inside was still and thin. The temperature had dropped without warning, and even though the heater clicked on occasionally, it only spat out cold air, like the machine itself had been compromised.

Kira sat on the edge of the bed, fully clothed, legs tucked up, arms wrapped around her knees. Her hair was pulled back loosely, and she hadn't spoken in nearly half an hour.

Miles had given up pacing. Now he lay on the other bed, staring at the cracked ceiling, counting shadows. Amy was curled in the far corner of the room, against the window, knees pulled tight against her chest. She hadn't moved in a long while. The lamp beside her cast a halo of yellow light around her feet. She sat in the space just beyond it, like she didn't want to be fully seen.

Kira finally shifted and whispered, "Should we take turns?"

Miles didn't look at her. "Take turns doing what?"

"Keeping watch."

He laughed, short and humourless. "Sure. I'll stare at the walls and listen to the fridge hum. That'll keep the demons out."

Kira didn't reply.

Miles shrugged. " It's cool, I'll take first watch."

Amy spoke softly, eyes still fixed on the black glass of the window.

"I think we're safe for now."

Miles sat up. "What?"

Amy blinked slowly. "They're still watching but they won't come tonight."

"How can you be so sure?"

Amy shook her head. "I just feel it."

Kira stood. "We need sleep. All of us. Just a few hours."

"Easier said than done," Miles muttered.

Kira lay down on top of the covers, jacket still on, walkie-talkie clutched loosely in her hand. Amy stayed where she was, head against the wall, eyes drifting closed. Miles eventually rolled to his side and let exhaustion drag him under.

But one by one, they gave in and let the darkness consume them.

The dreams came quickly.

....

She was back in the square. All alone.

The town was lit by lanterns instead of street lights. Old oil lamps hung from hooks driven into every post, flickering wildly in the windless air. The buildings around her were twisted, warped versions of themselves. The motel was gone, replaced by a dark house with too many windows to be practical. The church loomed impossibly tall, its steeple lost in the clouds.It's imposing visure casting an almost unending shadow across the town.

Kira turned in slow circles, heart pounding.

From every corner of the square, people emerged.

Dozens of them. Hundreds. Faces blank, movements synchronized. Like dolls wound up on the same invisible key. They walked in a wide circle around her, slow and soundless, their feet not quite touching the ground.

She called out for Miles and for Amy but her voice made no sound.

Then the church bell rang.

Each ring felt like a heavy thud in her chest, again and again, like someone beating on the inside of her ribs. It felt like the ground rumbled with every beat.

The crowd stopped.

Every head turned.

Every eye focused on her.

And then, from the steps of the church, a single figure descended.

A man.

Face shadowed by a deep hood.

She wondered if it was Richard?

It looked like Richard but it wasn't him. Something was off, it felt like something had taken his form.

When he looked up his smile stretched too far and blood dripped from his hollow eyes.

He walked toward her and raised one hand.

Not in greeting.

In command.

The crowd surged towards her.

……………………

Kira woke up with a gasp, heart slamming in her chest, her top dripping with sweat.

She looked around the motel room, it was dark. Still. The heater clicked again and blew some cold air into the room.

Amy was sitting on her bed awake too, sweat beading on her brow. Miles stirred beside her, muttering something in his sleep. She slid off the bed and stood, legs unsteady.

Kira looked at her. "You too?"

Amy nodded.

They didn't need to compare notes.

The town had touched both of them and gotten into their minds.

Kira stood and moved toward the curtain. She pulled it back an inch. Outside the window, something passed under the streetlamp. Too fast to identify, too slow to be ignored. A figure walked across the lot. A man dressed in dark clothes, face turned toward the door. He paused. Looked at the building. Then kept walking.

Kira stepped away from the window.

Amy turned. "Was it him?", she shook with worry.

Kira didn't answer.

Miles stirred again and sat up. "What time is it?"

"Just after five." Kira said.

He muttered something indecipherable, rubbing his eyes.

Amy crossed the room and sat on the edge of Kira's bed.

"I think I saw myself," she whispered.

Kira looked at her. "What?"

"In a dream. But not me now. I was younger and hurt. I was burning. But I wasn't afraid. Not exactly. I felt strong."

Kira picked up the journal from the table, opening it again to the page marked with the tunnel map. Her finger hovered over the circle beneath Cathy's house.

"The tunnel has to lead somewhere important."

Amy touched the circle. "We could just leave. It's not safe here."

"Nor is it out there. If they killed Cathy, I need to know why."

"But..."

Kira placed her hand on Amy's thigh. "We need to go back. You know we do."

Miles groaned. "Can't we just go when the suns fully up?"

"We're not going to sleep," she said. "Not after all that's happened and if someone's been inside Cathy's house, then whatever was sealed down there… probably isn't sealed any more. Anyhow if the tunnels spread under the whole town maybe they also lead out of it. They could be out best route of escape."

She slipped on her jeans and zipped her jacket as she moved toward the door. Miles ran a hand through his hair and said, "Great! The town's screwing with our heads now."

He stood and crossed to the window. Pulled the curtain aside.

Then froze.

Kira looked up. "What?"

"Come here."

Amy stood with her. All three of them gathered at the window. The street outside wasn't empty.

People moved through the mist slow, quiet, deliberate. No voices. No chatter. Just bodies, wrapped in coats and shawls, stepping carefully along the side-walk. Headed towards the church.

It was still dark.

Kira stepped back. "Where are they going?"

Amy answered before she could stop herself. "The church."

Miles blinked. "What the hell are they doing in there at this time?"

Kira didn't answer.

"We know there's something going on. We're following them and this time we're not losing them."

Miles's head whipped around. "What? No. Absolutely not. What happened to going to Cathy's house to find and exit?"

Kira was already pulling on her jacket. "Plans change."

"Yeah. They change when you realize you're suicidal." he shot back.

Amy reached for the walkie-talkie and tucked it into her pocket. "You're scared."

"Damn right I am," Miles snapped. "This town's acting like a beehive after someone kicked it. You two want to just stroll through it like nothing's wrong?"

Kira walked to the door. "If something's happening before dawn, it means they're trying to keep it secret. That means we need to see it."

Miles stared at her. "So what? We go on full spy mission? Sneak up behind them and hope no one notices? Why can't we just leave now? What is your obsession with following them? What do you expect to find."

Amy was already at the door. "It's OK, they won't see us."

"Why not?"

She looked back.

"Because they're not awake."

Outside, the air was heavier.

Still fog-drenched, not cold now but thick and damp.

They stuck to the side streets.

The townsfolk moved slowly, but purposefully in a line of silent figures in coats and gloves, heads bowed and eyes glassy. Not speaking. Not blinking. Not aware of anything else around them.

"They're so quiet" Kira whispered.

"They're not conscious. Not in the way we are. They're moving through instructions, not decisions."

Miles muttered, "You're scaring the hell out of me. How do you know all of this?"

She shrugged. "I just feel it."

They ducked behind a trash bin near the library and waited for another group to pass.

Amy's hand found the walkie in her pocket without thinking, her thumb hovering over the side.

No static, no signal, just dead air.

They moved again, this time cutting behind the diner and crossing through the alley behind the hardware store. The closer they got to the church, the more people they saw converging from every direction.

"Look," Amy whispered, pointing at the wide open doors of the church.

Candles lined the steps. The townspeople stood, shoulder to shoulder, heads down, facing the doors but not moving inside.

Miles crouched low beside them behind the hedge. "What are they waiting for?"

Amy blinked slowly then pointed, her hand shaking. "Him."

A man in an all black cloak stepped out of the church holding two pictures in his hands.

"Shit." Miles sees who the pictures are of. "Why do they have pictures of you two? It's like they're hunting you like some 'Running Man' shit."

Kira's nerves hit her. "I don't know but I've changed my mind."

Miles glanced surprised. "That was easy. What about going to Cathy's?"

"Screw the mysteries, we need to leave now." She glanced at Amy then back at the church.

Satisfied, Miles started to move away. "You sure? After all that talk at the motel about needing answers? You said the tunnels could be a way out."

"They'll know that's where we'd go. They've been a step ahead this whole time. Lets not play into their game. Let's go back to the garage."

Miles and Amy nodded.

They didn't speak again until they were three blocks away from the church.

Even then, it was only in short whispers.

Kira stopped beneath the skeleton of an old lamppost and turned to Amy and Miles, her voice trembling from more than cold. "Did you see their eyes?"

"It was like they were asleep, like they were dreaming," Amy said.

Miles exhaled. "What the hell? It was like some town-wide trance?"

Amy's eyes flicked toward the east. Dawn was only now beginning to threaten the sky, a thin line of light blooming above the treeline.

"We need to get back to the garage. We need to get out of here and I'm hoping one of those cars starts." Kira looked to the others.

Amy looked down the road that led back to the motel. Then to the path winding east toward the garage. Kira saw it in her posture, she was about to break away.

"No!" Kira said immediately. "We're not splitting up. Not now."

Amy looked at her. Calm. Firm. "We need Cathy's journal. It's still on the table."

Kira frowned. "We already went through it. It's not worth our lives."

"There's more. There's something she left in it... something I didn't understand before. But I think I might now. I need to see the book."

Miles interjected, "The motel's only a few blocks. Let's all go. Then we get back to William."

Kira looked between them the weight of decision heavy in her chest. But something in Amy's voice, her stillness, her clarity it told her she'd already made up her mind.

"We don't all have time to loop back. Not if we want to get out before sun-up" Amy said. "Not all of us. You two head to the garage. William might have more answers. Hopefully he has the car working."

"What if it's not?" Miles said.

Kira hesitated. "Amy..."

"We'll meet at the garage. Give me half an hour."

Kira's instincts screamed against it. Some part of her felt the town was trying to split them apart. Maybe this was inevitable. She reached out and touched Amy's shoulder. "If you're not there by sunrise, we'll come find you."

Amy nodded and then, without another word, she turned and headed down the motel road at a fast jog, swallowed gradually by the mist curling low across the asphalt.

Kira watched her go until she couldn't see her any more.

She took a deep breath then turned to Miles.

"Let's go."

....

They moved fast, not running, but close.

The town had changed again. Not physically. The buildings were the same, the roads unchanged. But the feeling had shifted.

It felt like they were in a cage with external forces moving and pushing them in different directions. It felt like they were pawns in a much larger game.

Miles kept scanning every alley, every shadow. "You know splitting up was a terrible idea, right?"

"She's right, though." Kira said. "That journal… I don't think Cathy told us everything in it and Amy's the only one who seems to *understand* it."

Instead, she asked, "Do you trust her?"

"What? Amy?"

"Yeah. She's my sister, I trust her with my life. What's wrong with you?"

Miles took a few seconds to reply.

Then. "I don't think she's lying. But I don't think she's telling us everything, either."

Kira frowned. "What makes you say that?"

He stopped walking for a second, his voice lowering. "Back at the house, when she saw the wallpaper, the rug, that trapdoor... she didn't react like someone seeing something for the first time. She reacted like someone remembering it."

Kira's stomach tightened.

Miles added, "And that photo, the girl, Willow was it? Red hair? She looks just like Amy."

Kira looked away and continued down the road.

....

Back at the motel, Amy moved quickly. She'd made it in good time and had luckily avoided bumping into any townsfolk. The air was colder and still. Like the calm before an upcoming storm.

She unlocked the door to the room. Inside, it looked untouched. She moved to the night stand and picked up Cathy's journal. The smaller one. The one she hadn't finished reading.

She flipped to the page Cathy had marked with a ribbon a simple red thread, frayed at the end.

Words in her Cathy's fluid handwriting:

> *If she finds this, it means I've failed again.*
> *But maybe I've bought enough time for her to*
> *understand.*

Amy flipped the page.

A drawing.

It showed the town from above, not a map, but a *vein-work* of buildings and tunnels and roots. The centre of it was marked with a single symbol: a triangle, filled with ash.

Then, in Cathy's shaky script:

> *They need the girl.*
> *She holds a role.*
> *It's always been her.*

Amy closed the book with her trembling hand. From somewhere nearby outside the motel she heard the sound of a door creaking open very slowly.

....

At the same moment, Kira and Miles reached the garage.

The bay door was cracked open slightly. The light inside was on, flickering yellow through the fog.

William's tools were laid out across the workbench like he'd stepped away mid-project.

Kira stepped in first, calling out softly, "William?"

No response.

Miles moved to the Buick he'd been working on. It hadn't changed. Still lifted, still half-disassembled. But something felt wrong.

There was oil on the floor but smeared, not spilled. A shape that looked like a handprint dragged crossed through it.

Kira walked toward the far corner, where the radio bank sat. Every single unit was on, their lights illuminating the darkened corner. All of them crackling with white noise.

Kira looked back to Miles.

His face was pale. "I think we're too late."

"No," she said. "We don't know that. Check the cars, I'll keep looking for William."

She reached for the walkie-talkie that sat on the table. It had blood on it.

………………..

Back at the motel, Amy stepped outside the room, the journal clutched tight to her chest.

Across the road, near the edge of some trees, three figures stood. They were dressed all in black. Watching and waiting. One of them turned and looked directly at her and raised their arm to point. The other clutched a burning candle to their chest.

Amy's heart pounded in her chest as she started to move. She saw them start to follow, causing her to break into a sprint.

Footsteps followed her through the haze.

110

CHAPTER EIGHT

The air in William's garage no longer smelled like oil and old rubber. A new smell had taken over with a visceral iron-like odour to it. Miles covered his nose with his sleeve.

"You smell that?"

Kira glanced over and nodded. She stood in the centre of the room, one boot in the smudge of oil that had been streaked across the concrete. Her eyes moved over the dark smear, long and curved with slight grooves tracking through them like nails trying to grip for purchase.

Miles crouched beside the workbench, fingers ghosting over the scattered tools. "I don't see anything over here. No blood." he muttered. "No signs of a struggle."

Kira didn't move. "There's blood on the walkie over there." She pointed. "There's also these handprints. Looks like someone was dragged."

That made Miles look up. "It makes no sense. Why would they attack William?"

"Maybe they knew he was helping us try and get out of here."

She turned and stared at the back of the garage, where the walls had been lined with stencilled signs each a make or model of some car he'd worked on: CADILLAC... FORD... CHEVY... MERCEDES...CHEVY...

She froze.

There were two Chevy signs. One wasn't stencilled it was hand-painted. As she looked closer the V in the 2nd Chevy sign looked almost like an arrow.

She stepped closer.

Kira glanced over her shoulder. "Miles."

He walked over. "What?"

"These signs. They're repeating."

He looked at them. "Maybe he just had extras? It doesn't automatically mean there's some hidden agenda."

111

"No," she said. "Look at the wall. The nails. This one was moved. Recently."

There were faint dusty outlines around the other signs. But the second Chevy one was different. Fresh. Sharp. Clean.

Kira lifted it from the wall and stepped back, taking in the wall again.

Then she noticed something.

Beneath the sign scratched into the drywall was a symbol. Not letters. Not numbers. But a shallow carving. Like someone had dragged a nail through the paint quickly and desperately. It matched one of the symbols from Cathy's journal. It was a gate mark.

Kira touched it and pieces of the wall flaked off in her hand.

Miles stood beside her now, watching.

"You think William put that there?"

"Or someone wanted us to think he did."

"Okay, well, I'm not fluent in ancient graffiti, but that looks like something we shouldn't be touching."

Kira turned to the radio bench and stepped towards it.

All of the radios were still on. Static humming, gentle but constant. Then, slowly, the frequency shifted. Words began to form.

A voice. Muffled. Warped. Low and rhythmic.

It repeated a phrase over and over:

> "One to open... one to hold... one to feed."

Then silence.

Kira backed away from the radios.

Miles stared at them, pale. "What the hell was that?"

"I don't know," she whispered. "But it wasn't William and it sure as hell wasn't Amy."

They turned at the sound of footsteps, soft, just outside. Kira reached for the wrench on the table, lifting it without thinking. The metal was cold and heavy in her hand. The footsteps stopped.

Then came a knock.

Just one.

Miles moved to the door, motioning for Kira to hold still. He peered through the gap between the garage door and the wall. A woman stood outside. Not someone he recognized. Elderly, in a black shawl, her eyes were like dark marbles. She just stood there motionless, staring. Then, without blinking, she turned and walked back toward the square.

"Okay," Miles said slowly. "I think we're officially being stalked by funeral ghosts now."

Kira lowered the wrench. "I don't think she was just here for us."

"Then who?"

Kira looked around the garage again and then it hit her. "She was checking if someone was still here."

Miles frowned. "William?"

Kira nodded "or Richard."

Miles ran both hands through his hair, pacing again. "Where the hell is he?"

"I think he was taken," Kira said. "Maybe into the tunnels beneath the town."

He looked toward the rear wall. "You think there's an entrance here?"

Kira nodded. "I think so. The symbol over there was one of the ones from the journal. It's got to be hidden somewhere."

She crossed to the other side of the garage, pushing aside a low shelf packed with old hubcaps and fuses. Behind it was a wall of what looked like solid concrete. But one panel was darker than the rest. Pressed into it, barely visible in the shadows, was a handprint.

Kira carefully and hesitantly pressed her palm to it.

"What the hell are you doing?" Miles stood behind her.

She was about to answer when suddenly the wall clicked then shifted. A small square panel recessed with a groan, revealing a narrow chute angled downward not quite stairs but not quite a slide. More like a maintenance access tunnel, lined with iron rungs.

Miles groaned. "You've got to be kidding me."

"Get a flash light."

Miles went rummaging and eventually retrieved one from a toolbox. Flicking it on he aimed it into the chute. It disappeared a few metres into the darkness. Kira turned back toward the walkies and noticed the static had stopped.

She looked at Miles.

"I don't think this is a good idea."

"Me neither."

....

Meanwhile, across town, Amy ran with the journal held against to her chest. The figure with the candle hadn't followed her for long, but she noticed others watching from windows and porches as she passed their properties.

No-one moved, they simply watched as she passed.

She reached the edge of the square and ducked behind the fountain, breathing hard. The sun still hadn't risen but the sky was slowly brightening up.

Amy stopped behind a low wall and desperately flipped open the journal to the drawing of the town's veins. Her finger hovered over the image until it settled on the triangle of red ash at the centre.

....

The tunnel yawned open in the back of the garage, a narrow vertical shaft lit only by the trembling beam of Miles's flash light. Cold air breathed from within, carrying with it a scent that made Kira's throat tighten. It wasn't rot nor damp.

It was ash.

They stood frozen for a long moment, the silence pressing tighter with every second. Then a sound broke it. The slow groan of old hinges. The hinges of the garage door.

Kira spun. Miles clicked off the flash light. instinctively. They backed into the darker rear of the room, behind the Buick's shadow.

Another sound echoed throughout the room.

Footsteps. Deliberate and slow.

Kira crouched low. Her heart hammered so loud in her chest that she was certain the intruder would be able to hear it. Covering her mouth with her palm, she backed further into the shadows.

The footsteps stopped and a taut silence.

Then a voice rang out. One that was eloquent and well spoken.

"Isn't it strange..." it said, calmly, "... how the night feels more awake than the day?"

Kira's stomach dropped as Miles mouthed the intruders name silently: *Richard.*

She nodded and motioned for him to stay quiet.

The mayor stepped fully into the garage, a tall silhouette against the shifting glow of the outside streetlamp. He wore a long black coat, buttoned perfectly. His posture was impeccable. He looked like a man returning from a church meeting but his face was hidden behind an ornate mask. His eyes sat recessed and black.

"I used to come here..." he said conversationally, walking further inside. "...William did good work. Reliable. Uninterested in gossip. Those are rare traits in a town this old."

He reached the workbench and ran a hand across the tools.

He lifted a wrench, examined it, then set it back in it's place with surgical precision. Behind the Buick, Kira and Miles didn't move. Richard cocked his head slightly as he studied the room. Miles clenched his jaw tight.

Kira's hand slid slowly into her pocket gently touching the old photo.

Richard turned. He was closer now. No sound had marked his steps. His voice softened.

"William made the mistake of thinking he could change the inevitable. It was an honourable thing he did, trying to help you. But he should've known better then most that there is no escape."

He walked toward the rear of the car.

"I know you're still in here."

Kira's breath caught.

"We've been watching," Richard said gently. "From the moment you returned. The town doesn't forget it's own. You're one of us even if Cathy tried to bury any evidence. The town has put a lot of energy into keeping you here."

He stopped a couple of feet from their hiding spot.

Then, quietly: "The problem is, everything buried eventually digs its way back up."

He lunged around the Buick.

Kira shoved Miles backward as Richard's hand swept down like a striking serpent unnaturally fast, with a knife in his hand. The Buick shuddered as his knife slammed into the bodywork.

They scrambled away.

Miles grabbed a crowbar from the workbench as they bolted toward the side door. Kira hit it first, yanking it with all her might. She heard a chain on the other side rattle as it kept the door shut.

"No!" she gasped.

"Back!" Miles shouted.

Richard stepped into view again.

His coat shifted with the movement beneath.

"What do you want?!" Miles shouted, holding the crowbar between them.

Richard didn't answer. He only stared at Kira. Not at her face but inside her. It didn't feel like he was even looking at her, more that he was looking inside her soul, trying to see something hidden deep in the darkness.

"I only want what I require. What the town requires." he said.

He stepped forward.

Miles swung the crowbar but Richard caught it in his free hand. He shouted in pain as Richard twisted the metal, wrenching it from his hands and sending him stumbling backward. Kira grabbed a can of brake fluid and hurled it striking Richard in the side of the face. He barely flinched and turned and looked at her again.

Kira bolted for an escape. Miles was close behind her, bleeding from the hand where the metal had cut him open. They rounded the Buick again and dove for the tunnel hatch in the rear of the building.

Kira went first, down the rungs as fast as she could go.

Miles followed.

Behind them, the sound of footsteps resumed. Slow and patient.

....

The rungs were cold and wet with something that clung to Kira's hands, like oil but smelled faintly metallic. She descended quickly, breath ragged in her throat, the metal shuddering under her weight. Behind her, Miles cursed as he descended one-handed, his other arm pressed under his armpit.

Kira reached the bottom of the slope and felt it drop away as she dropped into the tunnel below.

It was narrower than she'd expected. The air stale, and the dirt walls were wet with condensation. Wooden support beams arched overhead every few yards, marked with symbols burned into the grain. The ground sloped downward steadily.

Miles stumbled beside her a second later with a grunt.

"You okay?" she whispered.

He held up his hand. His fingers were streaked with blood, the veins already darkening just beneath the skin.

"I'll live." He lied a fake smile and continued onward. They moved quickly down the ever darkening tunnel.

A sudden echoed thud made them turn in panic. Someone else landed on the tunnel floor behind them.

Miles spun. "Go! Move!"

They ran. The flash light beam jittered with every step. Roots jutted from the ceiling like crooked fingers and water dripped from the roof. The dirt turned to old stone under their feet, then back to dirt again as the tunnel twisted once, then again. They were no longer on a straight path, the tunnel had turned into a maze that was guiding them somewhere.

"Where the hell does this go?" Miles hissed under his breath.

Kira didn't answer.

They passed a wall of sigils carved into wood. The flash light caught something; a child's handprint, smeared in soot, beneath one of the symbols. Kira stopped for a second.

Miles grabbed her arm. "What're you doing?"

Behind them, something scraped along the wall. Like someone dragging metal across rock.

"Look at the handprint."

"What?" Miles grabbed her arm. "We need to keep moving."

Kira hesitated before relinquishing behind him.

The tunnel opened into a small open chamber, circular, with a shallow pit at the centre. Other tunnels led off in other directions. Burn marks ringed the floor. Bones; animal or human, she couldn't tell, had been arranged in spirals, leading inward.

Kira skidded to a stop.

Miles looked around. "This looks like a ritual site."

The flash light flickered, then steadied.

Kira paused as she looked at chains bolted to the pit. "No. It looks more like a holding room."

She hesitated then looked at a rock where names had been scratched into the stone, layer upon layer. They looked like they'd been carved using rock. One jumped out at her.

WILLOW.

Not once. But over and over, scratched again and again into the surface like a child practising writing their name.

"She's been here," Kira murmured.

Miles looked at her. "Who?"

She shook her head. "The girl from our dreams." She turned to Miles then gasped. Behind the rock was the body of William, his face cut and his body broken. Miles tried to shield her but she pushed past.

"What did they do to him?"

Miles grabbed her shoulder. "We need to find a way out."

A sound came from the tunnel behind them. Richard's voice rung out from the darkness.

"Everything worth burying has roots."

Kira turned fast as Richard stepped into the chamber. He was still in his long coat but his face was no longer hidden behind a mask.

He raised his hand.

"I told you," he said. "The town isn't cursed. It's protected."

Miles grabbed a rock from the floor, small enough to swing but big enough to do some damage.

Richard stepped closer with no hesitation.

"The deeper you go," he said, "the more of yourself you forget. Until the town fills in the missing pieces."

Then, he moved… Fast. Too fast.

He crossed the chamber in seconds. Miles swung and smashed the rock into Richard's shoulder.

Richard grabbed Miles's arm and pulled it with a crack. Miles screamed as his wrist snapped as it twisted the wrong way. Kira charged and slammed the flash light into the side of Richard's head. It shattered in an explosion of plastic and a brief spark. The room was swallowed in darkness. Miles collapsed to the floor, cradling his ruined hand.

Kira backed up blindly. Then a voice beside her ear;

"You never were the one I wanted. But you were the one the town craved."

A hand reached for her.

"I should've never have let you get away."

The chamber filled with new smells. Fire, ash and something like burned honey.

Richard hissed.

Kira frantically reached around until she grabbed Miles. "Let's go." She dragged him back to the tunnel they came down as Miles turned the light on his phone on to give them some semblance of light.

Richard wasn't done with them.

They scrambled through the tunnel until they reached the chute. The metal shook under Kira's hands as she hauled herself and Miles back into the garage. They emerged gasping, filthy, slick with blood and dirt. The morning light should have greeted them through the open garage door, but the sky was gray and still. Kira helped Miles to his feet but he stumbled and fell against the Buick, groaning.

"You're okay," she whispered, wrapping an arm around his waist. "We're out. You're okay."

He didn't answer. His breathing was shallow. His face had gone paper white, and the blood soaking beneath his hand holding his shattered wrist still ran dark.

Kira scanned the garage. There was no-one else there.

The hatch slammed shut behind them. Kira whirled around expecting to see Richard but he wasn't there. Her eyes darted to the ceiling as the lights flickered, settling into a dimmed, rust-colored glow.

She backed toward Miles. "Something's wrong."

"I noticed," he muttered, voice weak.

Footsteps sounded from behind the Buick.

Kira grabbed a screwdriver from the nearest shelf and turned face to face with Richard Carson.

He stood unnaturally observing them. His arms hung at his sides, a large hunting knife gripped tightly in his hand. Richard's presence reeked of evil.

His voice, however, was still warm. Still rich and even.

"You put up a good chase. I must say I'm impressed"

She held up the screwdriver like a blade.

He stepped around the Buick.

Kira backed away.

Miles struggled to stand, then collapsed again.

Kira shouted to him. "Stay back!"

Richard paused. Kira could make out a faint smile beneath shadows of his face.

"My little Willow, I never thought you'd come back but I'd hoped. You can't hide from your fate. It was always going to end this way."

He moved suddenly.

Kira stabbed the screwdriver down quickly, sinking it deep into his back as she twisted around him but it wasn't deep enough. He didn't flinch. Instead, he grabbed her by the elbow and squeezed shattering it in his palm.

She screamed.

Miles shouted something, unintelligible, choked in pain and panic as he pulled himself up with his good arm. He frantically fumbled around trying to find anything to use as a weapon. He hurled a toolbox at Richard but it clattered at the mayors feet.

Richard turned slightly.

"Loyal until the end." he mused. "It's admirable. Misguided. But admirable."

Kira yanked her arm free and shoved a metal cart between them knocking him backwards slightly. She grabbed a wrench and swung wildly. Richard caught it mid-air and twisted it from her grip like it was a toy.

His voice dropped, colder now.

"You don't belong here. I can give you freedom."

He stepped forward.

Kira stumbled back, shielding Miles with her body.

Then he moved. So fast she didn't see the hit. She only felt it.

A sharp stabbing sensation in her chest.

She looked down.

Richard's hand gripped his blade. It was buried deep into her sternum. She feebly tried to grab it as she coughed. Blood spattered her lips as her life quickly started to drift away.

Miles screamed her name as he reached out to help her. Time felt like it paused in that moment. Kira felt everything around her fading but something caught her eye. She turned. Richard's anger faded as his eyes followed hers, panic shot through them.

A silhouette stood in the door way watching them.

....

Amy stood framed in morning light. The journal clutched tight to her chest. Her eyes wide. Her mouth slightly open.

She saw Kira first. The blood dripping from her mouth and the expression of stunned pain. Then she saw him and something inside her froze. Not because she recognized it as Richard. But because he seemed to recognize her.

Richard's eyes widened just slightly as he studied at her.

His blade withdrew from Kira. Her body collapsed to the floor like a discarded sack, as she choked on her final breath.

Amy froze.

"No," she whispered.

Richard didn't move, didn't speak. For the first time, he simply stared, speechless.

Not like a killer and not like a predator. But like a man who'd just seen someone he'd been waiting for all these years and had just realised he'd made a big mistake.

"Amy," Miles rasped from the floor. "Run."

But she didn't run. She stepped forward.

Her knees trembled. Her breath shook. But her feet moved anyway, eyes locked on Kira's body.

"Kira?" she whispered.

Kira didn't answer. Her body lay in a crumpled heap amongst her blood.

Richard turned toward Amy fully now. His head tilted slightly.

"Impossible." he murmured.

Amy took another step.

"You..." he said, voice quieter now, reverent even. "You can't be her."

"I don't know what you're talking about."

He stared at her and for a moment, he seemed truly confused. He looked down at Kira's body then back at Amy.

"Cathy took her in. She was…" He was panicking. "What did you…?"

Amy's breath caught. "I didn't... I didn't do anything."

Richard stepped forward once.

Amy backed away.

"Get away from her!" Miles screamed.

He tried to stand, but his arm crumpled again under his weight .

Richard stopped and looked down at Kira's body, then to Miles.

Then back to Amy.

"I thought she was the vessel, the one that got away." he said, almost to himself. "But you..."

Amy clutched the journal tighter.

"I don't know what you mean." she said again.

Richard smiled. Not mocking. Almost… apologetic.

"Deep inside you know what you are."

He took another step toward her.

Amy's hands trembled. Just faintly.

Richard saw the journal in her hands and stopped.

His smile vanished.

"You don't even know what you're holding." he said.

Amy looked down at the book.

Then back at him. He seemed to be panicking.

"It's too soon. I need to change things now." he said.

Then he turned and walked into the shadows of the garage before vanishing. Like a curtain had been drawn over him. Just like that he was gone.

Amy dropped to her knees beside Kira and began to cry.

PART II:

Sometimes, you only hear the truth once the door is locked behind you.

CHAPTER NINE

Amy cradled Kira's head in her hands, tears cascading down her cheeks.

Miles dragged himself closer. Kira's eyes were half-open, staring at nothing. Amy touched her hand. It was still warm but the warmth was fading.

"I'm sorry," she whispered.

Miles said nothing as he looked at Amy.

Kira coughed blood and began to choke. Amy held her close.

"What can I do?"

Kira tried to move her arm but it dropped feebly by her side. The choking stopped and her head rolled to the side. Amy tried turning her head back.

"No! You can't leave me. No!" She pulled Kira into her chest tight and cried.

Miles looked on, tears of his own forming in his eyes. They sat in silence for a while until Miles broke it.

"Amy! What was that?" he asked. "Why didn't he attack you?"

She looked up from Kira's body. "I don't know."

"You're not telling me everything."

Amy didn't respond because she didn't know what to say. She didn't fully understand it either. What was so special about Cathy's journal? Special enough that it seemed to stop Richard from attacking. She didn't know, nor did she know why Richard, the mayor, the killer, the thing in a man's skin had looked at her like she wasn't prey…but more like a prophecy. He'd been shocked.

Amy didn't move for a long time.

The garage was quiet. The echoes of Richard's retreat had faded into nothing. The only sounds were the slow, uneven breaths of Miles and the faint buzz of one dying light above them.

Kira's body was still. Her limbs limp by her sides and her face frozen mid-breath.

Amy sat beside her, knees drawn to her chest, hands locked around them. The journal lay on the floor nearby, untouched.

She had no more tears to shed. Her body was still full of shock, her mind tangled. The image of Richard with his knife inside Kira's chest and his voice like silk over steel refused to fade. His words spiralled in her mind;"You can't be her."

What did that mean?

Who had she been supposed to be?

Why had he looked so confused? So… reverent?

Amy looked back at Kira. Her friend, her sister, the one who had always protected her and the one Amy thought was going to get them out of this place.

Gone.

Just like that.

Miles groaned nearby. He'd crawled and propped himself against the wall, blood drying on his shirt, his broken wrist held gingerly in his lap. His face was drawn tight, pale with shock and pain.

"I should've done more," he muttered.

Amy looked at him.

"You couldn't have," she said.

He looked up, eyes glassy.

"I tried," he said.

"I know."

They fell into silence again. The light above them flickered once then died. In the quiet, another sound crept in. Faint and distant.

Footsteps. Lots of them.

Amy stiffened and Miles pushed himself upright with a hiss of pain. "They're coming."

Amy looked around worried.

"What do we do?" he asked.

She didn't answer right away. She looked at Kira one more time, then reached down and gently closed her eyes.

Then she stood.

"We hide," she said. "Then we find a way out of this place."

··················

The footsteps grew louder by the second. No voices accompanied them. Just shoes on pavement, boots on gravel. Heavy and purposeful. Amy grabbed the journal and slid it into a discarded satchel on the workbench. Then she moved quickly to the far side of the garage, scanning the walls.

"There has to be somewhere to hide or a way out."

Miles limped behind her. "What about the tunnel?"

"What tunnel?" Amy looked back at him confused. Miles pointed to the back wall and the chute he and Kira had traversed.

"Back there. It leads to a chamber. There's tunnels branching off in all directions. Richard chased us down there."

She turned back and ran her hand along the concrete wall.

"If Richard knows what's down there, I'd put money on the others knowing too. We need to find another way, fast."

Symbols had been scratched on the wall, shallow and faded like William had tried to record something before it'd all gotten worse. Amy didn't recognize them, not consciously, but her fingers trembled as she touched them. She moved aside a pile of stacked tires and found a narrow wooden panel, barely distinguishable from the wall. No handle. No hinges. Just a seam.

She found purchase with her fingers and pulled. It shifted slightly revealing a space behind, barely three feet wide.

"Help me with this," she whispered.

Together, painfully, quietly they pulled the panel free and saw a narrow passage that ran behind the garage wall. Dust filled the air and the ground sloped slightly upward.

Miles hesitated. "Where does it go?"

"I don't know. But it doesn't seem to go down to the tunnels you mentioned."

She nodded towards the front, just as shadows moved past the garage windows. Dozens of figures were coming for them.

Amy frantically grabbed a worn satchel from the table and threw it over her shoulder. With one glance back they ducked inside the crawlspace and pulled the panel closed behind them, sealing themselves into darkness.

....

The crawlspace was tight. The air stale and thick with dust.

They crawled slowly, Amy first, dragging the satchel, followed by Miles, whose breathing grew heavier with each yard. The narrow walls scraped their arms and backs. Branches hung down like wires, piercing the shell of the garage.

Amy and Miles didn't speak. Every sound they made, the rustle of fabric, the catch of breath, the groan of a joint echoed through the darkness.

After what felt like an eternity, the crawlspace bent sharply to the left and ended with a grate.

Amy pressed her face to it.

Beyond it was another room unfamiliar, but wider than the garage. A workroom of some kind. There were old tools, blueprints on the walls, boxes stacked high. She couldn't see the whole thing, but it looked safe, or at least safer then the garage.

She pushed gently on the grate. It creaked, freezing her in place as she waited for any other noise.

Another push and the grate gave way.

She slipped through and helped Miles squeeze after her, groaning as he collapsed to the floor.

Amy pulled the grate shut behind them. The room was lit by a single high window, slanted and narrow. It was barely dawn now, the first true light of day they'd seen since entering the town. At the far side of the room was an old wooden door with a frosted

130

glass window, the kind she remembered from her days in the orphanage.

They sat in silence.

Amy pressed her hand to her chest. Her heartbeat felt like a war drum going a hundred miles an hour. Miles looked at her.

"I'm sorry I couldn't help her."

Amy shook her head. "She died protecting me."

Closing her eyes, the image flooded her mind. She hadn't been able to move. Hadn't even *screamed*. She just stood there as Richard struck, as Kira crumpled to the floor. She saw Kira's blank face in those last moments as the life drained from her.

"I should've done something," she whispered.

"You couldn't," Miles said. "It all happened too fast."

"I don't know what's happening to me," she said.

Miles looked to her slowly.

"I don't think it's your fault."

"I feel like all of this is my fault," she whispered.

He didn't press her. Didn't demand answers she didn't have. He just reassured her, "Whatever it is, we'll figure it out."

A sound outside the room made them both stiffen.

Muffled voices. Distant and searching.

Amy stood and moved to the door at the back of the workroom. She cracked it and looked through.

Another hallway sloped downwards but this one felt strangely familiar. She'd seen it in one of the dreams. She knew at the far end was a door marked with a sigil. A perfect circle which held a tree with red leaves inside.

Amy closed the door and turned to Miles.

"We have to keep moving."

Miles leaned heavily on her. "Where... are we going?"

"I don't know, but something is telling me we need to go this way."

She looked back at the grate.

"We're not safe. Not in town."

Miles stood with effort.

"And Kira?"

Amy closed her eyes. She saw Kira's blood on the floor. The empty look on her face.

"She deserved more than this," Miles said.

"Then let's survive this and get out." Amy replied. "For her."

....

Outside, the people of New Grayson gathered. They stood shoulder-to-shoulder in the fog, surrounding the garage. Not shouting. Not angry. Just present and waiting.

Sheriff Barker stood near the front, arms folded.

His face was blank as he looked through the door at Kira's body. His hands were clenched in his pockets, knowing he could have stopped all of this.

....

Amy had expected the door with the sigil to lead into another tunnel, or a shadowed chamber that smelled of ash and memory.

Instead, it led into a narrow stairwell layered with dust and cobwebs, rising toward a square of weak light above. The steps creaked beneath their feet as she and Miles moved upward, slow and cautious. Every sound felt like a scream against the silence of the town.

At the top, a rusted door stood seemingly untouched for many years.

Amy pressed her ear to the cold metal but heard nothing from the other side.

She glanced back at Miles, who nodded as best he could, though he was still pale cradling his arm.

132

The door opened with a groan, cold morning air rushed over them, heavy with dew and a sense of relief. They stepped out into a narrow alley behind the bakery. The smell of stale flour and burnt crust clung to the air.

Amy helped Miles across the alley, keeping low as they reached the back corner. She peeked around the edge. The town square was a few blocks ahead. In the distance Amy could see it was filled again. Townsfolk stood, still and silent, in precise rows outside the church. No one moved. No one spoke. They faced forward, toward the doors. Waiting.

"It looks like they've given up looking for us… At least for now." Amy whispered.

Miles coughed softly. "Feels more like… they're waiting for us."

Amy stared at them.

"They're not waiting for us." she murmured. "They're waiting for someone else."

Miles pressed his good hand against the brick wall to steady himself.

"If Richard killed Kira," he said, "but then didn't touch you… what does that mean?"

Amy looked down at the satchel.

"I think… he was expecting her to be someone else. I think he thought she was me."

She opened the flap and pulled the journal free.

It felt heavier now. Like it held secrets no-one else knew.

She opened to the last page Cathy had written. Her handwriting ended a few lines down but beneath it lay more in different handwriting. It looked fresher, like it'd been written a few days ago in ink;

> *I knew it was her, as soon as we got here I knew*
> *why Cathy told me to keep the secret. I'm scared of*
> *what will happen when they find out who she really*
> *is. Willow.*

Amy's heart twisted. Kira had written this.

"Willow," she whispered.

Miles looked at her. "That name again."

Amy spoke quietly to herself. "I can't be."

"You walked into a room with a monster and he walked away."

"That doesn't mean..."

Miles cut her off.

"Amy," he said gently, "What if it does?"

………………..

They moved along the backstreets, avoiding windows, moving as quickly as Miles could manage.

Each turn they took seemed to twist back on itself. Each corner led them closer to the square, no matter how much they tried to skirt around it.

"It's like the town's folding in on itself." Amy said, breathless.

Miles leaned against a lamppost. "I don't know how much longer I can keep this up. It's like we're being guided where the town wants us to go."

Amy helped him across the street into another alley.

A figure stepped out in front of them making them recoil. A woman in her early 40's with brown hair pulled into a frizzy bun. A long coat covered a black sweater and muddy boots. She stood with her arms out, not threatening.

"God. I thought I'd never find you. I've been looking for you all over."

Amy blinked. She remembered her from somewhere.

With slight hesitation Amy stepped forward. "Who are you?"

"I'm Sophie, I knew you and your mother. We need to move now."

Something about her demeanour comforted Amy.

"Why are you…"

"I'm sorry, I can fill in the blanks when we're safe but if you want to live, follow me."

Sophie didn't wait. She turned and walked with pace.

Amy looked back at Miles for an answer.

"We don't have another plan," he said shaking his head with a slight shrug.

....

Sophie moved fast. She didn't speak as she ducked through the alleys and vanished behind a warped wooden gate Amy barely noticed. The wind shifted as soon as they passed through; colder, wetter, like descending into an unseen pocket of the town. Sophie dropped to a crouch.

"Keep close," Sophie snapped. "And don't speak unless I ask you to."

They weaved between dumpsters, fences, and overgrown hedgerows, cutting through yards and neglected backlots. Amy's head spun. The path made no sense, it felt like the town was a maze with no end point. Finally they stopped in front of a crooked door hidden behind a leaning trellis strangled with dead ivy.

Sophie unlocked it with three keys. No hesitation, no pause.

"Inside." She ordered while glancing nervously around.

Amy helped Miles through the narrow doorway and into Sophie's house. The air inside was thick with the scent of herbs and old wood. Dust hung in the lamplight. Bookshelves towered over them, filled with faded journals, candles, and small wooden boxes covered in carved symbols.

Sophie slammed the door and threw two deadbolts, then a heavy latch.

Finally Sophie exhaled.

"Please sit."

They collapsed hesitantly onto a long velvet couch, the upholstery cracked with age. Sophie moved to a side cabinet and poured a tea-like liquid into two chipped mugs.

"Drink this. It'll help you think."

Amy took a sip. It was bitter and earthy.

Sophie crouched in front of them and looked into Amy's eyes.

"You don't remember, do you?"

Amy blinked. "Remember what?"

Sophie studied her. "Not even a flicker?"

Miles groaned. "Can we stop with the cryptic crap? Just say it."

Sophie ignored him. Her eyes remained locked on Amy's.

"The fire? The room? The red tree?"

Amy's hands trembled slightly.

"I've been dreaming of a hallway," she whispered. "Pictures on the wall. A door at the end. A girl. She looks like me."

Sophie nodded slowly. "She is you. Or should I say she was you."

Amy's voice cracked. "Why don't I remember?"

Sophie stood and began pacing.

"You weren't supposed to come back. Not like this. Cathy tried to stop it, tried to protect you. She hid you, renamed you. But fate… fate always rethreads the cord. Especially in this town."

Sophie stood an began to pace.

Amy clutched the satchel to her chest. "What do they want from me?"

"They want what they've always wanted," Sophie said. "A vessel."

Miles sat forward. "That's what Richard called her."

"Because that's what she is," Sophie said then looked to Amy. "What you've always been. Only now they need her more then ever. The town's collapsing in on itself and they're determined to stop that from happening. Richard wants to open the gate once and for all."

Amy shook her head violently. "I'm not her. I'm not this... Willow."

Sophie walked toward a shelf and retrieved a framed photograph. She handed it to Amy. It was aged showing a little girl with red hair and wide pale eyes. She was standing beside a woman with curly dark hair; Cathy.

Amy touched the glass.

"I've seen this picture before," she whispered.

Sophie nodded as she tapped the picture. "That's you."

"I don't..."

"You don't remember because your mind closed the memories away. It was safer that way. But the town... the town knows how to unlock it."

Amy shook her head. "Richard didn't want to kill me. He looked surprised. Like... like I wasn't who he expected."

"Because you weren't," Sophie said. "Cathy had another step-daughter; Rebecca. She was 9 when your mother was killed. Cathy took you in and with my help she kept you safe. When she got the chance she got you both out of the town. She knew you'd need each other. Shortly after, the town closed off. It was like you leaving was the catalyst."

"Kira? Was she Rebecca? Did she know about me? Who I was?"

Sophie nodded.

"We thought it'd be safer if she too changed her name. Cathy told her to keep you safe. Such a big ask for a young girl."

Miles said nothing.

Amy looked at him, eyes wide and terrified, then back to Sophie.

"Why me?"

Sophie's expression darkened.

"Because long ago, this town made a deal. Power for blood. Vision for sacrifice. The key to all of it was the sacrifice of vessels like yourself. Richard wanted to push it one step further. Your mother tried to stop them."

"My mother?"

Sophie give a bittersweet smile.

Amy backed into the couch, clutching the journal to her chest.

"I didn't choose this."

"No one ever does," Sophie said. "But now you have to choose something else. Whether you run... or finish what Cathy started."

"And what was that?"

"To bring an end to all of this."

Miles shook his head.

"Even if we wanted to leave. The town doesn't want to let us."

Sophie ran her fingers through her hair. "There is a way, but the window to get out is small. I fear it may have already closed."

A loud thump hit the front door interrupting Sophie and causing all three of them to jump.

Another hit. Then a third.

"I thought we'd have more time."

Miles stood with purpose. "How'd they find us?"

"Nowhere's safe. As long as your in this town, They'll find you." Sophie said. quickly

Miles grabbed a fire poker from beside the hearth.

Amy stood."What do we do?"

Sophie moved to a large bookshelf and pushed it to the side. Beneath sat a hatch, much like the ones they'd seen around the town.

"Help me with this."

Amy ran over and helped lift it. The damp smell of aged dirt hit them. A narrow stone stairwell led into a darkness illuminated by lanterns linked to some old circuit.

"Down," she said. "It'll take you beneath the garden and into the woods. There's an old shed near the northern perimeter. You can hide and restock there. When they find you, there's a hatch at the back it'll take you back to the tunnels."

"And you?" Amy asked.

"I'll buy you time."

"No," Amy said. "We're not leaving you."

"You have to. You're the reason they're here and I can't let them get hold of you. I might be able to convince them you got out of town already."

Amy flinched as she was guided to the stairs.

Sophie softened.

"I don't blame you. But you need to live long enough to understand. And right now, that means running."

"But how will I know what to do?"

Sophie stroked Amy's cheek. "When the time comes, you'll know."

Amy looked to Miles. He nodded.

"We need to go."

They stepped into the stairwell. Sophie quickly placed a small key in Amy's hand.

"You'll need this."

Amy closed her hand around it. "Thank you."

Before the door shut, Sophie nodded with a sad smile and whispered, "The red tree will bloom again. Whether you like it or not."

"What's the red tree?"

"You need to go now."

The hatch slammed closed and Sophie struggled moving the bookshelf back. She stood and turned to face the door and her visitors.

CHAPTER TEN

The hatch above sealed tight with a muted clunk, leaving Amy and Miles in cold, damp darkness. The stone stairwell swallowed them in shadow. The air was thick with the scent of mould and soil. A single dim lantern, strung to a hook in the wall, cast trembling shadows along the narrow corridor ahead.

Amy held the journal and satchel in both hands, tightly to her chest. Her breath was short. Each step downward felt heavier than the last.

Behind them, silence reigned.

Then came the voices. Muffled. Distant. They were coming from above; Sophie was talking to the others.

Amy froze on the stairs.

Miles, just behind her, whispered, "We need to keep moving Amy."

"No. Listen."

They crouched low, just inside the arched tunnel that branched off from the stairwell. The walls were uneven stone, carved generations ago, when the town was younger or perhaps older than anyone remembered.

The voices echoed through the tunnel; Sophie, clear and angry.

"No! You've done enough! They're not here!"

Amy clenched her jaw. Another voice replied; male, steady, and eerily calm.

"The choice was made long ago. It's not you're place to stop it."

A pause.

"They're innocent," Sophie snapped. "You look at her and see prophecy. I look at her and see a young girl who's terrified."

Then another woman's voice; softer, breathless.

"Where are they?"

They heard Sophie laugh. "They'll be long gone by now."

"He'll find them. If not now, then soon. You can't keep them from him."

The silence that followed was worse than the words. Amy pressed a hand to her mouth as she realised she was almost audibly gasping.

The woman spoke again.

"The town needs her. It needs the vessel."

"Everything he's promised is a lie. You know that. All he wants is power for himself."

The man spoke up. "Everything he does is for the good of New Grayson."

Sophie's voice dropped, just above a whisper.

"If you need to take someone, just take me."

The man spoke up. "He needs nothing from you. You're a traitor to this town."

Something big smashed into the bookshelf above the hatch. They heard Sophie's scream muffled by a wet cough.

Amy gasped and started back towards the trapdoor. Miles reached forward and grabbed her arm.

"Don't." he whispered.

"They're going to kill her" she choked out.

"I know but we have to..."

Amy shook her head cutting him off, trying to push forward. "We can't just leave..."

"She gave us time," Miles said. "Let's not waste it. You heard what she said. We can't allow them to get hold of you."

She stopped with the realisation. Tears pricked her eyes, but they didn't fall.

She stood and nodded.

………………..

142

The tunnel ahead was low and narrow, lit only by rusted lanterns spaced unevenly along the walls. Each one flickered with a weak light, as if the town's rot had even seeped into them.

They moved as quickly as Miles's injuries would allow, careful not to trip over roots or uneven stones. The floor sloped slightly downward, then turned. Amy could feel it spiralling, taking them further beneath the town, into much deeper layers.

"I think we're going in circles." Miles said after a few minutes, panting.

Amy nodded. "It's guiding us somewhere."

"But where?"

Amy simply shook her head in response.

The tunnel spilt in two.

Amy looked down both. "Which way?"

Miles shook his head and shrugged, then pointed right. Amy nodded and headed down the fork. After a while, they reached an iron gate wedged into the corridor, half-rotted and streaked with rust. Amy shoved it open with her shoulder, and it groaned like a dying animal. The sound of it's strain bounced off the walls throughout the tunnels. Beyond it was a wider chamber. A service tunnel, maybe. Bits of old piping lined the ceiling. Metal grates rattled underfoot as they walked.

They both slowed.

"I've been here before," Amy whispered.

"In your dreams?"

"No I don't think so. Well yes, but I think I came here when I was young."

She touched the satchel gently, like checking for a heartbeat. Calmness washed over her, knowing Cathy's words were inside like a beacon in all of the darkness.

A faint hum reverberated around them. Amy knelt and placed her hand to the cold metal grate underfoot. A sound seeped into her mind. Like a whisper. Unintelligible but repeating.

Miles crouched beside her.

"What is it?"

She didn't answer. She just listened as it repeated over and over. She couldn't make it out but it felt like it was telling them where to go. They continued through the sparsely lit darkness slowly heading upwards, until they reached the end.

………………………

The tunnel ended with a metal hatch tucked beneath a slope of thick moss and rotted leaves. When Amy shoved it open, daylight hit her face like a slap; sharp and cold. She blinked fast as she pulled herself out, adjusting to the light after so much time in the darkness.

Miles climbed out after her, teeth clenched, every movement stiff and laboured. His makeshift bandage was dark now, the bleeding had slowed but not fully stopped. He looked like he was running on adrenaline alone. They emerged behind a dense thicket on the far northern edge of town, far enough from the centre that they could barley see any buildings. Trees stretched high, knotted and heavy with damp air. Everything smelled of rain-soaked wood and old bark.

Amy scanned the treeline and paused when she saw the silhouette of the building. A structure half-consumed by vines and shadow, its metal roof warped with rust, the wood faded gray. She moved toward it quickly, supporting Miles as he limped beside her.

The door was padlocked. Amy reached into her satchel and pulled out the iron key Sophie had slipped into her hand before they'd left her to die. The teeth of the key were jagged. Not manufactured. Hand-forged. It slid into the lock with a perfect, practised fit. The padlock dropped with a thud to the floor. Amy pulled the door open.

Inside: a single large room, cold and dark.

Dust hung in shafts of sunlight slicing through narrow slats between warped wooden boards.

The inside felt much larger then the outside. Along with a bench and a rudimentary cot, a worktable lined an entire side. Upon it lay dusty tools, some knives and a few bedrolls. At the far

144

end, beneath a threadbare blanket draped over a low chest. Amy walked across the room and lifted the blanket.

The chest was marked with a symbol burned into its surface; a tree, roots spread wide beneath its trunk. Amy examined it and pressed the catch.

The lid rose exposing documents with yellowed pages and photographs. She could see from the photos that they must've been special to Sophie. One showed a young Sophie and Cathy together, young, innocent. Beneath them were pages torn from Cathy's journal in a bundle.

Amy sat heavily on the cot.

Miles leaned against the door-frame, holding his arm with his good hand. "What is this place?"

"I think Sophie built it," Amy said. "Just in case."

Amy untied the twine on some papers and spread them across the cot.

Her eyes scanned across them quickly, desperate for meaning.

One page caught her immediately.

Written in Sophie's tight, slanted script:

> *There's no stopping the town now. Not unless she.*
> *But the girl isn't ready. Cathy made sure of that. She buried the fire deep. Hid it under skin and time. For better or worse if this town is ever to heal, we need her back.*
> *Fire doesn't die and when it breathes again, it devours all in it's way.*

Amy's hands trembled.

She found a torn map of the tunnels beneath New Grayson, each marked with small red X's. It was similar to Cathy's map but it marked things other than the gates. One circle was drawn in thicker ink than the rest, labelled in a different hand.

> *THE ROOT.*

Miles stepped closer glancing at the papers. "That mean anything to you?"

Amy stared at the page.

"I think they've been preparing this for years," she said softly. "Cathy, Sophie… maybe even people before them. They knew this day would come."

"And now they think you're the one who has to stop it?"

"I don't know but it feels like both sides are trying to use me for something."

Amy picked up the photo of Sophie; young, sharp-eyed, standing in front of the church.

On the back, a line had been written in faded pencil.

Protect the tree.

Amy looked up.

"What's the tree?" Miles asked.

Amy was quiet.

Miles hesitated. "You said you saw it in a dream?"

She nodded.

"It's not just a symbol," she whispered. "It's… alive. Rooted somewhere beneath the town. It's part of the gate they're trying to open."

"A gate to what?"

Amy shook her head. "I don't know. But I bet it's nothing good."

She looked down again at the map. The thick circle. "The Root," she murmured. "It's not a metaphor. It's real. A place. A doorway."

"And they want you to be the key?"

Amy nodded once, slowly.

Miles exhaled. "Then we've got two options. Run."

He nodded toward the knives.

"Or fight."

Amy didn't answer. She reached down and pulled a knife from the table. Held it in her hand. The weight was clean, balanced, familiar in a way she couldn't explain.

Then another memory flared;

A woman screaming.

A burning room.

A hand covered in soot gripping a knife just like this one.

Amy dropped it quickly.

Miles stepped forward. "You okay?"

She wiped her hands on her jeans, as if that could scrub the memory away. "Yeah. Just… flashes of memories."

They sat in silence.

The wind rattled the shed door. Outside, birds had begun to return as if something had shifted again in the town's rhythm.

Miles picked up a knife and felt it's weight in his palm.

"What's the plan now?"

"You heard Sophie. She told us to regroup up here."

Miles rubbed his head. "And then what? What are we waiting for. We need to get out of here now."

"We're in no state to go now. We need some rest. Even if it's just a little. Anyway, Sophie said the exit was likely shut by now."

Amy stared at the lock box, at the pages, at the words written in someone else's hand. Miles hobbled over and placed a hand on her shoulder.

"Okay," he whispered. "But I take first watch".

Amy rested her head down on the cot until her body finally gave in and darkness consumed her.

. . . .

Amy stood barefoot in the dark.

The earth beneath her feet was warm, not with sunlight, but with a buried heat. Around her, the woods were quiet. The trees were wrong. Not the pines and oaks she knew, but tall, skeletal trunks that bled red sap like old wounds. Their branches twisted like antlers, and their bark was etched with crude shapes: eyes, teeth, flames. The air shimmered around her as fog rolled across the forest floor, thick and gray, curling around her ankles. Her nightdress clung to her like wet paper. When she breathed, the fog moved with her in and out.

Then she heard it.

Crack.

A branch breaking underfoot.

She turned. In the distance, light. Faint. Scarlet. Pulsing.

With each step towards it the light grew brighter. The trees leaned inward, not like walls closing, but like watchers kneeling in reverence and then the woods ended.

She stood at the edge of a clearing.

A circle of scorched earth stretched ahead; wide, hollow, smoking faintly. No grass grew here. No life stirred. In the centre of it stood a large tree.

It was enormous, taller than the church steeple, its bark dark as iron, its leaves a wild explosion of red. Not autumn red, not brown or burgundy, but vivid arterial red, like blood held upto sunlight. The leaves swayed, though there was no wind and they shimmered as if they were burning at the edges.

Beneath the tree, the ground cracked in spirals radiating outward from the base of the trunk. Carved between the roots were symbols. Some she recognized from Cathy's journal. Others were older.

At the base of the tree a small girl knelt. Her face was hidden, but her hair, tangled and crimson, fell like a curtain across her shoulders. She wore a pale dress, smudged with ash. Her fingers traced the root line like a blind person would read Braille.

Amy took a step forward.

The girl froze. Then, slowly, she stood. Amy's mouth went dry as the girl turned.

She was maybe eight. But the moment her face caught the glow of the tree, Amy saw it.

Her face. Her eyes. Her mouth. She knew those features.

Amy gasped and the girl looked straight at her.

"You left me here."

Amy shook her head. "No... I..."

"You burned everything, and you left me behind."

"I don't understand."

The girl took a step forward.

Amy couldn't move.

"You left me in that room," the girl said.

Amy trembled.

"You locked the door behind you and left me alone." The girl whispered.

"I was a child."

Amy dropped to her knees. "I didn't ask for this."

The girl walked closer, unblinking.

"You're the key," she said. "But you're also the lock. You're the thing they tried to hide with a borrowed name."

"Then why do I feel like a ghost?"

The little girl crouched in front of her, face to face now. Their eyes locked, mirrors across time.

"Because you're not dead yet and you're not done either."
Amy swallowed hard.

The Red Tree pulsed behind them and the leaves rained down, each one sharp-edged, glowing at the edges like coals.

Amy flinched.

The girl whispered something again.

Amy leaned in.

"What?"

The girl opened her mouth. But instead of words, ash cascaded out. Behind her she saw the town forming in the smoke. New Grayson was constructing itself in reverse. Buildings rose from ash and fire, windows blinking open, the church steeple growing like a bone out of the cracked ground.

The townspeople lined the streets, their faces empty, each holding a candle and chanting.

Amy couldn't understand the words but heard the rhythm. Like a heartbeat.

Then the ground opened.

A chasm beneath the tree split open revealing a staircase of burning wood, spiralling downward into nothing.

The little girl walked to its edge.

"Come with me," she said.

Amy took one step forward but the sound of her name pulled her back to reality.

... ...

Something yanked her back to the waking world.

A scream. Not from the dream but from reality.

"AMY!"

Amy bolted upright, heart hammering, lungs dragging in damp air like drowning lungs clawing for the surface. Her hand shot out, gripping the edge of the cot. The shed door shuddered under impact. Then came another thud and another.

A low grunt of effort followed.

She turned. Miles was at the door, bracing it with his body, his good arm pressed against the frame, sweat streaking down his face, his bandaged arm hanging limp.

"What's...?"

"They found us," he grunted.

Amy swung her legs off the cot, she was soaked in sweat, her skin crawling. The dream still clung to her like smoke, red leaves drifting behind her eyes. She staggered upright and ran to the window.

Shadows moved through the trees. A dozen, maybe more. Figures advancing through the fog-drenched woods. Silent. Steady.

"What do they want?" she breathed.

"Pretty sure we both know the answer to that." Miles said without turning.

The shed shook again. Something slammed into it from the side.

Amy grabbed knife from the table, then scanned the room. "There's a back hatch, right? Sophie said there was an escape."

"Corner maybe?" Miles growled. "Floorboards. Near the cot."

Amy scrambled across the room, dropping to her knees. Her fingers clawed at the dusty boards.

Another blow rattled the door. This one harder.

"We have no more time," Miles hissed. "They're almost in."

Her hands found purchase as they pried a board up. Beneath it, a narrow tunnel no more than shoulder-width wide leading down into dark.

"Found it!" she called.

Amy grabbed the satchel with the journal and slid it over her head. "We're not dying here."

Miles gave a grim smile, still braced against the groaning hinges. "You're damn right we're not."

Then...

CRACK.

The door frame split near the top. A pale hand reached through. Miles turned and slammed the knife he held into it. A hiss of pain came from it's owner as they pulled it back taking the knife with it.

Amy pulled open the rest of the hidden hatch. "Let's go!"

Miles stumbled back from the door but not fast enough.

Another blow landed. The top hinge buckled and splintered.

"GO!" Amy screamed.

Miles dropped into the opening. Amy followed, yanking the trapdoor shut above them just as the shed door burst inward.

Darkness swallowed them whole.

. . . .

They tumbled down a steep dirt incline, landing hard in a narrow tunnel. The air was moist and heavy. Roots dangled from the ceiling, brushing against their faces as they scrambled forward. The tunnel quickly compressed in on itself forcing them to their knees.

Amy led the way through the darkness. Miles dragged himself behind her, one hand clutched to his injured side. The tunnel angled downward with every metre taking them deeper beneath the ground.

Further from fresh air.

Further from the light.

"Where does this lead?" Miles panted.

"I don't know." Amy admitted.

But the truth was, she knew that somewhere in the back of her skull, behind the panic, the pain, and the afterglow of the dream, where it would take them. To the tree. To the place where the young girl waited.

They crawled in silence for several long minutes, guided only by the faintest glow ahead from the trickle of lantern light through the tunnels. The passage opened slightly, enough for them to crouch instead of crawl. Miles collapsed against the curved wall, panting hard.

152

"We can't keep doing this," he muttered.

Amy turned and crouched beside him. His face was pale, feverish. The cloth on his arm had begun to leak again. Amy touched his cheek gently.

"I'm going to fix this," she whispered.

He gave a weak laugh. "With what? A knife and a bunch of someone else's memories?"

"No," she said. "With fire."

Miles blinked at her.

Behind them, from far up the tunnel, they heard the sound of wood crashing down. Then voices with following footsteps. Amy stood and looked down the tunnel. The air smelled different now. It smelt like dry smoke.

She knew that smell. It was ingrained in her bones.

CHAPTER ELEVEN

The tunnel narrowed again before opening up.

It happened gradually with the dirt walls pulling back, the low ceiling stretching upward into a space that felt carved by something older than tools. The passage widened into a vaulted chamber lined with broken stone and collapsed beams, half-consumed by plant roots.

Amy stepped forward, raising a lantern she'd pulled from the wall of the chambers opening. Its flame trembled in her hand, barely touching the edges of the dark.

Miles limped behind her, pale and sweating, his breath shallow. Still alive. Still moving. But only just holding on.

"I think we lost them. I heard them go down one of the other tunnels." He took a deep breath.

They stood now in what looked like the remnants of a buried structure. Not a natural cavern.

Amy turned slowly, the light catching fragments of what remained; Shattered support columns, scorched and blackened. Half a staircase, now leading nowhere. The curved outline of an archway, swallowed by dead vines.

She paused as she saw the silhouette behind the building.

The tree, or at least what was left of it. What was once a breathtaking vision, was now the burnt discarded remains of a severed trunk.

Miles leaned against a jagged post. "Is that the tree?"

Amy nodded, silent.

Miles looked closer. "It looks like there was a monastery around it."

It had the shape of a sanctuary, but it reeked like a tomb. She stepped deeper into the ruins. The ground crunched beneath her boots, bone dust, ash, and rotten wood. Her breath caught as she passed what looked like the charred remains of a pew.

Her stomach turned. She recognized this place and her body instinctively moved.

Amy lowered the lantern and knelt. The floor here was cracked, blackened from long ago flame. The damage spread outward like the epicentre of a blast. Something caught her eye. A shape, curled in the darkness, almost perfectly preserved in the shadows.

She moved toward it, breath tight. She knew it before her fingers touched it; A toy rabbit. Hers.

It was missing an arm and much of the body was charred but it was still recognizable. It's once white fur now stained black with soot. Amy's hands trembled as she picked it up. Her breath left her in a single, ragged sob.

She remembered holding it on the night she ran.

She remembered the room on fire and the screams of a woman. Her mother?

Amy crumpled and dropped to her knees, arms wrapped around the doll, breath coming in short, panicked gasps.

Miles limped to her side. "What is it?"

She couldn't speak. The weight of it hit her all at once. The little girl in the dream wasn't a ghost. Wasn't a vision. She was a memory. She was her.

"I was here," Amy whispered, voice cracking. "I... I was here."

Miles knelt beside her. "What do you mean?"

"This place," she said, barely above a whisper. "They brought me here. They tried to do something to me... I watched him kill her. Watched him kill my mother."

She held up the rabbit up to Miles.

"This was mine."

Miles went still.

"Sophie was telling the truth?"

The silence between them stretched long and painful.

Finally, he said, "So you're...?"

Amy nodded. "I'm Willow."

The words left her mouth like a weight escaping from inside her.

"I don't know how. I don't know why I forgot. But it's coming back now."

She ran her fingers over the rabbit's fur.

"I used to sleep with this every night."

Miles sat back against a stone slab, breathing hard.

"Jesus," he whispered.

Amy's eyes filled with tears, not from grief but from clarity. Clarity of who she was.

"I'm not just tied to the town," she said. "I'm the reason it still breathes. I'm the thread that never got cut."

Miles reached for her hand. "That's not your fault."

Amy looked around the ruined space. "Then why do I feel like this fire started with me? I did all of this." She motioned to the tree and the ruins.

Amy didn't know how long she kneeled there on the scorched floor. The rabbit rested in her lap, its charred limbs curled inward like it, too, remembered. Miles sat nearby, head tilted back against a cracked stone pillar, eyes shut. His breathing had steadied, but he was still pale, lips dry and colourless. Every few minutes he blinked like someone half-dreaming, but Amy knew he was staying quiet for her.

She needed silence to think.

The chamber they'd stumbled into, what was left of it, had once been a special place. That's what they'd called it when they led her there.

The fire had started here. It had started when she knocked over a lantern as she ran. She could still hear the way the wooden beams creaked amongst the heat.

Her mother had screamed for her to run with her dying breath. She'd turned and kept going until she got out.

Into the woods. They'd been close behind, but she was faster. She'd kept running until a man let her into his house. What was his name? James! Yes. Cathy's house.

Amy turned to the satchel and unbuckled it. She drew out the journal Sophie's pages and placed them with Cathy's original entries. She flipped through, scanning her mother's, no, her adoptive mother's handwriting, then Sophie's sharper, more anxious scrawl.

Two entries stood out.

She reread the first one, underlined in pencil:

> *She wasn't just a child. That's the lie we told ourselves to make it easier.*
> *The ritual won't just preserve the gate, it's to reinforce the vessel.*
> *From ash. From blood. From lineage.*

Amy swallowed. "Sophie was there that night."

Miles rubbed his head. "You're sure?

Amy nodded as she frantically flipped back to the next page.

> *I let her run. I knew she'd find help. Thank god it was Cathy who found her. She thought she could protect her. That if the girl escaped, she could cheat the cycle. We owed that much it to Ali. But fire doesn't go out. It smoulders dormant, until the fuel returns. The tree may be gone but she still holds the power.*

She stared at that last line. Her dreams hadn't just been memories. They'd been warnings. Glimpses through time's manipulative filter. Not just of what happened but what could happen again.

Miles stirred beside her.

"What did Sophie say again?" he murmured. "About you?"

"That I was the key," Amy said. "But that I didn't know I was."

Miles frowned. "And now you do."

Amy nodded. "Yeah."

She tucked the rabbit into her satchel, gently, like laying a child to rest, then opened the journal again and flipped toward the back. There, tucked between two pages she hadn't read yet, was a loose scrap. A different parchment, rough-edged, hurriedly torn. The writing was fainter.

> *The child's blood can open the root. But it also holds the power to close it forever.*

Amy whispered the words aloud.

Miles leaned closer. "That mean anything?"

She shook her head. "Not yet."

They sat in silence a moment longer. Then Amy stood, her legs trembling beneath her. There was more down there. She could feel it.

"This whole level is part of the ritual site. Somewhere special. I remember him saying it had to be here," she said slowly, scanning the space. "Because there's something below it."

Miles raised an eyebrow. "More tunnels?"

"Or something else," she said. "The town built over it. Tried to bury what happened here. But the roots… they never stopped growing."

She moved toward a collapsed corner of the room. A beam jutted from the wall at a sharp angle, bent like a broken rib. Dirt spilled from between its joints not fresh, but disturbed recently. Someone had passed through.

She knelt and pushed aside the debris. A narrow path curved downward, partially hidden behind collapsed shelves and blackened brick. It looked almost too narrow to crawl through.

Amy stared into the dark beyond. She heard a whisper pulling her. Low and rhythmic like a chant.

She stepped back.

"We're going deeper."

Miles didn't have the strength to argue. He simply nodded and stood.

"Then let's find out what they buried."

....

The tunnel descended at a steep angle.

Amy crawled first, her shoulders brushed against rough stone and exposed root, her lantern throwing twisted shadows against the low walls. Miles followed close behind, quiet except for the soft scrape of his boots and the occasional cough that echoed too loudly in the tight space.

The path was suffocating. Amy felt the air thicken with every foot forward they crawled. It was damp and sour. When the tunnel finally widened, it did so suddenly.

Amy emerged into a low, circular room carved from stone and blackened by fire. The soot on the walls wasn't recent, this room had escaped the flames above. This fire had burned long ago, long before she'd been above, but it had scarred everything. The walls. The floor. Even the air. Smoke clung to the stone like it had never left.

Miles dropped in behind her, landing with a grunt. Then they both went still. At the centre of the room was a shape.

Not an object but an imprint.

A child-sized outline, scorched into the stone floor like a shadow permanently seared into the world. Arms slightly raised. Legs curled. The mark was darker than the rest of the room, untouched by time. From the ceiling the roots of the tree cocooned the room. Smaller veins had found their way to the outline. Amy stepped toward it.

Her breath caught.

This was where it had happened. Where all the others had been killed and where she was being led to that night. The shape in the stone was around the size she'd been when Willow had vanished and Amy had been born.

She knelt beside the outline, her fingers trembling as they hovered over the blackened surface. How many had come before her? How many children had they burned in this place?

The roots that adorned the walls were marked with symbols; some carved, some painted in ancient flaking red. They ringed the space like a grim mosaic: eyes, trees, spirals, flames and runes she couldn't make out.

There were chains embedded in the walls too. Rusted now. One hung loosely, its iron cuff still open, as if the thing it once held had slipped free. Miles leaned close to the wall and traced one of the spiral marks with his finger. Beneath his breath he mumbled something.

Amy looked up. "What?"

He nodded toward the symbols. "This place has been here a long time. Just think how long it would've taken to build."

Amy's hands clenched at her sides. She rose slowly, looking again at the outline on the floor.

Miles crouched beside her and placed a hand on her shoulder.

Amy flinched. "I don't want to be this Willow."

"But you are," he said gently. "And Richard's going to try and finish what he started. He has the whole town under his control. That is unless you and I stop him."

"How do we do that?"

Miles took a breath. "We fight."

Amy stared at the burned outline again. It was her and it wasn't. It was the intention of her. The mould made for her and those who'd come before.

She moved to the far side of the chamber. A section of the wall was blackened, but beneath the soot was a mural cracked, faded, but intact. It showed the red tree above. If she was the key then the tree must've been the lock.

The mural showed the trees roots spread down into a burning house and it's branches reaching into the sky, wrapping around a large star. At the base, a child, faceless, arms outstretched. Amy touched the child's figure and felt an internal whisper echo through the chamber. She turned from the mural and stepped toward the far corner of the room.

Something felt… wrong. Felt different.

The stones were uneven and slightly raised. Not just cracked like the rest of the floor but disturbed, as if someone had opened something once and forgotten to put it back perfectly. She crouched and brushed soot away with her sleeve.

Glancing at Miles. "Help me."

He limped over and knelt beside her. Together they dug into the stone, fingers scraping against rock and ash, until Amy's hand struck something in a void below.

She retrieved her hand, pulling out a bundle of rolled papers, old and brittle. Although some had crumbled with age, a few were still readable. Amy's fingers shook as she gently lifted a sheaf of them free. Miles leaned close, holding the lantern.

At the top of the first page she read.

18th February 1759

Her pain calls the flame. Her silence binds it.
Her death seals it. But if the death is incomplete, the
fire will remain open. Unshaped.

Miles read aloud, voice low. "Incomplete death?"

Amy nodded. "This is nearly 300 years old. How has it survived all this time?"

She opened another page. This one was less damaged.

At the top, in rough, aggressive handwriting:

29th May 1822

We failed….

Amy read slowly;

Miles looked at her.

"It looks like this has been going on for a long time. Look, these papers are hundreds of years old." She carefully showed the pages to Miles.

"So if you were meant to be one of these sacrifices and escaped, is that why they lured you back here?"

Amy nodded slowly, stomach turning. "They thought it was Kira but I guess it was twisted fate I came back too. That's why they let us walk through the town without stopping us. They weren't chasing to catch us. They were leading us here. Guiding me back to the tree."

She reached for the next page but it crumbled in her hands.

Miles shook his head. "They want to complete whatever ritual they were performing."

Amy nodded.

"Then we can't let them," he said.

Amy stared down at the papers in her hand. "We won't."

They moved to the far edge of the chamber and with one final look at the room they ascended out of the chamber.

"If we can't find a way out of this town, we need to work out how to stop it. We need to get back to Sophie's, she must have something more that can help us."

Miles shook his head.

"What if they're still there? Hell, how do you even know there'll be anything useful there?"

"We either we risk it up there or we die down here. Personally I don't want to die doing nothing."

Miles sighed and gave her a nod.

"Let's go."

. . . .

They spent a long time retracing their steps until they finally emerged from the tunnel. They'd encountered no-one on their journey out and had seen no signs that anyone was waiting for them.

The sky was red; dusk or dawn, Amy couldn't tell. It didn't feel like either. It felt like the world was no longer what she remembered.

Amy supported Miles as they headed up into the trees. In the distance they could see the town. Standing still and silent, the church stood tall and cold. Lights glowed from within, flickering like candle flames in the darkness.

Townspeople moved through the streets again. They no longer looked like they were searching. It looked more like they were preparing.

Miles leaned heavily on Amy. "What's your plan?"

"I don't know," she said looking at him. "Not yet. Let's get back to Sophie's house and work this out."

She reached into her satchel and pulled out the burned rabbit.

"I was made to be a key of some kind. They called me the fire," she said quietly. "But maybe I'm just the match."

Miles gave her a tired smile.

"If you are, then light the whole damn place up."

CHAPTER TWELVE

The path back to Sophie's was overgrown. The townsfolk had destroyed the tunnel they'd previously used. Branches clawed at her arms and coat sleeves, as if the town itself didn't want her retracing old ground. Each footstep through the woods behind New Grayson echoed too loud in the humid air.

They'd left Sophie's too quickly that night. Fleeing the blood, the townsfolk, the certainty of death and in their panic, it felt like they'd left behind the final piece to stop all this.

"We should wait until dark," Miles said beside her, his voice strained. He limped heavily, his injured arm hanging loose.

Amy didn't stop.

"They'll expect us to wait. If we wait, they'll move it. Or destroy it. Or use it."

"Amy..."

She turned sharply. "Stop calling me that."

He froze. "What?"

Her jaw clenched. "That name. Amy. Am I even that person any more? I don't know who I am."

"You're the person who saved me. You're the person who wouldn't let Kira die alone. You're still you."

"I'm a lie wrapped in someone else's skin," she snapped. "And the only reason I haven't torn it off yet is because I didn't know it until now."

Miles didn't argue. He just kept walking.

They crossed the eastern perimeter of the town, keeping low behind fences and abandoned cars. The streets were emptier than they had been, no more silent observers watching from porches. No slow processions.

"Do you think they're watching?" Miles asked.

"They're always watching from somewhere," Amy said scanning the surroundings. "But something's different now."

He frowned. "How?"

"I think they're afraid."

They moved through the alleys, toward the curve of the hill that led to Sophie's house. Amy's heart beat louder the closer they got. Sophie had tried to protect her. She'd saved them and in return Amy had left her behind to die, just like she'd left her mother, like she'd left Kira. She didn't know if she was ready to face what was to come but knew she had to.

They paused beside the rusted fence that bordered the rear of Sophie's yard. Miles winced as he leaned against a post, catching his breath.

"Amy," he said again, voice low. "Willow. Whatever name you want to go by. You don't have to become what they want you to."

She gave him a sharp look. "Yes, I do."

"You don't," he said. "They built a trap around you. They want you to believe this is who you are. That you're part of this towns sickness but you're none of that. We just need to figure this all out and not act on impulse."

"Figure out what?" she said, stepping through the weeds. "Why I wake up sweating with a burning under my skin? Why I can't remember my childhood except when it's bleeding through nightmares? Why I'm apparently the only one that can stop whatever is going on in this town?"

He stayed quiet.

Amy's voice softened. "I know you're scared. I am too. But there must be some writing or a notebook that has everything Sophie didn't get a chance to tell us. If I'm going to survive this, if either of us are, we need to know what she knew."

They reached the edge of the garden. What had once been a tangled collection of herbs and overgrown hedges now looked flattened, and trampled. A path led from the back steps toward the woods, but it was muddied and fractured by deep boot prints.

Amy held up a hand. "Wait."

She crouched low, scanning the shadows. The wind blew faintly through the cracked windows of the house. Nothing moved.

Miles joined her. "Looks clear."

Amy wasn't so sure.

They approached slowly, creeping toward the broken porch steps. The house loomed above them, darker than she remembered. Amy reached the door, her fingers pausing over the warped frame and for a moment, just a breath, she thought she heard Sophie's voice.

A whisper or a warning.

Then it was gone.

She pushed the door open. The air inside smelled of blood. The hallway stretched ahead like an abyss ready to swallow them. The floor creaked beneath their steps, and each groan of the old wood made Amy's skin crawl. Ahead they could see the front door now broken and discarded. Objects littered the floor where they'd been knocked over in the attack.

Creeping through, they passed the living room and glimpsed a crumpled body laying next to the hidden passage. Amy quickly looked away. They slowly made their way upstairs onto the landing and crept along the corridor until Amy stopped outside what appeared to be Sophie's study.

The door was battered and the lock had been smashed in from the outside.

"Ready?" she asked.

Miles gave a grim nod, bracing himself against the wall.

Amy pushed the door open.

The study looked like it had been ransacked by storm winds. Papers littered the floor, scattered from desk drawers that'd been torn free of their runners. The curtains had been shredded. One chair lay on its side, legs broken. The other had been pulled backward and pinned into the far corner by a tall, toppled bookcase. Ink pooled on the carpet from an upturned ink-well. Amongst the chaos the floor was littered with books. So many books. Some intact, others ripped at the spine. Sophie had filled this room with knowledge. Secrets she had gathered over the years like weapons.

Amy stepped over a fallen volume of some old tome and made her way to the desk.

Miles stood in the doorway, keeping watch.

The desk was unlocked and most of the drawers littered the floor. Amy started pulling the remaining drawers, one by one. Most were empty but the roof of what had once been the top drawer felt like something was attached. Reaching in she touched something taped tight; a sealed envelope and a thin book bound in faded leather. A piece of fabric bound them both together.

Amy took both items out, hands trembling, and backed away towards the wall. Miles entered and moved to see what Amy had found. She set them down to the desk and opened the envelope.

Inside was a single page.

She unfolded it;

> *My darling girl,*
>
> *I don't know what you remember. Maybe pieces. Maybe more.*
>
> *You were never supposed to be born this way. He used your mother and when you came into the world, he tried to make you more than human. More than a mere child. He wanted you to be the key.*
>
> *I only know this from years of whispers and research.*
>
> *Never did I expect you to turn up on our doorstep that night. You spoke in riddles but I knew there was something special in you.*
>
> *I hid you away in plain sight. I changed your name, I buried your past and I raised you as Amy. When I started to learn the truth I sent you and Rebecca away. I hoped you'd keep each other safe.*

*The town believes it needs you. They believe
you'll keep the town safe, keep it protected, but the
ritual's true purpose is transformation. It'll turn the
town into a conduit. A permanent door to a place of
pure evil. Richard has deceived them all.*

*You are the key. Not just to open it. But to close
it forever.*

*I love you and always will. You'll always be my
daughter,*
Cathy

. . . .

Amy sat frozen and laid the letter back down.

Miles stirred beside her. "What does it say?"

Amy handed it to him, eyes wide, mouth dry. As he read she
lifted the leather book.

Miles moved forward. "Is that what you were after?"

She nodded. "Sophie's notes. Cathy's too. All of them."

Amy stood slowly, brushing dried ash from the cover.

Inside were more journal entries Cathy's hand again. Some
longer, some hurried. She moved past the torn pages and settled on
one with her name at the top.

*Willow is safe. I've sent her away. I hope she can stay
away from here and live a good life.*

*It's not safe for anyone here now. I hope Rebecca will
forgive me.*

But one page near the centre had been rewritten over and over,
as if she'd been trying to find the clearest way to say it. Amy read
it aloud.

*The ritual was never about saving the town.
It was about making a place a conduit, a point
where a hellish domain could push through forever.
A wound in the world. Willow was the scalpel. New*

168

Grayson is the skin and Richard thinks he's the doctor.

Miles looked up, expression dark. "So if they finish the ritual..."

"...the whole town becomes the gate," Amy said. "This place becomes Hell's front porch."

She flipped to the final page.

One last line written in red ink.

To close the wound we need to return the fire to its source.

"Let's go," Miles said, moving to the door and glancing down the hall.

"Miles," she whispered.

But her voice was drowned by the sound. A thud from downstairs.

Both turned.

Then another heavier one. Footsteps.

Miles moved to the door. "We need to go now."

Amy nodded, gripping the journal tight. They slipped into the hall and began down the stairs, moving quickly now, each creak of wood beneath their feet echoing too loud.

Amy's breath caught.

The hallway was darker than before.

They reached the bottom of the stairs and headed for the open front door.

Then a weak voice rang out from the living room.

"Amy?"

Amy froze and turned.

Miles grabbed her arm. "No, we don't have time."

But she was already moving. In the centre of the floor, half-covered in blood, barely breathing was Sophie. Amy dropped to her knees beside her and placed the journal on the ground. Sophie's eyes fluttered.

Her mouth twitched.

"You're too late," she whispered. "He's coming."

Amy reached for her hand. "We're here. We're going to get you out."

Sophie shook her head. "No time. No time... He followed you. He waited until you were close... so he could finish it in front of you."

Amy's heart pounded.

"Who?"

Slow methodical footsteps approached from behind them. Miles turned and stepped backwards into the room with Amy. Richard stood in a long flowing robe with knife in hand.

His face calm and serene.

"Hello, Willow," he said.

Amy rose slowly. Sophie gasped for air once more and then went still.

Richard smiled.

"Now," he said. "Let's finish this."

CHAPTER THIRTEEN

Richard didn't speak again. He didn't need to. His presence filled the room like smoke, thick, choking. The knife in his right hand glistened with dark steel. Amy's breath caught as she shifted instinctively in front of Miles, shielding him with her body. The blade twitched slightly in Richard's hand, like it was growing impatient.

Behind her, Miles whispered, "Amy…"

She flinched.

Not because of the name, but because hearing it now made her feel small and vulnerable again. But she wasn't Amy anymore. She was and always had been Willow.

She was the reason this monster was smiling.

Richard tilted his head with curiosity, like a predator examining it's prey.

"I've waited a long time to meet you again"

Then he lunged.

Amy didn't think. She threw herself sideways just as the knife slashed down, splitting the wooden table Sophie had used for drying herbs. Splinters flew. She slipped on a glass bottle that exploded underfoot.

Amy rolled then scrambled to her feet, snatching up the heavy looking book from the bookshelf. It was solid and it had weight.

She brought her arm back and hurled it with all the force she could muster.

It hit Richard's shoulder with a thud, sending him stumbling backward a half step. It wasn't enough to stop him but it bought them enough time.

"MOVE!" she screamed.

Miles grabbed the journal, his face pale and twisted with pain. He staggered toward the hallway as Amy backed up after him.

Richard came again, silent this time. No taunt and no theatrics. Just the cold, steady walk of a killer stalking their next victim.

Amy kicked over a tall wooden stool and sent it tumbling toward his legs as it broke into pieces. He stepped over it easily but it slowed him.

They ran.

The hallway twisted under their feet. Every board felt like it would collapse. The lights above buzzed violently, dimming and brightening in unnatural pulses as though reacting to Richard's breath. They ran for the front door but Richard cut them off. They turned for the stairs.

"Amy!" Miles tripped.

She grabbed his arm and yanked him upright. They reached the staircase and took the steps two at a time trying to create distance between them and their hunter. Behind them, Richard growled. Not like a man. Not even like an animal, but like something otherworldly.

Amy spun and grabbed a painting from the wall and flung it blindly down the stairs, hoping it would buy them even a second.

As they burst onto the upper landing they ran straight for the room at the back of the house which appeared to have been Sophie's bedroom. Amy barged the door open with her shoulder and almost threw Miles inside. She followed, turned, and kicked the door shut just as Richard's heavy footfall hit the staircase.

They locked the door then shoved a chest of drawers against it, one of the few pieces of furniture that occupied the room. Amy paused as the newfound silence encapsulated them. The hallway beyond was far too quiet.

Miles leaned heavily against the wall, panting, clutching the journal.

"I think..." he gasped. "I think he's enjoying this."

Amy didn't answer. She turned to survey the room. Sophie's bedroom was oddly intact, untouched by the violence downstairs. The walls were still lined with faded lavender wallpaper. A small writing desk sat by the boarded window, a cracked mirror resting atop it. The bed was neatly made. The comforter folded just so. A wardrobe stood open and was mostly empty.

The windows were boarded from the inside, unseen from the outside. Thick slats, nailed with heavy iron spikes.

No easy way out.

She crossed to the window and pressed her fingers to the wood. It was solid and heavy to her touch. Miles lowered himself into a sitting position against the wall, trying to slow his breathing. Amy turned back toward him.

"The door won't hold forever."

"No," he said. "But if we can stall him long enough, maybe..."

He stopped.

Behind them, the door shuddered.

Amy's hand curled into a fist. "I just want this to end."

Miles flinched as Amy readied herself.

"When he comes through, we don't run. We trap him."

Miles raised an eyebrow. "With what? A couple books and some sharp words?"

She moved to the desk and rifled through the drawers.

The door creaked again. A low growl. Then silence. Amy backed toward the bed.

She could feel it. He was on the other side waiting.

Miles groaned softly as he pushed himself to his feet. "I'm not going to be much help if he comes through."

"You'll be enough," Amy said without turning.

Miles limped over to the writing desk. He began pulling open drawers one by one, brushing aside papers, spools of thread, candle stubs, and other fragments of Sophie's quiet life.

"What're you looking for?" Amy asked.

"Looking for anything that shoots, stabs, or blinds," he muttered.

Amy moved to the night stand. It held a collection of old photographs in dusty frames, each one slightly crooked as if Sophie had straightened them over and over across the years yet they were determined to slip from the frame. One showed a younger Sophie beside two women. One was Cathy and the other... Her mother.

They stood side by side in front of a farmhouse porch, arms wrapped around each others shoulders. Her mother's hair was wild and windblown, Sophie was laughing and Cathy was pointing towards the camera.

Amy sat down on the edge of the bed and stared at the image. It was like touching a nerve that had been severed long ago. The women in the photo had all protected her. In the picture they all looked so alive and full of hope. Amy swallowed hard.

"They all died trying to save me."

"No," Miles said, pulling open another drawer. "They died saving you. That's not the same. I'm sorry but we don't have time for you to be getting all sentimental."

Amy blinked.

Then her eyes narrowed. "What did you find?"

Miles had gone still.

He pulled something slowly from the back of the lowest drawer.

It was wrapped in a faded cloth. He unrolled it revealing an old revolver. He turned it in his hand. The gun was old but well-maintained. Blue steel. Wooden grip. Sophie had clearly cared for it. He cracked open the chamber.

Three bullets.

Just three.

He glanced at Amy. "I'd say that's either just enough... or not nearly enough."

Amy stood, walked over, and took the revolver gently from his hands. She turned it over, testing the weight.

"Three's better than none."

He gave a weak grin. "Maybe we could play Russian roulette with Richard."

"Let's aim for something more productive."

She tucked the gun into her belt, grip ready. Then her eyes returned to the photographs.

She settled on one of her as a child. Amy touched the glass. She didn't remember that moment but some part of her recognized it.

A feeling. A scent.

"I was happy once," she whispered.

Miles moved beside her. "You can be again."

"I sadly don't think that's how this story ends."

A moment of silence passed between them.

Then came a knock on the door followed by two more.

Three slow, heavy beats that shook the frame. Not subtle. Like someone knocking on a coffin just to remind whoever's inside they knew they were in there. Amy froze and pulled the revolver. It felt too heavy in her hands now. Her finger hovered near the trigger.

Miles stepped beside her.

They waited in silence.

Amy inched forward. The wooden boards on the windows painted wild shadows across the floor.

The door creaked as if something was being placed against it. Amy moved closer and could hear footsteps retreating down the hallway. The sound confused her.

She turned to say something to miles but before any words could come out she was thrown off her feet as the door exploded inward.

The barricade gave way with a crash. The drawers split down the middle. Papers, glass, and wood erupted into the room like shrapnel. Amy fell backward, hitting the night-stand with her shoulder. Miles was flung to the floor with a force that knocked the wind from him. They glanced at the smouldering hole.

Richard stood in the doorway framed by darkness. Smoke curling around his shoulders like a cloak.

Miles pushed himself up. "Amy!"

Richard turned from Miles to Amy.

"Still hiding behind borrowed names?" he said softly.

Amy scrambled to her feet, grappling with the revolver in her hands. Her vision blurred and hearing pierced.

Richard lunged and she fired.

The deafening shot echoed through the room as the bullet struck him in the shoulder.

He didn't stop.

Amy fired again. It hit lower and the bullet entered in between his ribs.

Still, he came at her.

The third click didn't come. Richard reached for her, ready with his knife. He swung fast but stumbled as Miles slammed into him, knocking him into the wall.

Richard reared back, and slashed blindly.

Miles ducked as the blade carved a line through the wallpaper above his head.

Amy backed toward the desk, grabbing a lamp and flinging it at him.

It hit Richard in the chest and shattered.

He barely flinched.

His eyes focused on her.

Amy grabbed Miles and pulled him back toward the window. Panic crossed his face.

"We're not jumping," he gasped looking at the boarded frame.

"No we're not." she said. "But he on the other hand."

Richard turned again, knife raised and lunged at them.

Amy spun around him and slammed her boot into his lower back.

He stumbled against the boards knocking the breath from his lungs. Amy took a second then ran at him and jumped, kicking him with all her might in the stomach.

The wood cracked beneath his weight as he twisted on impact.

Miles charged at him hitting him in the back with his shoulder.

The wood splintered more then cracked as Richard's body smashed through the window. Glass exploded as he disappeared into the darkness outside.

Amy fell to her knees, panting.

The cold wind from outside blew into the room sending a chill up Miles' spine.

Amy crawled to the edge of the window, careful to not cut herself on the glass and peered down. The garden below was dimly lit by the crescent moon overhead.

"Do you see him?" Miles asked.

She was frozen and couldn't answer.

Richard wasn't there. The spot where he should have landed was empty except for shattered shards of glass. No body. No blood.

There was something else. A flaming symbol burned on the lawn. A shape she recognized from Sophie's journal. A ritual glyph.

Miles crawled beside her and stared down.

"Is that...?"

Amy nodded. "It's part of the ritual. All of this was planned."

In the trees they could make out silhouettes standing watching. Amy narrowed her eyes. They wore red ceremonial robes. Their arms and hands were clasped in front of them like in silent prayer.

She turned back to Miles.

"Richard will be back. He's not done."

Miles gritted his teeth. "Neither are we."

Amy nodded slowly then she looked down again at the burning glyph and made a decision.

"It's time to burn it all down."

She turned back to the room. The bedroom looked like a battlefield now. The door was a pile of scorched wood, the drawers had been blasted in half and the window gaped like a wound.

It was like a dream she hadn't quite woken from. Had Richard really been there? She'd shot him. She saw the bullets hit. She remembered the sound. The way he flinched.

But then he'd kept coming.

She shook her head, her mind trying to make sense of everything

No. He was real.

She felt the bruises forming across her ribs. She could still feel the weight of his knife slicing through the air. She turned around. Miles was on the floor, slumped against the wall.

"Hey," she said gently, moving toward him. "Hey Miles."

He didn't respond.

She dropped to her knees beside him.

His face was pale. His lips bloodless. His breath shallow.

"Miles?"

He stirred as his eyes fluttered open, glassy with pain.

"Sorry," he murmured. "I took the scenic route on the way to unconsciousness."

She smiled despite herself. "Please don't do that."

He tried to sit up and winced.

That's when Amy saw it.

His shirt was soaked through on the left side.

A deep, spreading red.

She pulled the fabric aside and saw the wound.

A ragged slash. Deep. Across his chest, under the collarbone, angling toward the ribs. The flesh had already started to bruise beneath the blood. He'd been hit during the fight and never said a word.

"Oh my god," she breathed.

She tore at the curtain next to them and pressed it hard against the wound. He grunted in pain.

"I need to get you out of here." Amy placed his shoulder around his neck and helped him up. "It'll be ok."

She guided him towards the door but slipped dropping him against the wall. Miles let out a noise as he slid down the wall, consciousness failing him.

"Stay with me," she said, voice suddenly tight. Blood seeped through the fabric.

"You know," Miles groaned, "for a town with so many demons and people being killed, you'd think someone would stock first aid kits."

Amy looked around desperately.

No medical supplies. Nothing but broken furniture, shattered glass and the journal.

She grabbed it and flipped through quickly, scanning Sophie's notes hoping for something.

A section stood out;

> *The man wears flesh like a mask. But beneath it,*
> *he's always been the same thing. A thing that feeds*
> *on control. He's no demon. Not yet. But close*
> *enough.*

Amy wiped the sweat from Miles's forehead with the hem of her sleeve.

His skin was clammy. Shaking.

"We need to get you out of here."

"Where?" he rasped. "Through the front door where our welcoming committee's waiting?"

She didn't answer.

He was right. They were trapped.

She looked back at the window. The glass was mostly gone. The fire had burned low, but the wind still blew in cool and sharp.

"We need to get out of here while we can." she said. "It's safer to keep moving."

Miles gave a weak chuckle. "Safe is relative."

Amy tore more fabric and bound it crudely around his chest as best she could. His skin color was fading.

She looked at him. "I need you to stay alive."

He gave a small laugh and nodded.

"You're okay," she whispered.

"Liar," he mumbled.

Amy managed a weak smile. "A little."

She looked back out of the window and looked down again. It was a drop but they could potentially make it. A guttural rasp made her turn back to Miles. Richard stood over him, his knife protruding from his chest

Amy's vision swam.

She wanted to run, to fight, to scream. But all she could do was watch.

Amy shook her head. "No… no…"

Richard crouched, then gently whispered something into Miles's ear. Amy couldn't hear it but she saw Miles laugh. A wet, coughing laugh, defiant to the very last second.

Richard lifted the blade and brought it down again.

Amy looked away, but the sound would never leave her.

Time stretched and folded like damp fabric. Her knees ached, her fingers had gone numb around the journal clutched against her chest. Miles was gone. Her last hook on world outside of the town.

The world felt quieter for it.

Her body finally moved without permission. She turned to the window then back to Richard. With a deep breath she jumped.

CHAPTER FOURTEEN

As Amy fell she managed to grab a drainpipe which broke in her hands, slowing her down slightly. Her leg crunched beneath her as she hit the ground hard.

There was no time to feel the pain as she pushed herself up. She scrambled to her feet, slipping in the mud before breaking into a blind hobbled run. Trees loomed in every direction, their branches skeletal and black against the sky. The woods no longer felt just like a group of trees but felt like something alive. With every step each tree trunk seemed to lean in closer, forming a cage around her. Every shadow felt like another bar walling her in.

Branches scratched her arms as she ran and roots grasped at her boots. She nearly fell, only catching herself at the last second. The pain in her leg was making it hard for her to remain steady on her feet but she pushed through it. Her breath tore in and out of her lungs like it was being ripped from her by some external force.

Then she heard them.

Footsteps amongst the leaves.

They weren't trying to hide. They wanted her to hear, wanted her to know she was being hunted.

Amy veered off the deer path and dove into a thicket, thorns scraping her palms and cheeks. She crouched low and held her breath. The footsteps grew louder. She held her breath with every bit of concentration she could. They passed close, then slowed. She could make out voices of the townsfolk but the tress muffled what they were saying.

She pressed herself deeper into the brush, heart pounding.

They moved towards her hiding spot and gently kicked the brush. Amy held her hands tightly over her mouth, masking any sign she may be there. Another kick made her let out a little gasp. There was a pause then more talking. "She's not here."

"Let's keep moving, she can't have gotten too far." They moved away from the brush and continued downhill toward a clearing.

Amy crawled out the opposite side and bolted again. She ran until her lungs burned and her legs screamed. As she glanced over her shoulder to see if she was being followed, her foot caught on a rock and she tumbled down a slope, rolling through mud and dead leaves until she crashed into a hollow between two trees.

Silence, pain and darkness consumed her.

Then light began to fill her vision, stars crossed through the darkness. A flicker of something approaching.

A torch?

Amy tried to move, but her ankle throbbed. She bit back a cry and crawled forward, dragging herself toward the light. It felt like it was calling to her like a beacon of safety.

A figure stepped into view. Tall. Familiar.

She flinched, grabbing a rock in panic.

"Amy?"

She froze and looked past the light. Sheriff Barker stood hand on his gun.

He stepped closer, holding up both hands. The Sheriffs face was drawn and his uniform torn down the side, one sleeve soaked in blood. But his eyes were alert, constantly surveying the surroundings.

"You're safe. I've got you."

Amy didn't speak. She knew she couldn't without letting out a pained scream.

The sheriff knelt beside her and checked her ankle, then looked her in the eye.

"We need to move. They're not far behind me."

"Richard…" she whispered.

He nodded grimly. "I know. Come on."

He helped her to her feet, wrapped an arm around her waist, and guided her through the trees. He was strong, steady, and careful not to ask questions she wasn't ready to answer.

"Why are you helping me?" she finally asked.

He didn't hesitate.

"Because you're not the monster they want you to be and you're the only one who can stop all this."

Amy leaned heavily on him, her ankle pulsing like fire beneath every step. She'd stopped trying to make sense of the pain. It was just a metronome now, with each step sending a bolt of pain up through her leg.

"They were behind me," she said hoarsely. "In the trees. I think they were circling."

"They were," the sheriff muttered. "I came in behind one group. Almost walked right into them but I held back until I managed to pick up your trail."

Amy looked to him with a thankful smile. She stumbled again, and he caught her weight effortlessly, adjusting her arm around his shoulder.

"You okay?"

"No," she whispered. "Not even close."

"That's fair."

They walked in silence for a while longer. She started to lose track of the path, if there even was one, until she saw something through the trees. It was a faint orange light, steady and warm.

The sheriff reached a patch of brush which had clearly been well-trodden.

"Come on. We don't have long."

They moved through shadow and dirt. Pine needles and dust stung her eyes. Wind rushed past her face. Every bump in the trail jolted her bones. Eventually, the forest began to thin and the faint light was getting stronger and then she saw it.

A low, boxy shape emerging from the dark, another police station.

. . . .

It was much smaller then the one she'd visited in the main town.

This one was older, tucked behind the woods on the north side, a backup outpost from a time when New Grayson had more logging routes than stop signs. It'd always been safer to have a small patrol stationed there in case anything occurred, which it often did. As the logging began to dry up, the station had been abandoned with only a few who actually remembered it existed.

Barker helped her along, and unlocked the heavy door with a set of keys that jingled loudly in the dark.

The interior was musty and cold with the overhead lights casting the orange light across the room. The walls were lined with filing cabinets, hunting maps, a dusty coffee pot. A metal desk sat in the centre. At the back next to a small store room were two holding cells behind an open reinforced steel door, old, but solid.

"You've been here before?" Amy asked.

"Not in years until today. When I heard you were headed in this direction I came and checked it was still here." Barker said, locking the door behind them. "But it's off-grid. Quiet. We'll be safe here for a while."

Amy collapsed into the chair nearest the desk, her body trembling.

"Thank you," she whispered.

He nodded once and moved to a small locked cabinet. From inside he pulled out a first aid kit and a a bottle of water.

"We patch you up first," he said. "Then we talk."

She nodded and didn't argue.

He knelt beside her. Pulling the boot away from her swollen ankle he gently wrapped it with gauze and tape, then he handed her the water bottle.

She drank in silence.

After a moment, she asked, "Why?"

"Why what?"

"Why are you helping me? After everything?"

He looked at her, and for the first time, she saw the cracks in his composure. The weariness in his face. The years of pretending everything was okay.

"I was born here. Raised in that church. Taught the myths, the beliefs, the stories. Most of us were. But I saw the truth too young. Saw what Richard was building. He says all of this is for the good of the town, but it's him that's benefitting. I even tried to leave once. They brought me back."

He looked at the door, his eyes distant.

"I've kept my head down for years. Pretended all was OK. I took the badge and played the part. But I never stopped watching. Never stopped waiting."

"For what?" she asked.

"For the answer to it all. For a way to stop him. I've been waiting for you."

The room felt colder.

Amy sat forward. "What do you mean?"

"The girl who burned and lived. The one they whispered about in secret."

Amy shook her head.

"I'm not her any more."

"Yes, you are. But you're also who you've become now. They hate that you've grown up. Richard hated you'd forgotten who you are. He needs you to remember."

Amy shivered.

He stood and placed a hand on her shoulder. "You're not what they say you are. You aren't some devil. But you're not nothing, either. You're the crack in their perfect mirror and they're terrified of what'll happen if you fight back."

Amy looked away, tears brimming in her eyes.

"I let him die," she whispered. "Miles."

"No," Barker said. "You lived. That's what he wanted. That's what scares Richard the most. There are people willing to die for you. He knows you won't be as easy to coerce as he expected."

She stared at the desk, fists clenched.

"They're not done are they? They're not going to stop until Richard has me?"

"No," he agreed.

Suddenly, a loud clang echoed through the woods outside.

Barker's hand dropped to his holster.

"Get in the back," he said quietly.

Amy moved quickly, limping toward the far hallway. She paused at the holding cells, unsure.

"This one," he said, opening the door to a storage room with no windows. He flicked on the light. "Stay quiet. Don't open the door until I give the all-clear."

Amy stepped inside. Her heart thudded as he shut the door and locked it.

Outside, the wind picked up and somewhere in the trees, voices echoed through the night.

....

Amy sat alone in the dim light of the storage room, her legs tucked beneath her, blanket wrapped tightly around her shoulders. The concrete beneath her was cold and unforgiving. Her ankle throbbed with a dull heat and her ribs ached with every breath. But none of that compared to the ache in her chest the kind that came from knowing she was still alive and Miles wasn't. She blinked hard, forcing the image of his last moment from her mind. It came back anyway, again and again, the pain in his face scarred her vision.

A key clicked in the lock.

Amy tensed.

Then the door creaked open, and Barker stepped in. His boots scuffed the ground softly. He looked tired. Older. His eyes sunken with worry.

187

"It's just me, I couldn't see anyone out there but they'll still be searching. It's only a matter of time until someone heads this way." he said quietly, then handed her a tin mug. "Tea. Not great, but it's warm."

She accepted it with a nod. The liquid steamed faintly. She sipped it without speaking.

He sat down beside her on a crate. For a long time, neither of them spoke.

The sheriff looked at Amy's hands. They were shaking slightly.

"I never thought I'd live to see this," he said. "Thought maybe I'd die before you came back. I have wondered though if that would've been better. Easier."

Amy said nothing.

He leaned forward, elbows on his knees. "When I was sixteen, Richard came to town. Not like a stranger. Like a preacher returning from a pilgrimage. Said he'd been called. Said the town had been chosen as the place for salvation. We were withering back then, small population, few jobs, nothing left. He offered us purpose. Unity. He offered direction to grow and thrive. No one asked where he'd come from, no one questioned who he was. People just accepted him. We had nothing to lose."

Amy frowned. "And they believed him?"

"Not everyone. Not at first. But he gave people something they hadn't had in a long time. Hope. Then the accidents started. People who didn't agree… they vanished. Got lost in the woods or worse. Folks quickly stopped asking questions. Then there were rumblings of secret services at night. The church put a curfew in place. They said it was to keep people safe but it was the opposite."

He paused, rubbing his face with both hands.

"Once, I followed Richard after curfew."

"Curfew?" Amy took another sip

"Yes. I saw him bury something in the church yard. Still don't know what it was. But from where I stood it looked like a body covered in a sheet. A small one. I tried to tell my father. He told me that we all serve something and I'd better pick the winning side before I ended up forgotten. It was then that I realised the curfew was simply a way of allowing Richard and his church to get away with whatever they wanted without questions or observers."

Amy wrapped the blanket tighter.

"What happened after that?" she asked.

"I played dumb. Played loyal. I did my job. Protected who I could. Stalled when I could. I thought maybe if I kept my head down, I'd have time to stop it when it really mattered."

He looked at her now, eyes dark.

"That time is now, Amy."

She swallowed hard. "It's too late."

"No," he said. "It isn't."

He stood and walked to the far corner, pulling a folded map from the back of a filing cabinet. He spread it on a crate between them.

"This town is rigged to pull you inward," he said, pointing. "Every road curves back to itself. The paths in the woods bend when you're not watching. Richard crafted it into a maze to keep those he wanted to here. It sounds crazy but he's used something in this town to turn it into a..."

Amy leaned over the map, she looked at the added sections that had been drawn on over the years.

"A trap?" Amy looked up at him. "He used the tree?"

Barker nodded. "The tree was the key to keeping the town safe he said. The tree became the centre of the maze. All roads led to it. There was something about it that was otherworldly, like it'd been here long before the town."

Amy stared at the map. He was right, the highways in and out were a spiral. The old rail lines cut straight into the centre. Everything fed the town. Nothing left.

"There's a way out though," the sheriff said. "One that not many know about. The old maintenance trail out near the quarry. Long since buried, but it runs under the ridge. That's how I tried to escape. It was Richard who caught me and gave me a choice. He needed my father so he couldn't just make me disappear. If you move fast, you can maybe get out before they block it."

Amy shook her head. "I can't just run. Not now."

"It's your choice," he said, firm now. "But the longer you stay here, the more you fuel the ritual. Every step you take inside this place get's him nearer his goal. That is unless you stop him."

She hesitated, thinking about the journal, Sophie's words, Cathy's drawings, the binding sigils and the markings.

"They already killed Kira," she whispered. "Then Sophie and Miles. It's happening exactly the way he wants."

"I know," he said.

"The final thing they need is me."

He didn't speak. Which meant he agreed.

She stood now, limping slightly.

"I can't run. Not any more. If I leave, he'll try and finish his ritual with someone else. Or they'll just find bring me and bring me back. I can't keep looking over my shoulder for the rest of my life and I can't leave knowing I could've done something."

He stepped forward. "If you stay, you may not get back out."

"But if I stop him..." she said, voice low.

"You won't get another chance to go if you don't."

The silence between them thickened.

She sat stiff, tea cooling in her hand, but still refused to run. The sheriff had tried to convince her to leave. Had pointed to the old maps, had muttered about maintenance tunnels and the trail, but she'd only stared at him. Finally, he'd gone quiet and now they sat in the cold police outpost together, silent except for the low hum of an ageing generator and the occasional creak of wood under the shifting wind.

"You want the truth," the sheriff said at last, leaning forward with a groan. "Fine. I'll give it to you."

Amy didn't look at him.

"I don't need another speech about running," she muttered.

"You won't get one," he said. "Not any more. You're past that."

She looked up.

His expression had changed. No longer just worry and tension but something else. A resignation like he'd dropped whatever mask he'd been wearing.

He stood and crossed the room to the far filing cabinet. From the bottom drawer, he pulled out a thick folder bound in twine. He set it on the desk and untied it slowly, his hands calloused and steady.

"I kept these here, kept them safe."

Inside were yellowed pages, some handwritten, some typed on fading paper. Photographs, black-and-white, grainy, some of them decades old. Newspaper clippings. Topographical maps.

He slid an old piece of parchment with a painting on across the table to Amy.

A church made of stone and brick. Grand, but stern. It appeared to be in a large cavern. Behind it stood the large red tree.

"This was the Church they built when the town was founded. Before they rebuilt it down town."

Amy picked up the painting. Something about it was wrong, the angle, the haze around the tree. It felt like the picture itself had been painted by someone who wasn't supposed to be there. It looked like the place she and Miles had found.

"This is the church under the town."

He nodded. "They built it in the caves when they found the tree. There was something special about it and the fact it grew underground led them to believe it was something worth worshipping. There were ideas about it and stories which transcended generations. Most sounded far fetched but now I'm sure most were real. This is what Richard had been searching for when he stumbled on the town."

He slid a photo of a man who looked like himself only older.

"My father was sheriff before me," he said. "My grandfather, before him. This town's always had someone to wear the badge and look the other way. But not all of them liked it."

He pulled another sheet and handed it to her. It was a scan of a diary entry.

> *June 14, 1959*
> *The Hollow Boys returned. All four this time. Caked in ash, mouths sealed. Tomlinson says it's a hallucination, maybe from tunnel fumes. But the Binding Flame folk... they lit candles. They celebrated. I think they brought those boys back on purpose. I think they let something else wear their skin.*

Amy's mouth went dry.

He pointed to the text. "That's my great-uncle's handwriting. He vanished three weeks after writing that. They said it was a hunting accident. They never found his body."

He handed her another and leaned back. Amy looked at it with fascination.

> *October 12, 1923*
> *The Bakers have been complaining about their livestock again. They keep saying they are vanishing at night. They say the devils are getting them. I've advised them there are no devils in this town.*

> *October 13, 1923*

> *It happened again last night. Livestock just vanished. It makes no sense. The Bakers are beside themselves. Note taken to put someone on watch tonight.*

Amy lowered the pages and saw the Sheriff straighten.

"I read this stuff when I was in my early teens. My dad caught me and beat me within an inch of my life. Not because I found it but because I started asking questions. I didn't understand then, that survival here meant silence. It was only after Richard that I realised there was far more to the town."

Amy's hands curled into fists.

"Why didn't you say something?" she asked.

The sheriff sighed.

"Because they own this town. The people. The ground. The air. You don't get it yet, but the truth is New Grayson isn't just where the ritual happens. It is the ritual."

He gestured at the maps.

"Even before Richard the streets were designed in spirals and with the town's help, shifted them further for the rituals. The buildings are aligned to astrological markers. They probably didn't realise at the time but the tree got them to build it this way. Even the damn power grid pulses in thirteen-minute cycles during the solstice. All of it's designed to feed whatever lives below."

Amy flipped to another sheet. A faded birth record, marked with the symbol from Sophie's journal.

"Some of these people… they were born into it?" she asked.

"Yes," the sheriff said. "But others came here. Chosen. Like your mother."

Amy's breath caught.

"She wasn't from here?"

"No. She came when she was in her late twenties. Just… appeared one day much like Richard had. All she had with her was a backpack and a kid. You."

Amy stared at him.

"She was scared out of her mind. Said she couldn't remember how you'd both gotten here. She remembered very little about before she arrived."

"I wish I remembered her."

Barker smiled faintly.

"She was the strongest person I've ever known."

Amy closed the folder slowly.

"This is all connected isn't it? It's not just about me or you. It's about the town. The land. The people who made it this way."

The sheriff nodded.

"They built it around a wound in the world and they've been feeding it ever since."

Amy stood, her legs still shaky but steadier than before.

"Then I'm not running," she said. "Not until I end it."

The sheriff didn't argue. He only looked down at his watch.

"We've got until sunrise," he said. "After that..." He paused.

"What?" she asked.

He didn't answer at first.

"Then it's too late. He'll get the gate open and it'll be the end of everything."

Amy's chest went still.

"How do you know?"

"Because they tried it once before. In 1983."

He looked at her and in his eyes, she saw the thing he had been carrying all this time and had hidden for so many years.

Fear.

"We covered it up. Blamed it on a storm. But for seven hours, there was no sound in this town except screaming. People saw things. Heard voices. And when it ended, there were twenty-three bodies missing. Gone. No trace. My dad said the town had to forget or it would happen again."

He turned to Amy.

"But it's not about forgetting. It's about repeating. Without you they'll force it open again and this time I worry it won't just be a small amount. It'll open fully."

Amy stepped back, stunned.

"Why now?"

"Because the town's dying and it's Richard's final chance. It's no coincidence you and your friends were brought here. No coincidence that they killed Cathy when they did. Everything that has happened has been guiding you to your destiny."

Amy's legs failed her and she dropped into the chair.

Then a low dull sound scraped the window.

The sheriff snapped to attention, hand on his holster. He suddenly realised that if everything had happened for a reason, so had them being there.

Amy froze.

"Is that?" she whispered.

He nodded slowly.

"They've found us."

. . . .

The sheriff reached into the cabinet again and handed her a small pistol.

"It's loaded," he said. "Don't shoot unless you have to and don't waste time with warnings."

Amy took it.

"I shot him before. It didn't do anything."

"I know. This is for the others. Or for yourself if all goes wrong. But I'm not going to let it get to that."

She stared at the gun.

The scraping grew louder.

The sheriff moved toward the hallway door, peeking into the main room. Amy followed closely behind.

"Get back in the storage room." The Sheriff said.

"No."

He looked at her. A tired smile. Amy's jaw tightened.

"Let them come."

A scrape then a hollow knock. Amy stood behind the sheriff, pistol clutched tight in her hand. Her throat was dry, her ankle still throbbing, but none of that mattered now.

The sheriff moved to the window. The silence of the woods outside was unbearable. The kind of silence that pressed in on your chest. Finally, the scraping ceased. The stillness that followed was worse.

"Barker?" Amy whispered.

He didn't respond immediately. When he turned, his face looked paler than before, washed out by something internal rather than fear. He pulled his gun and raised it in front of him.

"It's them," he said.

Amy swallowed. "What do they want?"

"You," the sheriff replied.

Amy stood beside him. "What're they going to do?"

In that instant glass exploded into the room as a log came tumbling through the side window. Barker and Amy stumbled backwards with guns raised as four intruders climbed through the window. They held knives by their sides like they were expecting a fight.

The sheriff moved in front of Amy.

"STAY BACK!"

The intruders paused briefly and looked at them.

"We just want the girl. If you hand her over now, they might let you live."

The sheriff glanced over his shoulder at Amy.

"Get behind the wall. NOW."

The leader of the group smiled then rushed at the Sheriff, who pulled the trigger. The gunshot echoed through the building as it struck the man's shoulder, sending him spiralling sideways. The others moved in. Barker fired again this time hitting one in the stomach and another in the chest. But they were too quick.

The first regained his balance and grimaced at he lunged at the sheriff, swinging his blade in a wide arc. It caught Barker's arm causing him to twist. He tried to fire again but the bullet went wide embedding itself in the wall.

The fourth attacker dashed towards Amy.

She backed up and pulled the trigger in panic. The first shot missed but delayed him enough that she managed to get a second one off, this time into the neck of the attacker dropping him to the ground.

Barker was still fighting with the leader. Amy watched as a knife penetrated deep into Barker's side causing him to scream out in pain. He turned and saw the one he'd shot in the stomach crawling towards Amy, like some zombie from an 80's horror film. He managed to raise his gun and fire, hitting him in the spine.

Three were down and it was just the leader of the group that was still breathing.

Barker smashed the butt of the gun into the attackers face but received a headbutt in response followed by a twist to the blade. They tumbled to the floor, grappling for their lives.

Amy watched as the bodies writhed with each other. She couldn't work out where the attacker started and Barker ended. Two gunshots bellowed out and the two were still. She kept her gun raised ready.

Time seemed to slow as she surveyed the chaos and the bodies. Suddenly the attackers body moved causing her to slightly pull the trigger but she relaxed when she saw it was Barker who was moving it. He pushed the body from on top of him and pulled himself backwards to sit up against a cabinet.

Amy let out the breath she'd been holding and dropped to the floor near the sheriff.

CHAPTER FIFTEEN

Amy sat on the floor, wrapped in the blanket, barely noticing the chill of her back against the cold wall. The pistol the sheriff had given her rested on the floor beside her, untouched since the attack.

Outside, the wind was rising and sent papers astray through the smashed window. It was like the trees were whispering secrets to each other, growing restless in their roots.

The Sheriff sat slumped against a filing cabinet holding some cloth to the stab wound in his side. The bodies of the intruders still littered the stone floor.

"There'll be more of them. When these lot don't return more will come." Barker said, looking to her. She didn't know what to do.

She blinked and looked over to him.

Amy shook her head. "I can't do this."

The Sheriff didn't look good. Blood dripped from the cloth to the floor.

"I've seen that look before," he said.

Amy didn't answer she just stared down at the pistol.

"I don't know what he is," she said. "Richard. I don't think he's just a man any more."

"He's not," the sheriff said coughing up some blood. "But he remembers what it feels like to be one and that makes him dangerous."

Amy's chest ached.

"I should've done more," she said. "I should've seen it coming. Kira. Miles. Sophie. You"

The sheriff didn't interrupt.

"I let them die thinking I was just Amy. But I'm not. I'm whoever this Willow is."

"You're friend Kira knew. I could hear it in her voice," the sheriff said. "Even though she knew, she still wanted to keep you safe. It was her choice."

Amy looked at him, tears burning her eyes. Her mind was circling in convoluted circles.

"If I don't try to stop him, I'll die anyway."

He didn't argue. Instead, he pulled something from his pocket, a small, faded photograph. He handed it to her. It was her mother. Holding a toddler in her arms. They were standing in front of a brick wall covered in ivy. Her mother wasn't smiling, but her eyes were full of life. Fierce and protective. Ready to fight.

"She didn't run," the sheriff said. "She saved you. She knew someone would keep you safe when she was gone. That's why he killed her. She wanted to stop him."

Amy stared at the photo until her hands began to shake.

"Where did you get this?"

He handed her another photo, his blood smeared the corner. This one was of Cathy standing next to a young Kira.

"I found them amongst Cathy's items. She believed in you too. Both of them did. They kept your secret and kept you safe," the sheriff continued. "So did Sophie and Miles. They didn't die to buy your obedience. They died to buy you time. Whatever your choice, it has to be yours or all of this was for nothing."

Amy wiped her face. Then stood slowly.

"Do you have any weapons? Knives, guns?" she asked.

The sheriff tilted his head. "Are you planning to fight him?"

"I don't know what I'm planning," she said. "But I want options."

He pointed towards a cabinet and she opened the bottom drawer. She retrieved a hunting knife from it, the weight felt solid in her palm. She hid it inside her coat, tying it off with the elastic from her bootlace.

The sheriff watched her for a long moment.

"Are you just going to walk right up to him?"

"it's what he's planned isn't it?"

"And you're not going there to surrender?" he said.

"I don't think I ever could. If I'm going to die, I may as well try and stop this in the process." she replied.

Then she looked him in the eye. His skin was already going pale.

"I'm going to Richard's office to finish this."

"What about the gun?" he said quietly eyes drifting to the weapon ion the floor. She glanced to it.

"The gun did nothing to him last time. I hope a knife to his throat might be more effective."

He nodded.

She turned toward the door. The sheriff called after her softly. "Amy."

She paused.

"Don't let him make you forget who you are."

She smiled sadly. "If I make it out alive, I'll come back for you."

"We both know I'm not going to make it. Make my death mean something."

She nodded and checked the knife was strapped tight to her body.

Amy felt its weight against her ribs with every step she took toward the door. The leather grip pressed close to her skin, grounding her. Not for comfort. Not even for protection. But because it gave her something real to hold onto, something solid in a world that kept twisting into nightmare.

She stood in the station's front hall for a long time, staring at the door.

The wind howled through the trees outside. The ritual was moving beneath the surface she could feel it in the air.

The cold hit her instantly as she opened the door. Not deep winter cold. Just sharp, still and unforgiving. The woods were darker than they should've been. She didn't see the moon, or the stars. Only clouds and the crooked black arms of trees swaying like slow dancers.

She limped forward, careful on her injured ankle. The path wound downward, toward the edge of town. Her boots crunched against old pine needles and gravel. Somewhere in the far distance, a bell rang once.

When the trees broke, and she stepped onto the first gravel road that led toward the edge of New Grayson proper, she expected to see people but she saw none. No townsfolk, no figures in red, no masked believers.

As she hobbled through the town she studied the buildings. Shutters creaked as if moved by unseen hands and curtains stirred. Amy knew she was being watched.

She passed the grocery store which was now boarded up, it looked like something with claws had torn through the front.

She passed the motel and saw no lights on.

Each step was slower now. Each breath colder.

She wasn't ready to be anyone's sacrifice. She wasn't going to die here.

The mayor's office came into view.

It stood at the far end of the square, past the church and next to the town hall. There was no-one guarding the building, there were no gates. She hadn't expected a full welcoming committee but had expected something.

As she stepped into the square, she noticed something that made her stop.

The air had changed. It felt thick but not humid. The pressure of her choice rested on her shoulders and it was weighing her down. She still clutched the journal tight beneath her arm. The pages felt warm. She'd brought it to keep a bit of Cathy and a bit of Sophie with her. They'd kept her safe in the past, maybe they'd do the same now.

The mayor's office loomed before her now. Its facade was smooth, too clean for a town this old. The flag above the door fluttered gently in the breeze. She climbed the steps one by one, each echoing behind her like thunder.

The doors weren't locked. She pushed one open and stepped inside.

The interior was quiet. Marble floors. An old wooden desk. Framed photos on the walls, images of past mayors, all stern-faced and identical in posture. Richard's portrait hung above the front desk. He was smiling in it, looking down on all that entered.

Amy stared at it for a moment then kept walking. The staircase was fully lit, leading and guiding her up. There were no people around, no noises other then her own heartbeat.

The halls were narrow, the walls painted red and gold. There were symbols carved faintly into the corners, they were noticeable enough because she'd seen them in the journals, but they would likely not have been visible to most.

She passed a set of double doors, their glass windows stained with something dark and finally, at the far end of the hallway stood a single open door leaking it's warm light like an invitation.

She stopped just before the threshold. Her hand found the hilt of the knife under her coat.

She breathed in once, deep and steady then stepped inside.

....

Amy entered slowly, eyes scanning everything. The room smelled like old paper and polished wood. It was a large, high-ceilinged office with ornate wooden beams, floor-length red drapes, and a fire burning low in a stone hearth. The walls were lined with old books.

There, behind a desk too large for one man, sat Richard.

He looked exactly as he did in the painting in the lobby. Not monstrous nor grotesque. Just calm and composed. Like a man who'd been expecting her for a long time.

The only thing that changed as she entered was his expression: curiosity.

For the first time he didn't look like he was in control. He genuinely wasn't sure what she'd say or do.

Amy stepped in the room and slowly closed the door behind her.

"You came," Richard said, folding his hands. "I wasn't sure you would. But I'd hoped."

Amy didn't answer.

"You can sit, if you'd like." He motioned to a high-backed chair opposite his desk.

"I'll stand." she said.

He nodded with a smile. "Fair."

The silence stretched for a beat, then Richard leaned back slightly, regarding her the way a scholar might a puzzle piece that was inches from finally falling into place.

"You look more like her then I remembered," he said.

Amy raised an eyebrow. "Cathy? Or my mother?"

"Neither," he said. "The girl before you."

Amy's stomach tightened.

"What are you talking about?"

"I imagine by now you know that you aren't the first?" he said softly. "There were many before you but they were all failures. They kept the gate alive but could never open it. You were created to be the answer to that but you're damn mother got in the way."

Amy didn't respond.

He tapped a finger on the wood desk.

"I'm not your ritual," she said.

"No," he agreed. "You're my key."

She frowned.

Richard stood, slow and deliberate, and walked to a tall cabinet. He pulled it open, revealing rows of hand-bound tomes wrapped in twine. He removed a small iron box and carried it back to the desk.

"You want to know what this town really is?" he asked.

"No," Amy said. "I already do."

He smiled faintly. "Tell me, then."

She stepped forward. "It's a wound. A scar that someone tried to stitch closed, but you keep reopening it."

Richard chuckled, not mockingly. More like someone genuinely impressed.

"Well said."

He opened the iron box.

Inside was a coil of black string, an old knife with symbols adorning its blade, and a very old mottled piece of parchment. The paper had yellowed, but the image was clear.

A baby, wrapped in cloth, held in the arms of a gaunt, pale man with a sunken face and eyes like deep wells.

"This was the first," Richard said. "The first child born at the convergence. Not to open the gate. But to keep it from closing."

Amy's eyes narrowed. "If it's been happening for such a long time, why you?"

He laughed. "The town and the gate have been here far longer than me, true. But I was drawn here by it's power. I was chosen. You are the one I..." He thought about his words.

"The one they've been waiting for all these years," he said. "You're mother stopped your destiny. With the tree gone there isn't much more time. We've kept it alive but the roots are dying. After all these centuries it was a little girl who almost brought an end to it. Now that girls stands in front of me ready to fulfil her purpose."

He gently closed the box again.

Amy stepped forward.

"You think I'm going to say I'll be your sacrifice?" she said.

Richard tilted his head. "I think you already did, somewhere deep inside, or you wouldn't be here."

"I came to understand." she said. "Not surrender."

"Then understand this," he said. "You are the key Willow. You were made from fire, ash and memory. They tried to save you, and in doing so, they gave us exactly what we needed. Someone broken and full of rage. I knew you'd be back. It's always been your path."

Amy shook her head. "Sophie and Cathy did what they had to. They made me human."

"And in doing so," Richard said, "they made you more then that."

From outside a faint sound of chanting had begun. Amy glanced toward the windows. The curtains swayed slightly but she could see people forming in the square. The smell of smoke threaded through the carpet and wallpaper.

"They're gathering," Richard said quietly. "They've been waiting for you a long time."

Amy's fingers twitched near the knife beneath her coat. It's weight was like a great pressure on her body.

"What happens if I say no?" she asked.

"The gate opens and you die anyway." he said. "They will be released. They will take over, destroy and burn this world to the ground."

Amy stared at him.

"And if I just accept my so-called purpose. Won't the same thing happen?"

"No," he said. "Because if you come willingly, you stay yourself. Awake. You'll feel the world. You'll help guide and shape it. You will stand by my side through what's to come. We will create a new world. I'll be like a king and you'll be..."

Amy's voice was ice.

"You want me to be your queen?"

Richard didn't flinch.

"I want you to be what you were always meant to be... Complete."

Another whisper from outside.

Amy took a single step toward him. "If I join you, what happens to the town?"

"They survive," he said. "The ritual ends. The gate remains open but we will be in control."

"And if I fight you?"

"Then the town is nothing but cinders and the world forgets it ever existed. Then eventually everything will burn"

Amy stared at him.

He stepped closer.

"I'm offering peace," he said. "One moment of pain, in exchange for a world we can be in control of."

Amy's voice came quietly.

"That's not peace," she said. "That's control."

Richard's smile faded.

"You don't understand what's coming," he said.

"I don't need to," she replied.

She unzipped her coat half an inch and her fingers closed around the knife.

Richard stepped around the desk.

Somewhere outside, a bell rang again. Louder this time. Dozens of voices joined it a chant

Amy felt it. The town. The presence. She was being pulled again, the centre of a wheel about to spin.

"You've felt it." Richard said. "The weight. The hunger."

Amy's voice didn't waver.

"I've also felt something else."

"And what's that?"

"Resistance."

She met his eyes. Not with fear. But with rage.

Miles. Kira. Sophie. Cathy. Everything had led to this moment.

She grinned and reached for the knife. Amy didn't hesitate. Her hand moved faster than she thought, sweeping the knife from beneath her coat and driving it forward in a tight arc. The blade sang through the air and found its mark just beneath Richard's ribs. She felt the impact and the give of flesh.

Blood spilled over the floor as Richard's expression shifted, not in anger but in approval.

Amy pulled back and slashed again, this time at his throat.

He dodged slightly and a wide red line opened through his buttoned shirt, slicing his tie in half and exposing his bloody chest. He staggered but she kept moving.

The only sound in the room was Amy's ragged breath, the fire behind the desk crackling, and the wet sound of the third blow aimed at Richard's shoulder.

It connected and knocked him backwards as he stubbled onto one knee.

Amy stood over him, panting, the knife slick in her grip imbedded near his collar bone.

"Is this what you wanted?" She hissed. "You asked me to remember. You wanted me to wake up. Well here I am."

Richard looked up, his eyes gleaming like coals in ash.

He smiled, then moved. Not like a man. Much faster.

His hand snapped forward, catching her wrist and he twisted. The sound of bones grinding made her scream. The knife clattered across the floor. She tried to pull away but his grip was like a vice.

"Very good," he said through bloodied lips.

He rose to his feet, dragging her with him. Amy kicked and punched. Her fist caught his jaw, but he didn't budge.

"I've waited years for this moment," he whispered. "But I never imagined it would feel this... Beautiful."

He flung her across the room. She hit the bookshelf with a sickening crack, wood splintering beneath her back. Books crashed to the floor around her. Pain lanced through her shoulder and down her spine. Her vision swam.

But she got up, staggering to her feet, blood in her mouth, ears ringing. Amy glanced to him. Richard was still bleeding heavily from the wounds. Even still he didn't stop smiling.

"You're not scared," she said, voice shaking.

"No," he said. "Because this is what it's supposed to look like."

Amy blinked and stepped backwards. "You wanted this??"

"I needed it," he said. "Pain is proof and resistance is a match. You just lit the fuse."

He walked forward slowly, no longer hiding what he was. His shirt hung open, revealing not just flesh, but scarred symbols etched into his chest like brands.

"They made you strong," he said. "But I made you necessary. I needed them to see what you are truly capable of. Only then will they accept us."

Amy spat blood onto the floor. "You're insane."

"No," he said. "I'm ready."

He lunged.

She dove aside narrowly dodging his grip. She rolled, grabbed the journal from where it had fallen near the desk, and scrambled for the door.

"You don't get to decide what I become." she said.

"I already have." Richard replied smiling.

He stepped between her and the door with a speed that caught her off guard.

Amy backed away. There was nowhere to run. Nowhere to hide.

"Your sorrow opened the first seal," he said. "Your rage broke the second. But your choice in this moment will break the third and will complete sequence."

He raised the dagger that'd once been in the box he'd pulled out. It was etched with the same brands carved into his flesh. In that moment Amy realised he'd grabbed it while she was on the ground.

Amy's eyes widened and she screamed.

Not in fear, but in a defiant war cry.

She lunged again with bare hands this time grabbing at his throat, punching, clawing, anything to stop what came next. He caught her and pulled her close.

She gasped as he drove the knife into her stomach. Her breath slowed. A soft sound escaped her lips. Half gasp, half sob. He held her there, pressed against his chest, the only thing between them was the blade.

"Don't worry. You're not going to die. I'll not let you." he whispered. "Soon you will be my bride in a new world."

Amy tried to speak but couldn't. The pain was bright and endless. He lowered her gently to the floor, the knife still buried in her gut.

"You did well," he said. "Better than I'd hoped. They'll be very pleased."

The room spun.

The fire roared behind him, casting shadows that didn't match his shape. The townsfolk outside began to move, now their hands raised, voices low. The final stage of the ritual was about to begin.

Amy felt herself slipping. Her hand found the edge of the journal and clutched at it like it could save her.

Richard knelt beside her, watching.

"Don't fight it." he said.

Amy's vision blurred. Her lips moved. One word exited.

"Liar."

Then everything went dark.

PART III

Sometimes the worst part of dying is waking up halfway through.

CHAPTER SIXTEEN

Warmth surrounded her. Not comfort. Not softness. Just a warmth like fresh blood on skin, or breath trapped beneath heavy cloth. Amy floated in it, mind half-lost, body somewhere far below. She didn't know how long she'd been weightless. She didn't even know if she was awake.

Light pulsed through her closed eyes, red, then black, then red again. A heartbeat. Was it her own?

Voices filtered through the haze, distant and muffled, as though spoken underwater. Some she didn't recognize. Others reached into her mind, pressing against memories she didn't want to see.

"She's almost ready."

Richard's voice coiled through the dark like smoke.

"But she still resists."

She didn't recognise the voice. Female. Measured. Cold.

"She'll break soon"

Amy twitched.

Someone touched her arm. Cold fingers. Gentle, but impersonal, like a mortician adjusting the limbs of the dead.

She tried to move, to fight, to scream.

Nothing.

Her body remained still. Her breath was slow and shallow.

"She dreamed again," said another voice. "Saw the flame. Saw the child."

"Good," Richard whispered. "That means the layering is complete."

More hands and water. They wiped her face and her arms, bathing her in silence. Not a ritual of reverence, but of purpose.

"She's stronger than the last one," someone muttered.

A pause.

"She's the key. She's the end of it all."

Amy fell again into darkness.

·····················

She was in a hallway.

Wooden floors. Flickering lights.

She knew this place.

Cathy's house.

But the colours were wrong. The walls too narrow. The shadows moved in twisting tendrils. They turned corners before the light caught up.

A child laughed and Amy turned.

A small girl stood at the far end of the hallway. Pale dress. Bare feet. Long hair matted with ash and eyes that were too old for her face.

"Amy," the girl whispered.

Amy tried to move toward her.

The girl turned and ran laughing down the hallway.

Amy followed.

The floor stretched beneath her feet. The hall lengthened with every step. The walls bent inward.

She ran faster.

The laughter grew louder.

Then... flames.

The house erupted around her. Walls peeled open like blistered skin. Smoke poured from the ceilings. The girl stopped and looked back.

"Don't forget," she said.

"Forget what?" Amy gasped.

But the girl didn't answer, she simply turned and stepped into the fire.

………………..

Amy gasped awake.

Her body still didn't move. Her gut burned and her arms ached.

She was lying on stone. Cold. Smooth. Something soft beneath her head.

A cloth? A pillow?

She smelled wax, blood and ash.

Chanting drifted through the room. Low and steady. Not forceful but rhythmic and Lulling. Hands moved again. She felt thin fabric being slid over her body. She realised in that moment that she had been stripped naked. Her arms were sticky with something.

Fingers smeared ash across her forehead.

"Willow," a voice whispered.

Not Richard.

This one was familiar. Female. Kind.

Sophie?

No, it wasn't real. The voice was inside her head. It had to be.

"Willow," it said again. "You have to wake up."

Amy's fingers twitched. Just once.

Someone noticed.

"She's stirring."

"Good," Richard's voice answered. "Lets begin."

The chanting grew louder as Amy drifted into darkness again.

Into another memory.

………………..

This time she stood on a hill.

Above the town.

The sky was red. The houses below burned. In amongst the fire she could she Richard standing in silhouette holding a knife.

Kira stood beside her, looking tired. Her clothes soaked in her blood.

"You're not supposed to be here," Kira said.

"I didn't want to be." Amy answered.

Kira nodded and chuckled. "That's the trick, isn't it? None of us did."

Amy reached for her. "I'm sorry."

Kira stepped back. "Don't be. It's not over yet."

"But I failed."

"No. You woke up and remembered. That's the first step to ending this."

Amy's vision blurred.

Miles appeared behind Kira.

Sophie stood at the edge of the hill slightly further along.

Cathy's shadow lingered at the treeline.

They all watched her and all stood with her.

"You're not done," Sophie said.

Amy looked down at her hands.

They were covered in blood.

·················

She woke again. Not fully, but closer. The voices around her grew clearer.

"She's ready for the next stage."

"Move her to the circle."

"Apply the final brand."

216

Amy's breath quickened.

Panic clawed at her throat, but still her body wouldn't move.

She screamed inside but nothing came out. Then the girl spoke again

"Willow," she whispered. "Do you remember your name?"

Amy tried to answer. *"Yes. My name is Amy."*

But her lips didn't move.

The girl stepped closer. In the haze behind her eyelids, Amy saw her clearly now.

She was her. Younger. Cleaner. Unscarred. The child from the fire.

"I remember," Amy whispered.

But the voice came only inside.

The child smiled.

"Then wake up."

Amy's heart slammed once.

Then again.

And then her finger twitched.

The chanting paused.

"She's waking," a voice hissed.

"Bind her," another snapped.

Hands reached out but this time Amy moved and they backed off. Her eyes opened partially and she saw them. They were terrified.

Then she saw the altar. The candles. The circle of ash.

They were in the cavern beneath the church. The cavern with the remnants of the red tree.

She looked down. A symbol was painted beneath her silk covered body. It glowed a burning red.

Amy's fully eyes opened. She was awake.

For a second, she wasn't sure they had. The chamber around her was dim and saturated in shadow. Her first breath was a gasp. Pain answered her. Sharp, stabbing through her side and gut, where Richard's knife had entered.

Her hands twitched again as the feeling began to spread through her. She felt the cold stone beneath her. Her arms were no longer restrained but sigils etched in blood and ash adorned them. She tried to move her legs, but found they were bound together with silk cords, tied loose enough to not injure, tight enough to hold.

She managed to turn her head. Around her, the ritual continued.

Candles lined the perimeter of the vast underground chamber. Dozens of them. Some tall and narrow, some melted to stubs. Their flames didn't flicker, even in the stagnant air. The walls were carved stone, circular, with claw-like alcoves and more newly painted symbols coating every visible surface.

She was at the centre, in the shadow of what was once the great tree. Around her stood four cloaked figures, each with a bowl in their hands and long knives at their belts. Behind them, the townsfolk formed the entire congregation.

All in red. All silent.

Amy blinked again, more of her thoughts returning. The room reeked of ash and sweet rot. Someone stepped forward.

Richard.

He was dressed differently now. No longer in a suit. He wore an open black robe, his chest visible beneath it. His wounds, the cuts she had given him were barely visible.

"I see you," he said softly. "For what you truly are."

She tried to speak, but her lips stuck together. A woman to her left dipped her fingers in one of the bowls and painted a spiral across Amy's lips with warm liquid.

Richard smiled.

"The gate stirs," he whispered. "It feels your resistance. It feels your pain, your sorrow and your rage."

Amy turned her head to the side. The motion took immense effort. No one stopped her. They wanted her awake and present.

Her eyes drifted across the chamber to the circle.

The outer ring of the chamber was marked in white ash, broken in thirteen places by her count by skulls. Within the circle, lines had been drawn in spirals, glyphs, and unnatural geometry. The lines didn't make sense in three dimensions. They appeared to move when she blinked.

The sigil beneath her burned red-hot but there was no pain.

It was the gateway. She was right on top of it

The entry point Richard had spoken of.

Amy tried again to move her hand. Her fingers twitched. This time more.

One of the men stepped hesitantly forward, dipped his hands in the bowl and painted Amy's feet with what looked like soot and salt.

Richard turned toward the congregation.

"Brothers and sisters," he said, voice echoing despite the low pitch. "Tonight we undo the exile. Tonight we unchain the memory. The flesh is bound. The gate will open and the world beyond will be revealed."

Amy's fingers curled into a weak fist.

He turned back to her.

"You know what you were made for. You've seen it in your dreams. The burning child. The spiral path. You were made from the fracture. You are the bridge and you will be my queen."

Amy rasped, "I'm not your..."

He cut her off by raising a hand.

"You are what happens when fire takes human form, it can be bent, it can be manipulated. But ultimately with the right fuel it can burn brighter then anything else."

He knelt beside her.

His voice dropped to a whisper.

"And now, fire will burn again."

Amy stared up at the ceiling. It pulsed with unseen energy. The lines in the stone bled light.

Then, from within, the voice.

Her voice. The child. Not screaming. Not begging. Just speaking.

> *"They don't know what you are. Not really. They only remember what they need to. But you remember everything now."*

Amy saw flashes.

Her mother's voice.

Sophie's words in the journal.

The names in the margins.

> *"You were made to open the gate"* the child said. *"But you can destroy it."*

Amy's breath caught.

Richard stood again.

"Begin the alignment," he said aloud.

The twelve townsfolk nearest the edge began moving to the skulls. They each took one, leaving the thirteenth unclaimed. That was for Richard.

Amy could feel the energy rising.

Pressure built behind her eyes as the altar began to hum. The sigils on her arms and chest grew warm and still, the child whispered from inside.

Amy strained to move. Not with panic but with will.

She turned her head and locked eyes with Richard.

"I remember everything," she said softly.

He froze. Just for a second.

A ripple spread from the altar across the floor, disturbing the ash lines.

One of the robed women gasped and quickened the chant.

Amy sat up. Only a few inches. But enough.

The energy surged.

Richard shouted to the closest men, "HOLD HER."

Hands grabbed her shoulders but she was moving now. She was awake and still alive.

Somewhere inside her, the fire lit by Kira, Miles, Sophie even Cathy, grew brighter.

Amy didn't yet know what she would do next.

But she knew one thing;

She was no one's gate. She was no one's vessel. She was herself. She was Amy.

Amy sat up fully.

The chamber quaked.

A tremor beneath the altar. The temperature in the air dropped. The flickering candlelight guttered for just a moment. Shadows stretched longer, moving against the shape of their casters.

Hands pressed down on her shoulders again, firm, trying to force her back onto the altar.

But she didn't yield.

She didn't scream or cry out.

Instead, Amy breathed in deeply. The air was heavy with ash, with salt, with blood. But beneath it… something else.

Something that tasted like iron and fire.

Voices started punctuating her mind.

Low. Rumbling. In a language she didn't recognize but somehow understood. Not spoken aloud, but inside her skull. Pounding through her temples.

> "She awakens. Flesh-bound. Soul-torn. Memory-made."

Amy squeezed her eyes shut.

Pain lanced across her mind. Like something was scraping at the inside of her skull.

> "The vessel cracks."

> "The gate pulses."

> "Let her see."

Her eyes snapped open and she saw it.

The true shape of the chamber.

No longer just a room of stone and ash and blood.

But something deeper.

The walls shifted, no longer solid. They pulsed like muscle, like tissue. The altar beneath her glowed from within and opened.

Just a sliver.

Beyond it, there was no world. Only a void with twisting shadows moving through it's darkness. Shapes, impossibly vast. Wings without form. Jaws made of ruin. Eyes layered in circles. Everything moving, writhing, pushing against the threshold.

Amy screamed inside her skull.

The creatures, the demons looked back at her.

They did not hunger.

"She was made by fire."

"She is the flame."

"She's strong."

"The world opens for us."

She felt her bones tremble as her chest seized. The chains around the gate rattled. The sigils on the stones blazed red.

Richard stood next to the altar now

His hands were raised, his voice lost in chanting.

He wasn't just summoning one demon. He was inviting all of them.

The gate was open and she was the bridge.

The ritual surged as Richard raised a blade high above her. She tried to scream but her voice failed. The knife came down fast into her stomach. Her scream was silent but the pain on her face was visible to all.

The ash circle lifted from the floor, swirling in the air like a cyclone.

The townsfolk knelt, heads bowed, voices joining in.

The red light intensified until the entire chamber glowed as if lit from a sun buried deep underground.

Amy writhed. Her restraints burned against her skin. Her pain kept her from moving.

Her arms bled from the sigils.

The voices in her mind continued:

"He calls us."

"He dares."

"He forgets."

"He will never be king."

Amy gasped as the words struck her.

They weren't meant for her. They were meant for Richard.

The demons were watching. Listening. But they weren't loyal to him.

She stared at the bone gate as she writhed on her side.

From within, something moved forward. A shape formed through the flaming void, bigger then a man, a monster. Amy watched in horror as the figure pulled itself from the hole half-formed, not yet across the threshold. Its body was made of smoke and stone. Horns curled like roots. Its eyes were black filled with a hollow emptiness.

It looked straight at Richard.

Amy turned toward him.

Still chanting. Still blind. The others didn't see it. Only she did.

The demon smiled. Not at her but at him.

"He thinks he calls us."

"He forgets who opened the door."

Amy realized something at that moment. She was the one who'd opened it. Not Richard. It was she who cracked the veil. Her memory. Her fire.

The air in the chamber thickened. Even the fire from below seemed to recoil. The demon pulled itself fully through the gate. Its body was not built for this world. It seemed to bend the space around it as it moved, dragging heat and shadow like a cloak as it's body morphed and writhed. Its head adorned with bone. Its arms hung long and heavy, ending in fingers made of smoke and razors. It whispered in languages Amy didn't recognize but instinctively feared. Its eyes remained focused on Richard.

The chamber fell into silence.

The chanting stopped. The ash cyclone fell still.

Even the townsfolk trained, conditioned and brainwashed, froze in place, suddenly aware they'd invited something older than worship and crueller than prophecy.

Richard didn't flinch as he took one step toward the demon.

"I am the architect of this ritual," he said. "I have opened the gate for you. I have fed it blood, memory, fear. I have given you the vessel."

He pointed back at Amy. The demon said nothing.

Then it spoke to all in the room. A voice that transcended description and rippled through the minds of all those who witnessed.

"You gave us nothing."

"She woke herself."

"You are a preacher to flames that will never kneel to a false prophet like you."

Richard's face twitched.

He raised his hands.

"You cannot be here without me," he insisted. "You are bound by sigil, by sequence. I summoned you. I opened the way. You will obey me."

The demon took another step.

Its foot struck the stone, and cracks splintered outward. The altar beneath Amy shivered.

"You are the one who lit the torch," it said, *"but you forget who the match is. The fire burns in her. Not you."*

Amy's restraints fell away as they melted with the demon's power. The bindings on her arms and legs had ignited, silent, controlled flames reducing silk to dust without touching her skin.

She rose slowly, bloodied and weak, but awake. Entirely awake.

Richard didn't notice. All of his attention was locked on the thing before him.

"I demand your allegiance!" he bellowed.

The demon's mouth twisted.

"You will not demand anything from us."

It raised one hand, a gesture that seemed small, effortless and the air exploded.

Five townsfolk standing near the western side ignited, not from the outside but from within. Their robes burst apart, skin blistering, bones shrivelling in an instant. They collapsed like ash-filled scarecrows, their screams muffled by the sound of wind rushing through a gate no longer closed.

The rest screamed and scattered.

Richard turned finally seeing Amy and his mouth opened in shock.

"You…"

But she was already stepping down from the altar.

The demon looked at her now and fell silent.

Amy stood tall. Her voice came out as a whisper, but it cut through the room like thunder:

"I brought you here."

The demon did not smile. It bowed.

Amy stared at it, heart hammering. Somewhere behind her, Richard began to scream.

CHAPTER SEVENTEEN

The chamber burned with quiet power, something deep like the simmering hum of judgment waiting to be handed down.

Amy stood tall at the foot of the altar, body still in pain, blood still ran from her stomach, eyes fixed on Richard. Her vision was crystal-clear now. Not sharpened by pain or adrenaline but with clarity. The kind that only comes when there was nothing left to run from.

The demon loomed behind her, still half-shrouded in its own darkness. Though the townsfolk scattered, screamed and wept, it remained still watching with ancient eyes. It didn't speak. Not yet.

Amy watched as other creatures pulled themselves from the void, not as big but just as monstrous. The air thrummed around Amy's ears. A low vibration. Like the ground itself was vibrating. Richard stumbled back from the broken circle of ash, the ritual blade dangling from one trembling hand. His face twisted between fury and disbelief.

"You..." he began, voice raw and scared.

Amy didn't answer but she stepped forward. Her bare feet touched the ash-inscribed floor. It no longer burned her. No longer resisted her. If anything, the stone warmed beneath her, like the chamber itself acknowledged her presence.

The remaining townsfolk parted like smoke.

Some dropped to their knees in prayer. Others turned their heads away in fear and shame.

Richard took another step back.

"I brought you here. It was me." he hissed, not to Amy, but to the demon. "I called you. I sacrificed for you!"

The demon didn't answer.

Amy did.

"You never understood what you were playing with," she said, her voice low, edged with something deeper than rage. It was history, prophecy and truth all combined into one.

Richard raised the blade, wild-eyed. "You're just a girl!"

"No," she said, stopping Richard in his stride. "I was a girl crafted into a flame. Isn't this what you wanted?"

She stepped closer and threw her arms out to the sides.

The knife he held shook in his grip.

She didn't flinch.

"I am the fire that remembers."

Then, with swift certainty, she reached for the ritual blade still slick with her own blood. Richard tried to stab her but she was too fast and caught his wrist. In one fluid motion she turned and drove the blade into his throat.

"Not this time."

There was no scream. Only the sound of blood gurgling from his mouth as his eyes widened, hands flailing, grasping at nothing. He dropped to his knees as Amy twisted the blade once. Not for cruelty but for finality.

Richard gasped then slumped forward onto the stone floor, choking on his own fear. Behind them, the demon began to laugh.

Not mockingly.

But knowingly.

It's mouth opened wide.

"There she is."

It stepped forward.

Taller now. More formed. Its limbs no longer coiled in shadow, but fully physical, obsidian skin, cracked with lava filled veins. Its hands opened like a priest giving a service. Then it hesitated and looked to Amy.

She nodded. "He's all yours."

It nodded and reached for Richard's corpse. Clawed fingers lifted the mayor's body like a rag doll.

The crowd watched, frozen. Then, without ceremony, the demon snapped Richard in half. Bone crunched and blood sprayed.

The remnants of Richard fell to the floor, no longer man or monster, now just an empty carcass.

The demon turned to Amy.

"You have broken the architect."

The voice echoed through her mind like an intruder. Amy stood at the centre of the chamber, the circle still lit beneath her, the bones of the old ritual glowing faintly.

The townsfolk knelt. Some in reverence. Others in surrender. Far above, beyond the gate, the shadows writhed, waiting and watching.

The demon overlord, towering, armoured in smoke and obsidian, fire threading through its skin like veins stared at Richard's torn body. Amy stood over the mayor, her hands no longer trembling, blood drying on her palms. The sacrificial blade still warm in her grip, but its work was done. Now the decision ahead of her was larger than the knife.

Behind the demon, the gate pulsed as more demons exited. Shapes, figures, impossibilities; A crawling thing with too many mouths and no eyes. A thin creature composed entirely of woven arms and weeping faces. Some walked on limbs. Others floated. One had no form at all, just a shadow cast where there was no source of light.

They did not stumble. They did not rush. They came because she had called them.

Amy felt them.

They saw her not with hunger, not with pity but with familiarity as if she were one of them, or at least, meant to be. The overlord turned back to her, black eyes reflecting her entire figure small and bloodied and standing amid the ruin of everything Richard had ever built.

"You have opened the gate," it said. *"and you have brought us here."*

She didn't speak.

Not yet.

She watched as more demons stepped from the gate, but none approached her. They kept their distance. They watched.

The overlord stepped forward again, crouching slightly. Its voice was softer now, almost reverent.

>*"You were born from ash and bound with blood.
>A child buried beneath memory. You were not meant
>to be one thing. You are many."*

It looked her in the eye and added;

>*"Queen."*

Amy flinched.

The word echoed in her skull in a way nothing else had.

"I didn't ask for any of this," she said finally, her voice hoarse.

The demon straightened, casting a shadow long enough to blot out the circle behind her.

>*"That is why you are worthy."*

>*"Those who seek thrones never survive them."*

It extended a hand.

>*"You can end the wheel,"* it said. *"No more false
>rituals. No more puppet priests. Only us."*

>*"Power. Without leash. Memory. Without loss.
>You can reign, child. And they will never harm you
>again. Together we will craft this world into
>something new, something terrifying."*

Amy turned slowly, scanning the chamber. The remaining townsfolk cowered on their knees. Some wept. Some stared at her like she was a storm they couldn't outrun.

One girl, no older than sixteen, whispered, "Please."

Not to the demon but to Amy. She turned back.

"What do they call you and what does reigning mean?" she asked.

The demon's mouth answered at once.

> *"They call me Eizrekel We will reshape the world."*

> *"We will unmake the false cities and birth new empires."*

> *"You will stand above fire and time."*

> *"They will pray to you and be heard."*

Amy clenched her jaw.

"And what happens to the ones who don't want to kneel?"

A pause.

Then Eizrekel replied;

> *"They will be given the choice not to exist."*

She stared at it. The words did not come with malice. They were simply unflinching truth.

The gate widened.

More demons were coming. Hundreds of them. None dared cross the boundary of the circle she stood in. She was not just the one who called. She was the centre of it all.

The scarred stone beneath her feet pulsed again. The fire around the gate shifted.

Her mind flickered to memories;

She saw Cathy holding her close as a child.

Sophie writing symbols in the journal by candlelight.

Her mothers bittersweet smile as she told her to run.

Kira laughing in the motel.

Miles holding her close in his arms.

"They gave you life," Eizrekel said. *"We offer you purpose."*

Amy stepped toward the gate. Just one step. The demons stirred. Hundreds of heads turned. They watched her breath, her pulse, her presence. One more step. If she accepted she'd have infinite power but would no longer be human. She would become something else. Something greater.

Amy took another step forward.

The air before her shimmered. The voices in her mind whispered louder now, not words, but feelings: the weight of knowledge, the taste of power, the quiet thrill of becoming something more than mortal.

Behind her, the town remained hushed. The townsfolk still on their knees. Some looked up in terror, as if they too sensed what Amy was now considering. The demon stood at the edge of the circle, arms still outstretched.

"Come," he said. *"You were made for this. You endured the burning, and the becoming. Now take your place."*

His voice had changed. Not demanding. Not coaxing. Just certain.

Amy stopped within a foot of the demon. Close enough now to see the texture of his skin. Not just smoke and obsidian, but layer upon layer of screaming faces trapped beneath the surface. Shrieking silently, eternally. Caught in the molten swirl of whatever realm it came from. She looked up into his eyes. Beyond them an endless void.

She didn't flinch.

"I want to understand," she said.

Eizrekel's mouth opened, speaking in a slow calming tone.

"You already do."

Amy raised her hand, slowly, reverently and placed her palm against the creature's chest. It was hot, pulsing with raw energy. She could feel the world behind the gate radiating through its being. She could see what she would become. Not a queen. But a god.

All she had to do was surrender.

In that moment she realised her hand wasn't empty. The ritual blade, still slick with Richard's blood rested in her palm. The demon noticed but it didn't recoil. Instead, it smiled.

"You would strike down eternity?"

Amy's voice didn't tremble.

"No," she said staring down at the knife.

"But I'll strike down you."

She drove the blade deep into Eizrekel's chest.

The reaction was immediate. Not a scream… a shock-wave.

The air ruptured with pressure. Symbols on the walls shattered like glass. The townsfolk were thrown to the ground as the ceiling began to crumble. Candles burst.

Eizrekel staggered back, a hiss of black steam pouring from its chest.

Amy held on to the hilt. The blade buried in Eizrekel's chest trembled with raw, unnatural power. The creature's molten blood began to weep around it, steaming and bubbling as it splashed onto the floor in thick, glowing droplets.

"YOU DARE!"

Amy stood her ground. The heat threatened to blister her skin, but she did not flinch.

"You chose the wrong vessel," she whispered.

The demon reached for her, fingers like coiling branches of obsidian lightning. But its arm trembled. Its form wavered. Still, it did not fall. She braced her feet, gripped the blade tighter, and with a cry that echoed across stone, she twisted the knife.

Eizrekel's body buckled and his chest split open enough to reveal a glowing, pulsing mass of heat and fire at its core. Images spilled into the air like smoke: faces of the murdered, the used, the lost. The girls who had come before her, the girls sacrificed, the children erased.

Amy stepped back, her hands slick with blood not her own. The demon dropped to one knee, but he did not collapse. He stared at her and for the first time looked afraid.

"You are one of us now."

Eizrekel reared back and roared, a howl that shook the chamber, that cracked the walls and sent terrified screams echoing through the underground. A deep claret erupted from it's chest covering Amy from head to toe. It was thick, hot, and full of power. As it ran down her face, soaked into her hair, and seeped into her wounds, Amy stood motionless.

It wasn't just blood. It was a baptism. She knew this wasn't the end.

Another roar echoed through the underground like thunder pressed against bone. Dust cascaded from the ceiling as veins of red light spread across the stone, reacting to the demon's wounded rage. The gateway behind it, once steady in its spiral of darkness and light, now trembled with instability, shadows clawing outward like storm-water through a broken dam.

The other demons went into a rage and began tearing at the townsfolk. The chamber was filled with screams. The blade trembled in her hand. Eizrekel hunched forward, his mouth gaping wide, black saliva dripping, hiss clawed hands pressed to the ragged wound in its chest. Its eyes locked onto her with fury and fascination. He had not expected this. The chamber no longer obeyed the laws of earth. Gravity tilted. Angles broke. The ash circle at her feet pulsed with slick light.

Amy backed up two steps, blood squelching under her bare feet. Her eyes never left the overlord.

"You wanted a queen," she said.

Eizrekel straightened slowly, blood leaking from the gash. One of his arms dragged limply now, torn by the shock-wave of her blow. Still, he towered above her.

"I wanted pain, rage and fear," it said.

*"You have brought that to me. This world will
make a great feast."*

Amy tore the blade free and raised it again. It glowed with the
same red-black energy that dripped from the demon's chest and
then she darted forward. No hesitation. No mercy.

Eizrekel lunged too, bellowing with fury.

She ducked beneath its arm, spinning, and plunged the knife
into its side aiming for the place where shadow thinned and light
pooled thick. It shrieked, clawing backward, crushing the stones.
She ran the blade through it's side and out the back.

Around them, the chamber was falling apart.

"LOOK WHAT YOU'VE DONE!"

Amy turned as the others moved in. Eizrekel turned,
staggering.

"You are not worthy," it roared.

"You are a flicker, not a flame."

"You are memory without shape."

Amy stabbed again right beneath the first wound and this time,
the demon screamed with fear. A high, jagged sound that shattered
one of the columns outright. Above, the ceiling exploded open
with a thunderous groan. Light from the world above poured down
through the widening rift. The church above collapsed into the
chamber below. Amy threw her arm up to shield herself the best
she could.

The town burst into flames. New Grayson had begun to
collapse. She could smell it now the scorched wood, the smoke,
the soot and grief. The gate behind the demon flared wide in panic.

The other demons watched as their lord was losing and they
knew it. Amy pushed the blade deeper.

Eizrekel crumpled.

> *"We will not end like this. You betray us. We will take this world."*

Amy turned toward the gate.

The chaos behind it tried to reach her, claws tearing at the void, tendrils trying to grip her but they stopped at the edge of the circle. Amy turned toward the fractured opening in the earth. Stone screamed above her. Cracks raced along the walls of the ruined chamber like lightning bolts. The entire town groaned under the strain of a reality no longer able to contain what had crossed its threshold. The gate fas fading as rubble fell into it crushing the demons underneath.

The other demons had not vanished. The gate, though flickering, remained open just wide enough for them to crawl through and they did.

A clawed thing slithered along the ceiling, a serpent formed from spines. A woman with no face hovered mid-air, her limbs folded into impossible angles. An insectoid beast with a skull mouth and dragging stingers stalked the edge of the circle. Their entire focus was on the demon overlord. They hadn't come to kill Amy but to consume their dying god. Eizrekel staggered, black-red blood pulsing from his torn chest, steam rising from its body in sheets. It stood, just barely, and hissed at them.

> *"I will not kneel."*

Amy took one slow step back as the chamber shook again. A massive chunk of the ceiling caved inward, crushing two of the emerging horrors. Stone and flame fell like judgment.

The gate sparked.

The walls split.

The ritual that held this place together the spiral of ash and intention could no longer bind it. She had unravelled it all. Now everything was collapsing. The demons shrieked as stone cracked above them. Another came through, a creature of bone wings, only to be immediately caught beneath a falling beam that impaled its body and pinned it to the ground. It writhed, screeching not dying, but trapped.

One by one, they were caught by the ruin of the place they had long waited to enter.

Amy turned and ran.

Smoke and ash choked the air. Her lungs burned. Her legs screamed with each step, muscles torn and bloodied. She slipped once, caught herself, then continued to climb up the shattered rubble that led toward the exit above. She dodged dying demons and the bloodied remains of the townsfolk

Behind her, Eizrekel howled with the realization that Amy wasn't simply sealing the gate, she was burying it. The bone sigil shattered and with a final, echoing shriek, the gate imploded crushing its children mid-transit. The demons that had reached through clawed at nothing as the stone crushed their forms, sending arcs of shrieking shadow into the dying air.

She reached the surface just as the church fully collapsed. Flames belched upward. The floor split. Part of the roof dropped behind her, and the hall crumbled into a yawning inferno. She burst into dawns breaking light.

The sky was soaked in fire. New Grayson burned like an offering. Rooftops collapsed, street-signs melted, windows burst. Screams echoed in the distance townsfolk trapped, fleeing, or already lost.

She kept moving. Down the front steps that still remained, onto the cracked side-walk, past the fire-engulfed square. Every step was a victory. Every breath earned. Her consciousness was beginning to fade with the amount of blood she'd lost.

Smoke followed and Ash fell like snow as she kept moving.

She didn't cry.

She didn't speak.

She just moved.

The town end came into view. Would it finally let her leave?

She stumbled past the sign: *Welcome to New Grayson. Where History Lives Forever.*

The irony wasn't lost on her as she crossed the precipice and collapsed. The heat from the fire behind her licked her back. She rolled onto her side. Her fingers dug into the cool, soot-covered gravel of the road. Her lungs heaved. Her body giving up. Blood still soaked her. Not just the demon's, but her own. Scratches, bruises, burns all layered into the shell of her.

She felt like she was changing. She'd walked through fire and made it out. Behind her, the demon's roar faded into crackling ruin. Amy closed her eyes.

Let the town burn. She thought to herself.

She was done with it.

CHAPTER EIGHTEEN

The world returned as light.

A flickering, sterile white that buzzed behind her eyelids like static. For a long time, she thought it was fire again; The flash of flame, the blinding glow of the ritual chamber collapsing above her, but it was too cold, too clean.

She tried to move but her body screamed in protest. Something sharp twisted in her ribs. A deep, electric spasm ran down her right leg. Her lips were dry. Her throat ached.

But she was alive. That fact alone felt absurd.

She dared to open her eyes. Only one responded. The other remained swollen shut, her face bruised and stitched in a place she couldn't quite feel. Her vision was cloudy, but she recognized the contours: a pale green ceiling, a small window half-covered with a blind, the quiet rhythmic beeping of machines. She was in a hospital.

Not a morgue. Not the pit of hell. But an actual hospital.

The room smelled of antiseptic, old linoleum, and cheap plastic gloves. Somewhere down the hall, she heard a door creak open and close. Muffled voices. The soft shuffle of rubber soles.

She turned her head slightly. The pain was immediate, a searing twist in the side of her neck and down her shoulder. She bit back a cry and squeezed her one good eye shut until the wave passed.

Memory stirred; *The gate. The blade. The demons. The burning town.*

She took another breath. This one shallower. More cautious.

Her mouth barely moved as she whispered, "I made it…"

A machine clicked beside her. Another beep. A shadow moved beyond the frosted glass window of her door. She froze and listened. Whoever it was didn't come in. She turned again, slower this time and saw her arm. IV lines fed into the crook of her elbow. Her wrist was bandaged. Her fingers still bore dried blood beneath cracked nails. Her entire body felt stiff, as though she'd been stitched back together piece by piece.

Which wasn't far from the truth.

The blankets felt too tight and her body itched beneath the gown. She moved her toes. Pain shot up her calves, but they obeyed. Her brain was returning in fragments. Like a puzzle dumped onto the floor, edges bent and pieces scattered. She tried to gather them, one by one.

Kira.

Miles.

Sophie.

Barker.

She winced.

She didn't want to remember all of it but she also couldn't let their memories fade away. She remembered the gate its heat, its voice, its pull. But what had she done to seal it? Had she sealed it? Had it collapsed on its own? Did she kill that thing?

No.

She remembered its roar. Its rage. It had still been alive when she ran. The others, the things from the gate must've been crushed. Some. Not all. She remembered wings. Chains. Screams. Fire.

The monitor beside her pinged softly, marking another steady beat of her heart.

How long had she been here?

She turned her head again, this time toward the tray beside the bed. No phone. No clock. Just a plastic cup half-full of water and a folded napkin. Her throat burned with thirst.

She reached out.

Her hand jerked short with a sharp metallic sound.

She frowned and turned her wrist.

Her left wrist was shackled to the bed. Steel handcuffs looping through the frame. The kind used for patients who were criminals or those on suicide watch. Willow stared at it. The sound of her heartbeat real and monitored felt louder now.

The water cup sat just inches out of reach. What had she done to be shackled to a bed?

Something was wrong. She wasn't safe.

Willow stared at the handcuff. Her fingers flexed slightly, the dull ache of inflammation biting at the joints. The restraint cut into the edge of her wrist, leaving the skin beneath it raw and slightly darkened. She tugged once to confirm it was real and that she wasn't in some nightmare. The cold metal clicked against the steel frame of the hospital bed.

No illusion.

She was very much restrained.

She blinked, trying to will clarity into her fogged vision but nothing came. Just the gentle *beep... beep... beep* of her heart monitor, like a soft ticking clock.

She closed her eyes for a moment, trying to remember the last real thing before this room. The road. The sign. Her knees hitting gravel. And then silence.

She must've passed out, but someone had found her. Dragged her here and then cuffed her.

Why?

Her stomach twisted. Not just from hunger, but from fear, memory and guilt.

Her other hand trembled. She tried to lift it and wipe her mouth, but it barely responded. Her entire body felt like a stitched-up sack of broken glass. She leaned her head back against the pillow and let out a small sound, not quite a sob, but more than a breath and that's when she noticed it.

A shape.

In the room.

A figure.

It hadn't been there when she first woke or maybe it had, and she'd simply been too dazed to notice.

Her gaze shifted to the corner, across from the foot of her bed, tucked between the shadow of the machine cabinet and the closed door.

Someone stood there. Still and watching.

He didn't speak. Didn't move.

Just stood with his arms crossed.

Dark slacks. A grey shirt rolled to the sleeves. A badge clipped to his belt and holster on the hip. He had a short, military-style haircut. His face weathered with deep lines at the jaw. He looked like a man who didn't need to talk to be heard. Amy's dry throat clicked as she tried to swallow.

He stepped forward slowly, just enough for the dim light to hit the hastily made name tag pinned to his chest.

OFFICER BRIGGS.

He gave a single nod, as if to confirm he knew exactly who she was and that he wasn't surprised to find her finally conscious.

"You've been asleep a while," he said.

His voice was calm and measured.

She opened her mouth, tried to speak, but only a rasp came out. He walked over to the table and picked up the cup of water. He held it in front of her for a moment, then wordlessly placed the straw to her lips. She drank, slow and grateful, each pull of water a tiny victory. When she finished, he set it back on the tray and stepped away again.

Amy licked her cracked lips and whispered, "Why… am I cuffed?"

Briggs didn't answer right away.

He watched her for another long moment, then finally said, "You were found outside of a small town called New Grayson. You were unconscious and covered in blood."

Amy's breath caught.

His voice remained level. "Fire crews responded to a massive blaze. The entire town of New Grayson is gone."

Gone.

Just like that.

The word hit harder than seeing the handcuffs.

"We've recovered…"he hesitated, as if choosing the right phrase…"pieces of bodies. Remains. Not many. Everything else was ash."

Amy closed her eyes.

Briggs continued.

"You are the only survivor. At least, the only one anyone's found."

He let that settle.

She swallowed hard. "And that makes me… a suspect?"

His lips pressed into a thin line.

"You're in protective custody," he said finally. "Which means until we understand more like who you are and what happened, you're under observation."

She turned her head slightly, her voice rasping. "You don't know who I am?"

He didn't answer.

Did he?

Or was he waiting for her to say it?

She looked at him again hard this time studying the angle of his jaw, the slight scar above one eyebrow, the way his left hand tapped faintly against his hip when he stood still too long. He wasn't nervous. He was curious.

"Why are you here?" she asked, quieter now.

Briggs tilted his head.

"To protect you," he said.

It wasn't a threat. But it didn't sound like a promise either. Amy let the silence stretch between them. It wasn't defiance, it was confusion. Her pulse echoed softly from the heart monitor beside her, the slow rhythm betraying how hard she was trying to stay calm.

He finally broke it.

"You remember your name?"

She didn't answer right away. The question wasn't about identity. It was about memory.

"Yes," she said softly. "Willow. No, Amy."

She saw the flicker in his expression brief, passing, but noticeable. Like a question had just been answered before he could ask it.

"Which is it?" Briggs tapped his foot gently awaiting a response.

Who was she? What name should she go by now? She sighed.

"Willow." It was her true name. Even if she'd lived most of her life as Amy. It was still the name her mother had bestowed upon her. She may as well accept it.

"Willow what?" he asked.

"I don't know," she replied honestly. "I don't think I ever had the rest of it."

He didn't write that down, but she felt the way he took it in.

Willow looked away.

"Do you know what happened?" he asked.

She turned her head to stare at the ceiling.

"I don't think you'd believe me."

"Try me."

There it was. The line. A test of trust. Or bait to measure her sanity. Either way, Willow wasn't about to give him demons, gates, and blood-thirsty townsfolk in one breath.

So she said carefully, "There was something wrong with that place. With the people. The mayor."

"Richard Carson?"

She nodded. "They were… following him."

"In what way?"

"Like he was something more than a mayor. It was like he was a cult leader."

Briggs uncrossed his arms and pulled a notepad from his back pocket.

"Cult?"

"Something like that," she said. "He had plans. Rituals."

She watched his pen pause mid-word.

"Rituals? Like sacrifices and magic?"

"You asked."

He studied her for a long moment, then continued writing.

"No one has found any survivors," he said. "None."

Willow swallowed. "There won't be."

"Why?"

She didn't speak.

"Why, Willow?"

She stared at him. Not angry. Not afraid. Just… tired.

"Because I saw what happened to them."

He tilted his head slightly. "You saw a town burn. But that doesn't mean…"

"I saw what burned them."

That stopped him cold. The room felt quieter. She didn't elaborate. And he didn't ask her to. Instead, he stepped forward, closer to the bed.

"You're the only lead we have," he said. "The only witness and depending on how this plays out, the only suspect."

Her eyes narrowed. "Suspect of what?"

He raised a brow. "You walked out of a town that's now nothing but smoke and ruins. You're covered in blood, weapon wounds, and half-conscious mutterings about fire and sacrifice. That buys questions."

Willow let her gaze fall to the cuff on her wrist.

"And chains."

"It's precaution," he said.

"Against what?"

He didn't answer. Which meant he didn't know. Or maybe he did, and just didn't want to say it aloud.

"I'm not your enemy," Briggs said finally.

"No," she replied. "But I'm not your answer either."

Another silence.

This one lasted longer as he waited for her to continue. Finally, he clicked his pen closed, slipped the notebook into his pocket, and stepped back.

"You're going to be moved soon," he said. "To a more secure facility. Official interviews. You'll need to start thinking about how much truth you're ready to share."

"I already am," she said.

Briggs studied her for another few seconds, then walked to the door.

Before he left, he paused studying her one last time then left. The door clicked softly shut behind him.

Willow was alone again.

She stared at the ceiling, chest rising and falling with shallow, steady breaths. The handcuff at her wrist tugged slightly every time she moved, a quiet reminder that freedom was still out of reach, even now, even after everything.

She closed her eyes. She told herself she was just tired. Just healing. But she couldn't stop the sense that something was off. She drifted back into an unsettled sleep.

She awoke but instantly realised the hospital was too quiet.

Hospitals, even at night, even when empty, had a rhythm. The creak of gurney wheels. The shuffle of nurses. The beep of IVs and monitors. Pages crackling over old intercoms. Doors opening, footsteps in the hall.

But now… nothing.

No sound beyond the soft beep of her monitor.

She shifted slightly, wincing at the pull in her ribs. The movement sent a light wave of nausea through her belly, but it passed. She exhaled, and that's when she heard it.

A whisper.

Too faint to make out. But there in her head.

Her eyes opened wider.

She waited.

Nothing.

A few more seconds passed, and then… a second whisper.

Closer.

Still indistinct.

Like two people talking just outside the door. But the tone wasn't calm. It wasn't medical.

It had a hollowness to it. A sound that slithered between syllables, like something trying to imitate speech, not form it.

Willow's breath caught. She'd heard these voices before. They'd found her.

She turned her head slowly toward the door.

The hallway light underneath the frame flickered once.

Then again. She strained to listen.

The whisper returned, clearer now.

A voice.

Low.

> *"You cannot escape us"*

Her stomach flipped.

Another voice joined it.

> *"She's ready."*

Then a laugh.

A third voice. High. Thin.

Mocking.

> *"She needs to feel suffering."*

Her mouth went dry.

"No," she whispered.

No one answered but the lights above her dimmed just slightly. The monitor beside her crackled with static before returning to normal.

Willow tried to sit up, but the cuff held her arm in place. She gritted her teeth and forced herself upright with her unbound hand, gasping as fire flared through her side. Her breath came fast now.

Her pulse quickened.

The monitor beeped louder.

A fourth voice whispered.

Right by her ear.

> "You thought it was over."

She recoiled violently, twisting in bed but there was no one there. Just the room and the click of the handcuff rattling against the frame. The pains of her body were beginning to fade.

She looked down at her wrist.

At the metal loop around it.

Her heart pounded.

The voices were all around her now.

A chorus.

A distorted echo of those she thought she'd buried. They hissed from the vents, from the walls, from the crack between the door and the floor.

"She bled them."

"Does she hear us?"

"The gate is damaged but never closed."

Willow screamed.

Short.

Broken.

Panicked.

Her back hit the headboard, her knees pulled tight. She tried to cover her ears, but her cuffed wrist stopped her. She thrashed, twisted, begged herself to wake up.

This wasn't real. It couldn't be. But the voices didn't stop. They pressed against her skull like fingers trying to pry open her mind.

Then footsteps. Fast and heavy.

She looked up as the door burst open. In the distance she heard screams and shouts.

Officer Briggs burst in. Dishevelled and pale. Gun drawn.

He slammed the door shut behind him and flipped the lock. His eyes found her, wide with fear. "You heard them?"

Willow could only nod, trembling, half-curled in the bed.

He rushed forward, dropped to one knee at her side, and fumbled with a keyring.

"What are you?"

"They're in the building."

Her blood ran cold.

He found the right key, jammed it into the cuff, and with a metallic snap it opened. Her arm was free.

She collapsed sideways in relief, but he grabbed her by the shoulder.

"Willow. Look at me."

He wasn't calm any more. He was sweating. Face pale. Shirt half-untucked. His voice was no longer measured.

"I don't know what they are, but they're killing people," he said.

A bang from the corridor. Both their heads turned toward the door. He raised for his sidearm.

"I came to check on you. Security said the lights were acting strange. Then the power flickered. Then… the screaming started."

Another sound. Closer.

The sound of something wet being dragged heavily along the ground crept into the room. Willow backed against the headboard. Briggs aimed at the door, his hands shaking now.

Silence.

CRASH.

The room window beside them shattered. Glass erupted into the room and through it came a body.

Not a demons. But the discarded body of a nurse. His body hit the floor like a sack of wet meat, face caved in, bones cracked, limbs bent and torn. Blood sprayed across the tile, warm and sudden.

Briggs spun round, gun still raised.

CHAPTER NINETEEN

The body hit the floor with a sickening crack. Glass cascaded down like sharp rain, glittering and deadly across the hospital tile. Blood sprayed the base of the curtain and pooled beneath the motionless corpse.

Willow froze when she saw the thing that followed behind the body.

From the shattered hospital window, something pulled itself through. It didn't move like a man. It dragged its weight across the jagged frame with limbs too long, bones cracking with each crawl. The skin wasn't skin, it was stretched tissue, semi-translucent in the flickering light, wet and glistening with rot. Its face held remnants of human shape, but melted. No eyes, no mouth, just a dark, gaping slit where a voice might once have lived.

The air around it thickened, filled with the smell of sulphur and decaying metal. The machines in the room sputtered. The monitor beside the bed screamed with static.

Briggs moved fast.

He shoved Willow behind the bed tearing the wires and needles from her arm, barking, "Move!" just as the creature's claws struck the headboard where she'd been.

Willow scrambled on all fours, pain still screaming in her side but nowhere near as bad as it was. She gasped but didn't stop. Her hospital gown caught on the edge of the bed frame as she dragged herself around the other side.

The creature lunged. Its body snapped forward like a whip, every joint bending wrong, every motion unnatural.

Willow screamed.

BANG.

A bullet tore through the thing's shoulder. Black fluid sprayed. The creature stopped mid-lunge, twisted, and reared toward Briggs. The officer stood his ground, eyes wide, both hands gripping his sidearm.

"Again!" Willow shouted, forcing herself upright.

She braced one hand against the windowsill, her vision swimming. Blood soaked through the gauze on her ribs, but she stayed on her feet.

Briggs fired a second time.

The round hit the creature again with a direct shot to it's chest.

It shrieked and stumbled sideways, crashing into the IV stand. Metal collapsed under its weight sending tubing and saline across the floor. Willow grabbed a shard of broken curtain rod, gritting her teeth. The creature turned back to her. It didn't leap this time. It studied her first. Its eyeless head tilted as if trying to understand what she was. What she'd become. In that moment of hesitation Briggs fired again.

The shot slammed into the base of its neck dropping it to the ground.

"GO!" he shouted. "RUN, DAMN IT!"

Willow didn't need to be told twice.

She stumbled toward the door as Briggs moved forward, placing himself between her and the thing. She could hear it growling now, a wet, gurgling sound that didn't come from lungs, but from somewhere else.

Another shot rang out. The hallway loomed ahead. Willow burst into it, one arm clutching her side. She didn't look back. She didn't need to. The creatures weren't done with her and neither was this nightmare.

The hallway stretched before her like a tunnel carved through chaos. Flickering fluorescent lights buzzed and snapped overhead, casting strobing shadows that warped the sterile white walls into twitching streaks of grey and red. Blood smeared across the tiles beneath her bare feet. Bodies lay discarded in heaps as she dashed past them.

Willow stumbled forward, pressing a hand to her ribs. Pain throbbed under her fingertips, sharp and pulsing but like the muscle and skin was stretching. Her gown clung to her damp skin, torn and stained from the fight.

The air stank of copper and antiseptic, as well as something else, something foul and unnatural.

She turned the corner and froze.

....

A nurse was slumped against the wall, throat ripped open, eyes staring blankly at the ceiling. Her name tag; *JANELLE* was still clipped to her scrubs, smeared with gore. The floor around her glistened with a crimson pool.

Willow's breath hitched. She stepped around her, careful not to slip.

Further down the corridor, chaos reigned.

Lights burst one by one above her.

A gurney was overturned, its sheets tangled like entrails. An overturned wheelchair blocked part of the path, wheels still spinning and a trail of blood leading down the hall. Screams echoed from somewhere deeper in the hospital, sharp and panicked, then silenced.

Another hallway branched left. Willow turned instinctively, her eyes darting.

Then she saw it.

Another one.

This demon was different taller, leaner, covered in slick black tendons that flexed like ropes under a thin membrane. Its head was bulbous, and its jaw stretched down past its chest, splitting open to reveal rows of rotating teeth.

It stood in the middle of the hall surrounded by the bodies of patients and staff. A man in a hospital gown lay face down with his spine exposed. A woman in a neck brace was pinned to the wall by a bony blade, eyes wide and lifeless. A nurse's arm twitched near the elevator doors, the body nowhere to be seen.

Willow choked back a sob as the demon turned toward her.

Its jaws clicked.

Willow didn't scream, there were no more screams left inside her. Instead she turned and ran.

A side door to her right stood half open. She dove inside, slamming the door shut behind her just as claws scraped across the tile outside. She collapsed to the floor, gasping, her back against the shelves.

Inside the dark room, she could hear her heart pounding.

She paused.

The demon was still out there waiting. She covered her mouth with both hands and slid deeper into the shadows, praying the metal door would hold. Willow's breath hissed between clenched teeth as she pressed herself back against the metal. The cold surface behind her dug into her spine. Her ribs screamed. Her legs quivered beneath her, but she forced herself not to move. Her body felt like it was regaining strength.

The room stank of bleach, gauze, and old rust. Shelves towered above her on either side, crammed with latex gloves, disinfectant bottles and blood pressure cuffs. A mop bucket sat in one corner. In another, a yellow sharps disposal bin.

The only light came from the flickering hallway outside, seeping in through the small wired-glass window in the door.

She could hear it. Just beyond the thin metal. A soft wet *chitter-chitter-chitter* sound, like claws dancing on the tiled floor. Her heart pounded so loud she was sure it could hear her. She clenched her teeth and curled tighter into the shadows. Sweat dripped from her brow. The pain in her side pulsed with every heartbeat.

The scraping stopped.

BANG.

The door shuddered as something massive slammed into it.

She bit down on a scream. Another crash. Then another.

The thin metal panel groaned under the assault, hinges creaking. The glass window spiderwebbed with cracks. Willow scrambled to her knees, her fingers flying across the shelves in blind panic.

Bottles. Wrappings. Scissors too small, dull and plastic. Nothing useful.

She opened a drawer. Cotton. Tape.

A Scalpel.

She froze.

There, nestled in the sterile tray, sharp, silver, surgical.

She snatched it up and backed away just as the window shattered.

A gnarled arm reached through the hole, four long fingers ending in curved claws, skin the colour of dried blood. It groped, twisting, trying to find her.

Willow backed toward the far corner.

The door collapsed inward as it lumbered in. The demon stood hunched, shoulders scraping the top of the frame. Its limbs twitched with fluid, jerking movements, like a puppet strung on invisible wires. Its body was ribbed, textured like muscle turned inside out, and its lower jaw hung open in a spiral of twitching bone and tendons.

Its eyes or what might have once been eyes were milky slits set too wide apart, glowing faintly with heat. It smelled the room. A low guttural growl crawled up from its chest.

Willow raised the scalpel. It looked like nothing in her hand. It looked to her like a toy. The demon took a step closer, claws flexing, jaw twitching wider.

She stumbled backward against the shelved wall with nowhere left to go and it lunged. Dropping to the floor she managed to dodge, rolling beneath its swipe. The creature hit the shelf instead of her with a screech of metal as boxes tumbled down. Gloves and gauze exploded around them like snow.

Willow crawled on her elbows, gasping, gripping the scalpel tight. The creature roared and turned, limbs cracking into place.

She had no time to think. No time to plan. The creature leapt at her again. She lifted the scalpel with both hands and drove it into its head right above where the eyes should have been. The blade sank in with a sickening pop, through thin bone, through thick membrane, into something soft. The demon shrieked. Not like before. This time, it was pain.

It bucked backward, slamming into the shelf again, howling. Willow flew with it, still clinging to the scalpel lodged in its skull. It thrashed, crashing into the mop bucket and sending it flying. The creature twisted violently, and she was thrown off, landing hard against the cabinet.

The air left her lungs.

She gasped, curling, then forced herself to stand.

The demon staggered.

The scalpel still jutted from its face. It reached for it with one hand but couldn't seem to grip it. Its claws flailed blindly, its movements erratic now. Willow grabbed the mop handle and swung it like a bat. The blow cracked across its chest.

It stumbled.

She hit it again and again. Every blow echoed through the small room like a gunshot. The creature finally collapsed, twitching, clawing at the floor.

Willow didn't wait. She limped past it, through the busted door, and back into the corridor.

The hallway beyond was still chaos.

Lights flickered.

Sirens wailed from somewhere below. But for now she'd survived.

Her breath came in ragged pulls.

Her ribs ached but not from pain now. It felt like new muscle was building and the nerves were realigning themselves.

She still held the mop handle like a weapon, blood and black fluid dripping from the tip and turned once more to look at the doorway. The demon's body twitched again. Not dead but not in the position to chase her.

She turned and fled into the next corridor.

Her body felt like it was burning from the inside.

Willow staggered through the hallway, leaning against the wall for balance, the mop handle clenched in her raw, trembling hand. Her body was a patchwork of bruises, blood, and barely clinging resolve. But her feet kept moving. Every corridor she passed was another scream, another burst of static from a dying intercom.

The hospital was a war zone.

She turned the corner and stopped. The hallway ahead of her was unnaturally quiet. No flickering lights. No overturned gurneys. No blood.

Just a stillness.

She hesitated. Something felt wrong. It all felt too deliberate.

Her breath caught.

She took one step forward, gripping the mop handle tighter. Then the air shifted.

Heavy and Familiar.

The floor beneath her trembled.

Then she heard it.

Not from behind her but from the shadows ahead. A deep layered voice.

"We are not finished."

Willow froze.

A shape emerged from the smoke and shadow.

Towering and shimmering with heat.

Its horns scraped the ceiling tiles, and its skin gleamed like obsidian cracked with veins of molten gold. Its chest still bore the deep wound where she'd plunged the ritual blade and from it, black smoke poured like breath from a furnace.

Eizrekel.

He had followed her.

Willow stepped back, her hands tightened around the mop handle.

"No," she breathed. "You're dead. I killed you."

"You think you can kill me," he said in a laugh. *"You broke the gate. But you did not break me."*

The demon took a step forward.

The floor cracked.

Willow raised her weapon, ready for what was to come.

It tilted its head.

"You are not our prey any more," Eizrekel said. *"You are one of us."*

"You walked through the fire. You woke the strength buried in your bones. I have come to take you back."

Willow shook her head, though her hands trembled.

"I'm nothing like you."

"But you are." Eizrekel grinned and this time its voice echoed truth and certainty.

"You felt it. When you struck down the others. When you stood in the gate's fire and did not burn."

He raised one massive hand, claws outstretched.

"Join us. Rise among us. Reign beside me."

Willow took another step back, her heel brushing the wall behind her.

"I didn't survive to to become you," she said. "I survived to end this."

Eizrekel didn't flinch.

And then, with impossible speed, he charged.

The hallway thundered.

Willow braced herself but she didn't run. She felt a strength deep inside her. She lunged to the side, the demon's claws raking the air where she'd just stood. She spun and swung the mop handle, connecting with the side of his head. The impact jolted her arm.

Eizrekel snarled.

Willow hit him again and again until the mop snapped in half. Eizrekel turned, catching her arm and flung her into the wall.

She hit hard, the impact knocking the air from her lungs but something was wrong.

No bones broke.

There wasn't any blood.

She stood up and stared down at her hands. There was no trembling, no cuts. Her side still ached, but it no longer crippled her. The bruises on her arms had already begun to fade and her vision crystal clear. Her breath came steady.

She looked up. Eizrekel loomed above her, mouth curling in a grin that split to the jaw.

Willow didn't answer. She didn't need to.

She moved a with a blur slamming her palm into the demon's chest, right into the scar she had made in their last encounter. He staggered. Not far. But enough. She followed it up with a kick, hard and precise that snapped his knee backwards.

Eizrekel growled. Not with anger but with glee.

"Yes," he breathed. *"You begin to understand."*

"You were made from us. You will return to us."

Willow snarled. "I'll never be yours."

She reached down and ripped the broken mop handle from the floor. With little pause she drove it through Eizrekel's neck. The demon screamed in pain. He slammed her backward with one arm and staggered, smoke pouring from his throat.

Willow rolled, rose, and charged again. Faster than she'd ever moved. Stronger than she should have been. She tackled him and sent Eizrekel crashing into the wall. She punched it once, twice, and on the third strike, her fist split the surface of his cracked obsidian armour.

The demon roared and shoved her away, retreating.

"You have power now," he hissed. *"But power must be used."*

"You will choose."

"And when you do, you'll remember who gave it to you."

And with that Eizrekel vanished into the shadows.

Gone.

Willow stood alone in the ruined hallway, breathing hard, heart thundering in her chest.

But she wasn't afraid.

Not now.

She looked down at her fists, at her healing skin, at the marks left behind. She wasn't sure what she had become. But she knew one thing:

She could fight them.

CHAPTER TWENTY

Willow stood alone in the wrecked hallway, blood streaking down her temple, the remains of her improvised weapon shattered beside her. Her breath came slow and even now, no longer shallow with fear or pain. The walls around her crackled with static pulses of unnatural heat. The fluorescent lights above popped one by one, dimming the corridor into shadow.

Silence settled.

But it wasn't empty. Not truly. Not anymore.

A voice coiled inside her mind. Low. Measured. Eternal.

"It's inside you. We are one and the same."

Willow didn't respond.

But the air around her thickened, like invisible hands brushing her shoulders.

"You can't run from this," the overlord whispered. *"You can't bury what you've become."*

"We'll keep coming. The gate was cracked not shattered. We'll keep coming for you."

Her jaw clenched.

"You bleed like us. Think like us. Move like us. You are one of the Fallen now."

She squeezed her eye shut, willing him to vanish but the voice wasn't behind her ears. It was inside her skull. She turned slowly and pressed her back against the wall and dropped the bloody handle.

"I buried the town. I'll find and bury you" she hissed.

Silence.

Then footsteps.

Real. Fast. Shuffling her way.

Willow snapped her head toward the sound just as a figure stumbled into view at the far end of the corridor. It limped, blood trailing from one leg, shoulder hunched. One arm cradled to the chest. The face came into view through the smoke and flickering light.

Briggs.

He looked barely alive but his will to live was clearly strong. One eye swollen shut, uniform ripped and smeared in blood. His service pistol hung limp in one hand.

"Will..." he rasped, then dropped to one knee.

Willow ran to him, catching him beneath the arms and lowering him gently.

He coughed once, his face pale. "They're still coming," he choked. "One followed me..."

Behind him, a growl.

Low.

Wet.

Hunting.

Willow looked up.

Another demon stalked out of the smoke, this one smaller than Eizrekel but faster and leaner, with bone colored ridges down its arms. Its face was long and narrow, its mouth stitched together with cords of black sinew. But that mouth twitched now, unravelling into a snarl.

Briggs tried to raise his pistol.

Willow stopped him.

"I've got this," she said.

He stared at her like she'd lost her mind.

She stood. No weapons. No armour. Just her.

The demon hissed, claws dragging against the wall as it charged. Willow didn't flinch. She walked forward. One step followed by another, speeding up each time until she was running.

The demon lunged and she caught it by the throat. Its weight slammed into her, but she held firm, feet planted like stone. Her hand closed tighter around it's neck, bone cracked beneath her fingers. The demon thrashed, claws slicing at her arms but she didn't let go. Instead, she lifted it from the ground and twisted.

SNAP.

Its spine broke like dry wood. The creature's body went limp. She let it fall. It hit the floor with a lifeless thud.

Briggs stared, mouth open.

"What..." he managed. "How?"

Willow didn't answer.

She just turned back to him, It's blood dripping from her hand. The voice in her mind returned.

"You see now."

She crouched beside Briggs and helped him up.

"You're not alone any more," she said.

....

The shattered emergency doors of the hospital groaned as Willow shoved them open with her shoulder, the weight of Briggs leaning heavy against her. Smoke spilled out like a curtain, curling into the night sky. Sirens wailed faintly from somewhere distant, swallowed by the roar of flames.

Outside was worse than inside.

The parking lot had become a war zone.

Cars sat upturned, their engines still ticking. Glass littered the ground in jagged constellations. A paramedic van burned in the corner of the lot, flames licking skyward like hungry fingers. Somewhere across the street, a streetlamp blinked in and out of life before exploding.

Lifeless, twisted bodies lay discarded across the lot. Discarded like broken dolls.

Some of them had been torn apart. Others still burned where they lay.

And in the middle of it all two demons stood.

One hunched over a man's torso, feeding, its claws sunk deep in his abdomen as it tore strips of flesh and viscera free. The other crouched on top of a car, scanning the lot, its tongue flicking in and out tasting the air.

They hadn't seen her yet.

Not yet.

Willow's breath caught as she ducked down, half-carrying, half-dragging Briggs toward a scorched and upturned police cruiser, the driver's side door lay shredded beside, the lights still flashing dimly.

She eased Briggs down behind it.

He groaned, coughing, blood spilling from the side of his mouth.

"You good?" she whispered.

He shook his head, eyes fluttering. "Does it… *look* like I'm good?"

A smile almost crossed her face. She was starting to like him.

Then her eyes caught something.

The back of the cruiser. The trunk hung open, the inner light still flickering and inside, a weapon in it's straps. A pump-action, matte black with spare shells hung from elastic loops gently scraping the ground.

Willow stood slowly.

Her wounds no longer throbbed. In fact… they barely hurt at all.

She looked down at her hands. The burns were gone. The cuts were healed. The swelling had faded.

Even the aching pull in her ribs had vanished.

She moved like someone reborn.

Not just alive. But ready for what was to come.

She stepped around the back of the car, silent and slow.

The demons were still occupied. The first continued tearing into the body, its teeth crunching bone. The second crouched, tense, its head cocked toward the flames but not yet toward her. Willow reached into the trunk. Her fingers curled around the shotgun grip. She pulled it free in one motion, loading a shell into the chamber with a satisfying click-clack.

She stood there for a second, letting the weight of the weapon settle into her hands. She didn't feel fear. She felt clarity. Willow took a breath then stepped forward out of cover, into full view.

The demons didn't notice at first. Then the one on the car turned catching her scent.

It shrieked, a sound like metal tearing in water.

The one feeding looked up, gore dripping from its mouth.

Willow didn't hesitate.

The first one leapt toward her. She raised the shotgun and pulled the trigger.

BOOM.

Its head exploded mid-air in a shower of black blood and bone fragments. The body hit the pavement a moment later, twitching once before going still. Willow racked another shell. The second demon turned from its meal and charged. It sprinted on all fours, limbs flailing, mouth wide open, a mess of fangs and sinew.

Willow didn't retreat, instead ran toward it. Each step thundered in her chest, the shotgun levelled like it was part of her arm. They collided with a shock-wave of motion but this time, she didn't fall. The demon reared back, slashing. Willow ducked and rolled under its swing, spinning and bringing the shotgun up to its side.

BOOM.

The shot tore through its ribcage.

It screamed.

She fired again. Its leg shattered at the knee, dropping it to the ground. Willow stepped on its chest and jammed the barrel under its jaw.

"You came to the wrong world," she said.

Then pulled the trigger.

BOOM.

Silence.

The second demon slumped, twitching, smoking. Willow stood over it, panting. The barrel of the shotgun steamed in the cold air. From somewhere deep inside her, the voice of the overlord returned before vanishing.

"You will be ours to use."

Willow stared at the carnage around her. At the ash, the blood, the destruction.

She whispered back, "No. I'm yours to fear."

Hot, black blood steamed on the concrete, evaporating in slow, curling tendrils. The shotgun in Willow's hands felt heavier now, her final shot still echoed in her ears.

The crumbling shell of the hospital behind her and two dead demons at her feet. The wind carried sirens in the distance. She turned her head slowly. Beyond the parking lot, beyond the crumbled entrance road, red and blue lights flickered like beacons on the edge of the smoke. She could hear the soft thump of rotors, helicopters maybe and the steady approach of engines.

Help. But too late for the dead.

But maybe… not too late for what came next.

Her arms ached with exhaustion, but her body still felt unnaturally intact. Whatever the demon's blood had done to her, it hadn't faded.

Not yet.

She turned and made her way back to the ruined police car. Briggs sat where she'd left him, slouched against the rear wheel well. His face was pale, but his eyes were open. Alert.

He blinked up at her as she approached.

"You came back," he rasped.

"I said I would."

He managed a half-smile. "That was… loud."

Willow knelt beside him.

"They're gone," she said. "For now."

He nodded, then coughed. A wet, painful sound came out of his throat.

"You're gonna be okay," she added, though her voice didn't try to lie too much. "Help's coming."

He gave a slight shake of the head. "Doesn't matter."

Willow stared at him. "It does."

Briggs reached up and grabbed her wrist. His hand was slick with blood.

"You stopped them."

"I killed a few," she said.

"But you're not done?"

"No," she replied. "I'm not."

He studied her a moment longer. "Something's different about you."

Willow didn't answer.

Not right away.

She looked down at her arms. Clean. Smooth. Not a trace of a burn or cut. No wound. No scar.

"I'm not who I was," she said finally.

"What does that mean?"

She met his gaze.

"It means I know where they are and where they are from. I know how to find them."

"You're… connected to them?"

She nodded. "More than that. I feel them."

A low wind picked up, sweeping through the lot, stirring loose paper and ash. In the distance, the sirens grew louder.

"They're not just in New Grayson," she said. "That was only the start."

"You can sense them?"

"I can *hear* them."

Briggs looked at her carefully. Not fearfully, but with something close to awe.

Willow stood again, staring into the smoke.

"They think they made me one of them," she said. "That they can use me."

"Can they?"

She turned back to him.

"No…. But I can use what they gave me. Their strength. Their blood. I can follow the cracks and I can stop them."

Briggs tried to sit up straighter. "You're going after them."

Willow nodded once.

"I have to finish this."

"You don't even know where to start."

"I do," she said softly. "They can't hide any more. I'm going back to the source."

He exhaled, slow and shallow. "You sure you're still… you?"

She considered the question.

Then said, "I'm more me then I've ever been."

Briggs smiled faintly. "Then go."

She paused, watching him for a long moment.

"You'll make it," she said.

"Probably not," he coughed. "But I'll slow 'em down if they come back."

Willow reached down and gripped his hand tightly once more.

Then she turned.

She walked across the parking lot, feet crunching glass, wind pushing the smoke behind her. As she passed the wreckage, the flames parted briefly, and beyond the rise of the road, the world opened again.

She didn't know what was waiting for her.

But she knew this:

They weren't done and neither was she.

EPILOGUE

You can survive the fire, but you'll always come out scarred.

The road stretched out like an open wound.

The pavement cold beneath her bare feet. Smoke hung low in the morning air, still rising in lazy coils from the blackened skeleton of what once had been New Grayson. Somewhere far behind her, the world stirred. Sirens faded. Radios crackled. Survivors, responders, maybe even reporters, late to the party they couldn't begin to understand.

Willow walked away from them.

Not toward safety. Not toward rescue. Toward the fire.

The shotgun rested across her shoulder, one hand curled around the grip. The heat didn't bother her anymore. Her skin, once raw and fragile, was now firm. Scarless. Her muscles ached, but not from weakness. She felt *alive* in a way she never had. Sharpened. Purposed. Reforged.

She wasn't sure when her limp had vanished or when her vision had sharpened but she felt it now, deep inside. Something had changed. Maybe she'd bled out the girl they once called Amy. Maybe what remained had always been Willow. Now, there was no doubt.

The cracked wooden sign at the town's edge creaked in the wind as she passed it once more;

Welcome to New Grayson. Where history lives forever.

Willow didn't glance at it. History was dead and she was what came after. Her feet crunched over broken glass, across the scorched gravel road, through the remains of police barricades and half-melted signs. She passed the empty husk of a fire truck, its lights still frozen mid-spin. The wreckage of a school bus, crushed flat. A scorched teddy bear lying face-down in the ash.

Her eyes stayed forward. In her chest, her heart beat with a calm, burning rhythm.

She walked through the outskirts of the town, through streets where bones still smouldered in the gutter, where blood had dried black on the side-walk. Some of the buildings were still collapsing slowly, inch by inch. A weakened beam groaned and fell in the distance.

The town had been hollow.

A shell of something once real, twisted into something malevolent.

Whatever Richard had opened hadn't sealed completely.

The gate had cracked and things were still trying to come through. She could feel them.

Not from the town. Not from Earth. But from the space *beneath* everything. From the place no god dared name.

New Grayson wasn't the source.

It was the reception desk for some place much older.

And she was the only one who had walked through it all and lived.

Crossing the destroyed remnants of the town square, now little more than a crater ringed by soot and bone Willow's mind took it all in. The flagpole lay twisted and blackened. The mayor's office or what had once stood as its facade had collapsed inward, stone crushed under it's own weight.

It was there she paused. The earth was cracked and still smoking.

She knelt slowly and pressed her fingers to the scorched stone. It pulsed faintly beneath her palm like a heartbeat failing. Or was it a call from them, a plea to help them escape? Willow stood again, the shotgun rested easy in her hands.

The sound of the wind brought a calm before the storm that was to come.

She never wanted to be different. Never wanted any of this. Glancing around, she knew she had to bring an end to the creatures. They'd taken everything from her. The demons and Richard.

Kira: Her sister in all the chaos. Her safe-space. The girl who'd bled trying to protect her.

Miles: The last tether to a world that might've been normal. The one who had hope even when everything turned to ash.

Sophie: Her mother's voice in ink. The woman who knew more than she ever said while protecting her all these years.

And there was Alison, her mother: Amy's mother. Willow's mother. The woman whose memories now echoed inside her like whispered lullabies in her dreams.

She had to do this for all of them.

She had to finish this no matter how far it took her, even if it meant directly walking into Hell itself. She glanced once more at the crater where the church once stood, then turned and walked on past the ashes, past the bones, past the scorched altar where her story had almost ended.

Beneath her feet she could feel them, could feel them on the other side. She'd find a way back. Her blood was the key.

Her next chapter had already begun and the girl they'd tried to burn had now become the fire that would destroy them.

Willow's story will continue...

ABOUT THE AUTHOR:

Aaron is a horror fan through and through. Books, films, art; he's always loved the idea of being scared. Two of his previous short stories have been published in horror compilations but 'Ashes of Her Name' is his debut novel. He's currently working on the follow-up, as well as collating a horror compilation of his own, made up of reams of short twisted tales he's created over the years.

Follow on:

Instagram: @anashhorror